DREAMLIKE

Vaughan W. Smith

Fair Folio

Sydney, Australia

Fair Folio
www.fairfolio.com.au

Dreamlike / Vaughan W. Smith. -- 1st ed.
ISBN 978-0-9874694-3-4

For Ana

CHAPTER ONE

STAGE ONE

Amy waved goodbye to everyone, checked that she had her keys, and walked over to the elevator. She pressed the down button and waited patiently. She made a point of not facing the tall glass panels, avoiding the spectacular view of the city. The problem was that it was too easy to look down to the street level, and even the memory of that was enough to make her sick. She adjusted her long blonde hair by using the reflection of the elevator call button panel. Soon after she heard the two tones of the elevator and waited for the doors to open.

She walked through the open doors to an empty lift. After pressing the ground button she zoned out a little, thinking of any groceries that she needed to buy. Suddenly a male hand thrust through the doors and forced them open. Startled, Amy looked up and saw a well-dressed man with brown hair, impeccable suit and dark brown suitcase walking into the elevator. She recognised him instantly, and subconsciously twirled her hair a little.

"Hey Amy! Glad I caught you. How are you going?" the man said.

"I'm good, how about you?"

"Way too busy, but to be honest I'd rather be back in the office tonight."

"Why's that?"

"A friend set me up on a blind date. He's been hassling me for a while, so I'm finally meeting her."

"Oh, well have a nice time."

"Thanks, I'll fill you in tomorrow."

"Bye David."

"See you later," David called back as he dashed out from the elevator. Amy smiled and waved, then when he had disappeared she sighed deeply. She walked out of the building, and paused, wondering which way to go. Left was to her home, right was to the bar where Samantha worked. Not wanting to sit at home alone, she headed right. It was just after five o'clock and the city streets were packed full of people. The dense crowds made Amy uneasy, so when she approached the traffic lights she stood back a little to have her own space. When the lights changed, she paused to let the others get ahead then walked in her own space. The crossing was a major one, so she went across diagonally to save time. However halfway across she spotted a man walking with a Great Dane and German Shepard and she changed her mind. She turned quickly and half retreated so that she still crossed the road but was on the opposite side to the man with his dogs.

Amy continued the crowd dodging the next few blocks until she arrived at the Golden Arms. The black sign of the two golden arms above the entry always amused her, but she didn't know why. Stepping in, the bar was busy but not full. The afternoon light and the heat outside wasn't strong, but the bar just felt a bit darker, quieter and cooler. She spotted Samantha behind the bar, and walked over.

"Amy, how was work?" Samantha asked.

"It was ok, the usual," Amy said.

"Your usual drink?"

"Sure, thanks."

Samantha smiled, and starting mixing a vodka and cranberry. When Amy tried to pay, she grinned, pushed aside the money and walked away to serve another customer. Amy picked up her drink and found a quiet table in the corner to sit down. Before she could settle down, a middle aged man with greying hair appeared next to her table.

"May I sit down," he said politely.

"Sure," Amy said, unsure of how to reply. The man sat down carefully right across from her.

"Hi, my name is Roger and I'll be out of your hair by the time you finish that drink."

"Ok." Amy was a bit stunned by the man's matter-of-fact manner. He also had intense green eyes.

"Please forgive me, but I spotted you out on the street and my professional curiosity kicked in."

"What do you mean?"

"I saw you on the street, avoiding people, animals and looking stressed. I see it all the time, you're carrying a lot of fears around."

"Well, it's nice of you to say so, but I don't need your help. I already have a therapist."

"How well has that worked for you so far?"

"I'm making progress," Amy said defensively, but they both knew she hadn't made any breakthroughs.

"That may be, but I have a solution for you."

"No thanks," Amy said. Roger leaned forward quickly and grasped both her hands in his.

"I can see that you are fed up with this way of living. Come and see me when you are ready to take your life back." With that, he withdrew his hands, took a card out of his pocket and placed it on the table. Amy watched him leave without saying a word.

"Who was that?" Samantha asked as she walked over.

"Some man who saw me on the street, he said he can help me," Amy said. She turned the card over in her hands and handed it to Samantha.

"Roger Butler, life surgeon. Sounds interesting," Samantha said, reading out the card. She placed it back on the table.

"What would you do?" Amy said.

"Sweetie men hand me their cards every day, but they never look like this. As much as this looks crazy, maybe you need to try a little crazy?"

"No, I'm not going to do it." Amy picked up the card and flicked it through her fingers. Samantha reached over, took the card and placed it in Amy's bag.

"I've gotta get back to it. Don't wait up tonight I've got the late shift, and this cute guy has been tipping me like crazy."

"Ok have fun," Amy said and waved as Samantha walked back to the bar. Amy sat, deep in thought. She pulled out a romance novel and read through it for a few hours, only stopping to get water from the bar. She looked up around seven thirty and decided to head home. She stepped outside, hailed a taxi and sat on the back seat. Directing the older male taxi driver to her apartment, she called a local Thai place and placed a take away order. Instructing the driver to wait for a minute, she went inside and paid for her food and got back into the taxi.

"Like clockwork, you do this a lot?" the driver asked.

"Yeah, it beats cooking for yourself."

"A pretty lady like you? Go get a nice fellow."

"It's not always that easy," Amy said, a little embarrassed but also annoyed at the driver.

"Yes it is, don't let this get in your way," the driver said, tapping his head. Amy nodded and turned to look out the window. Minutes later they arrived at a small block of twelve apartments. She paid the driver, who offered no more advice, and walked up the stairs into the building. She ate at her coffee table in front of the TV, and fell asleep on the couch.

A loud noise woke her suddenly. The apartment was pitch black, all the lights and the television were off. Wide awake, she crept over to the balcony and slid open the glass door. She stepped outside and had a look. A huge stroke of lightning illuminated the sky and a crack of thunder followed it seconds later. Amy trembled. The sky opened and torrential rain spewed from the sky at an alarming rate. A chill ran through the air and gave her goose bumps. She retreated into the house, allowing her eyes time to adjust to the darkness. Her anxiety was increasing by the minute, and her chest felt tight. She navigated her way to her bedroom and crawled into the covers.

Sleep didn't come as easily this time, and when she did manage to drift off it wasn't long before she woke up startled by a random noise. After several such events she finally fell into a deep sleep which was interrupted by the lights coming back on. Amy got out of bed, both happy at the lights being back on and annoyed at being awoken again. She walked around the house and turned off all the lights except for the one in the hallway outside her room then went back to sleep.

The warm sunlight tickled her face, and it felt strange. It was nice for a change. Then part of her brain ticked over, and noted that something was not right, her room never got full sun until late morning or midday.

She awoke suddenly, and scrambled around for her watch. The time said eleven twenty two.

"Shit!" Amy said. She rushed into Samantha's room and found her asleep. She turned and rushed to the bathroom. She found a post-it-note on the door.

Rough night? I called in sick on your behalf. Relax! - Samantha

The last thing Amy could do was relax, but the call had already been made.

"Maybe I can just go in for the afternoon?" she thought to herself. Amy quickly showered, skipped breakfast and dressed. She dug through her bag furiously, trying to find a lipstick without any luck. Losing her patience she tipped the whole bag onto the bed. On top of the pile was the card she had received from Roger Butler. She picked it up and looked at it again. She became aware of her anxious and stressed state, the way she had spent the night and how she was just about to rush back into work again. Something inside her snapped, and she wanted something different for herself. She carefully applied her lipstick, put everything back into her bag and left. She took a bus into the city and walked to the address on the card. It was a large building servicing many small companies. Just inside the main doors she found his plaque on the wall, showing his location as suite 407. She walked into the elevator and pressed the button for the fourth floor, butterflies in her stomach. Her decisive and rash mood was beginning to wear off and she was second guessing herself. However she also thought that since she was already there, it didn't hurt to see what he had to say.

There were many small glass-door offices on the fourth floor. One was a dentist, another a pathology lab, another a remedial massage establishment. At the end of the corridor she spotted his door and went inside. It was a small reception area with an older woman sitting behind a white desk.

"Hello, how can I help you today?" the woman said.

"Hi. I was given a card yesterday, but I don't have an appointment."

"Let me see. Of course, that's no problem. Mr. Butler is on a call at the moment, do you mind waiting?"

"Sure," Amy said and sat down at the nearest seat. She flicked through a trashy celebrity magazine and second guessed herself again. She had to be crazy, meeting this man.

"Have I really lost it?" she asked herself. Before that thought could be answered she saw a door open and Roger walk out.

"Oh hello! Please come in," he said pleasantly. Amy put down the magazine, stood up and followed him inside. Roger closed the door behind them and sat behind a giant wooden desk. Amy sat on the provided chair and felt another nervous flutter.

"I'm sorry, I don't believe I got your name," Roger said.

"It's Amy."

"Fantastic, well it's great to see you here today Amy. I had a good feeling about you."

"Well, I wanted to see what you had to offer."

"I'm a pioneer in both brain research as well as an avid supporter of alternate spiritual meditation. Few people plant themselves in both camps, so I have a unique perspective and have developed something revolutionary."

"What is it?"

"Before I explain the details, tell me about why you are here."

"Well, I'll give you the short version. I've always had these little fears, but they weren't really affecting my life that much. However a few years ago, I was involved in a fairly traumatic incident. I can't remember much about it, but essentially since then everything has been amplified."

"I understand. I believe I have a way to help you with this. Not only to help you conquer your fears, but to unlock your memory and be free of that event forever," Roger said, before launching into an explanation.

"Fear and anxiety, such as what you experience, arise from conflict in the mind. Conflict that is a result of your life experiences. The problem is, to clear the conflict you can't just talk about it, you need an experience to resolve it. Think of it like an experience mirroring what caused the initial conflict."

"That makes sense in a way."

"Of course it does. You've no doubt heard about many people offering radical experiences to confront people with extreme, and sometimes life threatening situations. I don't believe in that, it's hard to arrange, costly and you're essentially working in the dark. So I thought, why not have a way for you to tailor make your own scenario to conquer your fears."

"What do you mean?"

"Your mind has created these fears, anxieties and issues. Let your mind create the solutions too."

"How?"

"Dreams."

"Dreams?"

"Yes. How many times have you had a dream that felt so real that you were confused when you awoke? How many times has the feeling and emotion that you felt in your dream stayed with you for the entire day?"

"I can remember many times."

"Imagine then, if we can unlock your dreams and have them work for you. That's essentially what I am offering you."

"I'm not sure about that, doesn't that mean you are altering my mind in some way?"

"There is a drug involved yes, but it is just unlocking the capability. The rest is all you."

"I'll be honest, this sounds a little crazy," Amy said with uncertainty.

"I know, so here's the deal. I'll give you a pack today which has everything you need. Start whenever you want, or don't start. It's up to you. If you have any concerns down the road just come back and I'll be here to help you out," Roger explained. Amy was in two minds, but an opportunity was here and she could always opt out later.

"If I take it what's the cost?"

"No cost, if you are happy with the treatment then come back and we can fill in some forms to help me with my ongoing research." Amy hesitated for a moment, then felt a surge of emotion. A sense of energy and life, and hope.

"Ok sign me up, let's hope I don't regret this." Roger smiled and opened a drawer in his desk. He took out a small bag filled to the brim.

"Everything you need is in here. Good luck, I look forward to meeting the new you." Amy picked up the bag and Roger escorted her out of the office, waving as she left.

Amy walked down the street basking in the sunshine. Grabbing a sandwich from a local shop she headed straight home. Samantha was up and about and welcomed her heartily.

"Hey there girl, how are you doing?"

"Better now, thanks for the day off!"

"It was for the best. Now what have you got there?"

"Well I went and visited that strange man today, Roger Butler. He told me about his treatment, it's something to do with your dreams." Amy sat down at their small circular table and opened the bag. Samantha sat down with her, curious about the contents. Inside were a lined notebook, an artist's notebook, a pen and pencil, a note and a small white box. Amy unfolded the note and read it out loud.

"Instructions. Take the green pill to unlock your mind and record your dreams in the provided notebooks. Your treatment will end when it is completed."

"Your treatment will end when it is completed? That's a little vague," Samantha said.

"Yeah, well at least it is simple."

"Unlock your mind? I bet it's some kind of crazy hallucinogen!"

"You seem excited. Do you want to take it?" Amy asked.

"Nah it's for you, and they only gave you one so I don't want to waste it."

"Yeah that's true. So should I really go through with this?"

"Listen Amy, you deserve way more than you have in life. You're a fully qualified lawyer yet you're working as a legal secretary. Your life needs a shakeup, and if this is it then go for it. Worst case scenario, you have a crazy trip and move on."

"You're right," Amy said. She filled a glass with tap water and sat back down at the table. Opening the white box, she found a small pale green circular pill inside.

"Wait one sec," Samantha said and grabbed herself a glass and filled it with apple juice. She return and raised her glass.

"To new beginnings!"

"To new beginnings!" Amy responded and swallowed the pill with a gulp. She sat quietly waiting for a reaction, and Samantha stared at her intently.

"Do you feel any different yet?"

"Not yet."

"It might take time. Hey why don't you come hang with me at work tonight, I want to make sure you're ok."

"I'm not sure if that's a good idea."

"The note didn't say you couldn't have a drink, and I'll promise to leave on time."

"Ha-ha alright let's do it." Amy spent the afternoon lounging around, trying to relax. However she tried though, she kept thinking about what would happen. She had no idea what to expect. When Samantha was ready, Amy gathered her bag and together they went to the city and the Golden Arms. Amy had a drink with Samantha at the bar, then alternated between reading her romance novel and chatting with Samantha. She kept an eye out for the mysterious Roger Butler, but he didn't show up at the bar.

At the end of the night, Samantha sighed and turned down staff drinks, ignored the eager glance of a young tipsy man and left with Amy. They walked to the bus stop, taking care to use the street blocks that were well lit.

"Thanks for staying with me," Amy said.

"Hey that's what friends are for. Besides, I can get free drinks and dance with hilariously drunk guys anytime!" Amy smiled appreciatively at Samantha, and then got ready for bed. She placed the notebooks and writing implements on her bedside table and then got under the covers. She noticed Samantha pop her head through the partially open doorway.

"Sweet dreams!"

"Thanks. Goodnight!" Amy said. She tried to sleep but her mind was racing. She thought about what people would say to her at work the next day, what kinds of dreams she would have and if she would even remember enough to write any details. She couldn't remember her dreams normally.

"It's ok you can do this," she said to herself. A little while later she fell asleep.

CHAPTER TWO

DREAM ONE

I found myself walking down the street on a bright sunny day. The sky was a fantastic blue, there were no clouds anywhere and there was a faint breeze cooling me down. I was wearing a green summery dress and sandals. I didn't recognise the street, but it was tree lined and peaceful. The odd car drove along, but at normal speeds. Everything was very calm. A man walking a golden retriever came towards me and I jumped, startled. I quickly scanned the streets and crossed the road to the other side. It wasn't quite as warm, but was still nice. The man and his dog continued along without any interruption to their pace. It was as if they didn't care about my sudden evacuation or didn't notice I wasn't sure where I was heading, but I kept walking.

A block later I noticed an older lady walking a poodle. Hoping to avoid that, I stopped at the next intersection and pressed the button to cross the road again. However the lights just didn't change. The lady and the poodle came closer and closer. I pressed the button again, hoping the lights would change. They continued to be stubborn and stayed green. The crossing light for the lady was also green so she started to cross the street towards me. I felt very uncomfortable and started assessing the traffic to see if I could cross over to the other side.

The tightness in my chest was uncomfortable so I spotted a gap in the traffic and ran for it. I made it to the other side, and huffed and puffed a bit, regaining my breath. The older lady looked over at me, a little puzzled. It made sense, who would cross unnecessarily to avoid a poodle? They're such tiny dogs. I started to relax, then remembered that I was on this side of the street earlier, so looked back. Then I noticed that the man with his golden retriever had changed direction and were headed back towards me. I started walking faster to increase the distance between us. A car pulled up next to me and a teenager got out. I didn't really pay attention but then almost jumped out of my skin when he walked past me. He was wearing a dog mask. Only it was fluffy and covered his entire head, like it was for a mascot.

I slowed down a little to let him get ahead. Another person rushed past me, carrying a cat in a travel cage. The cat looked very content, but hissed at me as it passed. A car beeped its horn at a slow driver, and that car beeped its horn back. Only the second horn sounded like a dog barking. I felt something touching my legs, and it was a cat running through them. I jumped off to the side, watching the cat in amazement. It paused to look at me, then ran off. I noticed that I was walking alongside a park, so decided it would be better to move in that direction.

I stepped off the footpath and onto the grass. The sky darkened some, there were clouds rolling in. I felt like something strange was going on, but at the same time everything seemed as it should be. Having some space to myself, I felt a bit better. I continued through the park and sat down under a large tree. It was peaceful and the breeze resumed again. I heard the sound of the leaves slowly moving in the breeze and the trickling of nearby water. Only there wasn't any water nearby. I focused my hearing and it seemed like the sound was coming from nearby. I stood up and peered around the tree. There was a German shepherd urinating on the other side of the tree. It had no collar or anyone around in control of it.

Disgusted, I stormed off and looked back frequently to ensure that it wasn't following me. I saw another lady walking seven dogs at once, and gave her a wide berth. Soon I reached the edge of the park. The streets were full of people with animals. Cats, dogs, and even some pigs. All were on leashes. The sky darkened further and the clouds darkened more. There was a rumbling of distant thunder. I had to get somewhere under cover. There was a large building up ahead but I would have to pass all the people with animals to get there. I decided to go the long way, I could spot a deserted lane with nobody there.

I stepped into the lane and was greeted with dead silence. Then I heard the low whistling of the wind sweeping through, picking up the odd piece of discarded paper. I heard another noise behind me and saw a large dog. It was huge and I couldn't place the type. It shook its head and stared at me. Then the dog started walking towards me. I started picking up my pace, walking more steadily. It started barking, which seemed to echo all around me. It felt like there were five hundred dogs all barking at me in unison. I upgraded my walk to a power walk. The intensity and volume of the barking increased in pace with my speed. It was soon followed by howling. Then screeching cats. A whole menagerie of animal sounds were deafening me as I sprinted down the lane towards the building up ahead.

I closed the door behind me and noticed that it was quite dark inside. I found a light switch and turned it on. The only light was coming from the opposite end of the room. I walked closer and saw that it was illuminating an open door. It looked quite inviting so I wandered closer still. As I approached I noticed a giant dog in front of the door. I turned to return the way I had come and saw that the door I had come through was gone. I turned back to look at the dog again. It now had two heads and seemed larger. Knowing that something wasn't right, I closed my eyes and opened them. The dog was larger still, and had three heads. Each one was looking at me and growling. The more I looked around the room all I could see was the dog and the door.

Anxiety rose in me, but at the same time something else. I was stuck in this room and there was only one way out. I took a step forward. The dog remained as it was, snarling at me. I walked closer, slowly, a step at a time. I looked at the dog and the door from every angle. Once I was only a few steps away I had a dilemma. The dog was not moving, and there was no way to sneak past it. The angry, giant dog was completely blocking the way to the door. I was tired, I had been harried and harassed from the start. My day had gotten progressively worse and now there was a scary crazy dog stopping me from getting out. I had had enough. I turned and walked back, not with fear but with purpose. I took a deep breath, willed myself on, and then pushed forward. I sprinted towards the dog. As I got closer, it got scarier and louder. Ignoring it I continued my pace. I took one step closer than I had been before and then jumped. I soared above the dog, but could feel its jaws snapping at me. It was so close I thought I had been bitten. Somehow I maintained my momentum and less than gracefully toppled past it and through the open door. I was enveloped by a warm light.

CHAPTER THREE

STAGE TWO

Amy awoke in a slight haze. She sat up, grabbed the first notebook and wrote down her dream word for word. Then she sketched the image of a key in the other notebook. Moments later she appeared to be more aware of what was happening. She couldn't remember any of her dream, yet as she read the words she had written they seemed correct, and at the same time familiar.

"How strange," she thought to herself. Suddenly remembering the time, she glanced at her alarm clock and relaxed. She had awoken minutes before it was due to go off, so she disabled it. Instinctively she wandered over to Samantha's room and peered in. Even after going to bed at a decent time, she was still sleeping soundly.

"Some people just aren't morning people," Amy thought as she prepared herself for work. Everything she did was as if on auto-pilot. Her mind was entirely concerned with thoughts on what had just happened. She thought through it logically. What Roger had said was true, he had unlocked her mind. Last night her mind created a scenario for her to deal with. It was increasingly full of animals and forced many different confrontations until she had to face one. One that she would never encounter in real life. Just before she left, Amy turned back and looked at the notebooks. She didn't feel comfortable leaving them there, so she walked over and put them in her bag.

On her way to work, Amy saw a few different dogs on the street but didn't really pay them any attention. Only one came close and she managed to walk past it without incident. She was so proud of herself, that when she got into the elevator at work she had a little jump for joy. Only she wasn't paying attention and didn't time it well. The doors opened as she landed.

"Hey Amy feeling better today?" David said as he approached the elevator doors.

"Yeah, thanks for asking," she said in reply, feeling incredibly embarrassed. Thankfully her make up masked how much she was blushing.

"I'm grabbing a coffee downstairs, do you want one?"

"Yes please, skim cappuccino."

"Great, I'll be back in a minute." Amy watched him leave and hurried to her desk before she did anything else silly. She busied herself with some simple filing to zone out a bit. Her concentration was soon broken when David returned.

"Here's your coffee."

"Thanks again." When David lingered, Amy spoke up again.

"Busy week?"

"Not really, I think all my work will come through next week."

"That's a shame. Oh how did your date go the other night?"

"It went well, she seems nice."

"That's good," Amy said, unsure of what to say. Luckily she was rescued by another colleague calling David away. The rest of the morning passed fairly quickly. Just before lunch a senior associate, Margaret, stopped by Amy's desk with a small stack of documents. However judging from her conversation, it was not work she was there to discuss.

"You're single right, Amy?"

"Yes."

"David's quite a catch, you should drop some hints."

"What do you mean? He's dating someone now."

"Oh c'mon, I've been listening to how he's talked about her. Trust me, there's nothing serious there."

"Well…"

"Just let him know you're interested!"

"Maybe," Amy answered. Margaret wasn't impressed, snorted and walked off. Amy wondered to herself why married middle-aged women were always trying so hard to set her up.

She spent the afternoon doing a few mindless tasks. Her thoughts were elsewhere, wondering about what she would do next. As potentially valuable as the previous night had been, it was very strange and definitely concerning She decided to wait until next week before going back to visit Roger. One crazy dream a week was definitely enough. She was excited to talk about it with Samantha though.

As soon as work was done, Amy headed to the Golden Arms. The place was incredibly quiet, so she sat at the end of the bar and told Samantha all about the dream.

"That's incredible Amy. Although I won't believe it until I see you patting a dog."

"It's probably possible, but I'm in no rush to test it."

"Why not? If it was me I'd be kissing dogs to see what happened."

"Ha-ha one step at a time."

"So how's David doing?" Samantha asked knowingly.

"Not you too?"

"Too?"

"Yeah Margaret was giving me a pep talk today."

"Good on her. He's a great guy, good job and he likes you."

"I'm not so sure about that."

"Everyone else is, you'll join us soon enough."

"Sure. Well I'll be going, see you later."

"Bye sweetie, take care of yourself." With that said, Amy left the bar. Darkness had fallen on the street outside, so she automatically took her night time route. She had selected it some time ago to maximise the amount of street light. She heard a few dogs barking in the distance, but it didn't really disturb her.

Amy watched some television, read a book then felt sleepy. She felt strange about leaving the notebooks in her bag, so she took them back out and left them on her bedside table. Wondering to herself about a world without any of her fears, she fell asleep peacefully.

CHAPTER FOUR

DREAM TWO

I was walking up a strange staircase. The steps were perfectly clear and I could see the level below me. There didn't seem to be any people around. I looked ahead and couldn't see where the stairs were leading. I decided, it would be wiser to go back down the stairs. As I did so something was happening to the level below me. Each step I took towards it caused the ground to become more and more transparent. Once I stepped onto the ground, it was almost completely clear. Thankfully the next level below, which I could see through the transparent floor, looked normal.

Spooked out by this behaviour, I looked for another way to continue downwards. I found another set of stairs, only these seemed less stable. They made awful creaking sounds and shook enormously. The stairs went down in a spiral, over and over. Despite my earlier glimpses I didn't seem to be getting closer to another level. As I descended further the material of the steps appeared more worn, then rotten. Eventually there were whole steps missing that I had to skip over.

I had a little more presence of mind, and a part of me remembered having a similarly strange dream. The details were hazy, but suggested some kind of escalation of the dream against me. I paused, wondering if my descent was making things worse. However since it was just a hazy, almost insignificant feeling I ignored it. A thought about the strange transparent steps leading higher and higher convinced me that I was on the right path.

I started to see other people. None of them even looked at me, or acknowledged me, but they were all walking up the stairs. At first they were just an endless stream going up. Then their speed increased, then they started brushing past me. Soon every third person was bumping me in some way. It felt hostile. Suddenly my feet were on solid ground. I was on a concrete pavement outside a building. Ahead of me was grass, then a beach. I walked towards it with joy. I took off my shoes so I could feel the grass with my feet. Next I walked through the sand, feeling its texture and warmth. Then the coolness of the wet sand as I stood at the edge of the ocean, with small gentle waves lapping at my feet.

I looked out into the distance and could see nothing but endless ocean. A stiff sea breeze smelled fresh and whipped my clothes around. I thought that perhaps a storm was approaching, due to the change of humidity in the air and the increased motion of the waves. The memory of a storm of some kind flickered in the back of my mind, and then was lost. Looking down at my feet, the water had risen slightly. My ankles were now completely submerged. I scanned the ocean for any changes, but it looked the same. A chill ran up my legs and I looked down at them again. Now the water was up to my knees. Realising that something strange was happening I turned to walk away from the beach.

As I continued, I was no longer in water. However it felt like it was always a step behind me, lapping at my heels. I momentarily remembered leaving my shoes somewhere, but instantly lost the thought. I turned back to look at the beach, and noticed that it was completely underwater. I scratched my head, completely confused, then continued on my way. I was on a normal suburban street, but saw quite a few high rise buildings and skyscrapers along the street. I wandered along, not in any hurry at all. I jumped in a few puddles, kicked some water around and felt playful. I crossed the street, found a bench and sat down. I could see something on the horizon but couldn't make it out. A low rumbling and crashing sound was also coming from somewhere, and the volume was slowly building. I squinted more and then suddenly saw it for what it was. There was a giant wave on its way.

Feeling a new sense of urgency, I stepped into the nearest building. However once inside all I could see was an old rusty ladder. I started to climb it, then noticed the building around me disappear. I looked down and couldn't see the ground. There was no ladder below me, the only way I could progress was up. I looked around and saw clouds. I stopped climbing and a strong wind picked up, buffeting me violently. I felt incredibly isolated and everywhere I looked I was reminded of the extreme height that I was at.

I found a small wedge of courage, and used it to climb ahead a little more. The ladder I was on, started to sway. It sounded like it might snap at any moment. That or I would fall. My hands were frozen and holding on was difficult. I focused my eyes just on the ladder itself and continued. The ladder slowly morphed into polished silver. Every inch of it was reflecting the view around me. I closed my eyes and continued. My hands felt something different. I gripped onto something solid and textured. Opening my eyes carefully one at a time I saw that it was concrete. I pulled myself up a bit higher and surveyed my surroundings. I was on a concrete rooftop.

The rooftop was perfectly square with nothing visible around the edges and no ledges. I walked over to the nearest edge, crouched down and peered over. I could see the ground, but it was tiny and had no detail. I was short of breath, but didn't feel like I had exerted myself that much. Then I realised that my heart had been pounding like crazy for such a long time. I was so caught up in my situation that I hadn't noticed the enormity of my anxiety and physical reaction. I took a deep breath and tried to calm myself. I carefully stepped back from the edge and saw that it had changed colour and had a green tint. I looked around at the other sides of the rooftop and they looked the same as before.

Testing a theory, I crept over to another of the edges and looked down. The view was similarly insane, and I felt a little dizzy but I was ok. As I backed away it changed colour too. I seemed to be on to something, so I tried it for the other two edges. My experiences were the same, with the escalating unpleasantness but the colour changes. I closed my eyes for a moment to gather myself and opened them again. Something was different.

I saw an identical rooftop to the one I was on, fairly close. On it was a giant, partially opened door with light behind it. I carefully walked closer and realised that there was no way on to the other rooftop. If I wanted to go over there, I had to jump. Unfortunately, my expeditions around the edges of the rooftop I was on had somehow been constructed into a perfect three dimensional map in my head. I couldn't look at the other rooftop without seeing all the empty space around me all the way down to the ground. The ladder I had climbed up was also gone. The wind picked up and I felt freezing. I could feel the warmth emanating from the doorway.

I couldn't do it. It was too much. I could not leap over what was essentially a bottomless pit. Especially not with such a giant gap. I sat down cross legged and tried to shield myself from the wind. Rain began to fall and soon I was soaked. I was cold, shivering and stuck on a rooftop with nothing around me. I heard a large siren in the distance. It was getting louder and louder. The ground under me started to sway, and then I toppled through the air, falling. I fell for an age.

STAGE THREE

Samantha shook Amy again and again but there was no response. Finally Amy woke, incredibly groggy. Only instead of saying anything, she just picked up the notebook and wrote in it furiously. Samantha sat and watched with fascination. Amy stopped writing in one notebook, grabbed the other and started to sketch something, but stopped abruptly. Then her eyes lost that glazed over look and she stared at Samantha with confusion.

"What's going on?" Amy asked.

"You tell me, your alarm went off and you didn't respond at all. Even when I shook you, you were completely out of it. When I finally managed to wake you, the first thing you did was write in that notebook."

"Something feels wrong," Amy said. She opened the notebook and read the latest entry, with Samantha looking over her shoulder. A minute later Samantha spoke up.

"That's messed up." They continued reading.

"I failed," Amy said.

"That's strange, did you go take another tablet?"

"No."

"You don't think…"

"That once this has begun it won't stop?" Amy said, completing the sentence. A hush fell over them both. Amy was thinking about a future where she never slept peacefully again.

"Well if it's still working, maybe it just lasts a short while," Samantha said.

"I have to go back and see him."

"I agree, just go today."

"I can't miss more work without a good excuse."

"Just go on your lunch break then."

"Ok, good idea. Thanks."

"Don't worry, this will be dealt with," Samantha said reassuringly. Amy gave her a tiny smile, a quick hug and then got ready for work as quickly as possible. Even with skipping breakfast she arrived at work late. Sitting down at her desk she noticed a thermos mug with a note stuck to it.

"I didn't see you around when I got coffees, so I put yours into my thermos to keep it warm. Enjoy - David," Amy said under her breath, reading out the note to herself. She walked over to thank him personally, but saw that he was on the phone. When he looked up she waved at him, pointed at the thermos and mouthed 'thank you'. David smiled and gave her a thumbs up before returning his attention to the call. Amy's mood brightened a little, and for a little while she forgot about the events of the previous night and early morning.

Even though she wasn't particularly busy, midday came much sooner than Amy realised. She was dreading going back to that place, feeling uncomfortable due to her bad experience. Not only that though, but a part of her feared the news she might get. She might find out that there was no going back. She left a note on her desk informing anyone that she was out at lunch, grabbed her bag and reluctantly left the office.

Amy took her time getting to Roger's address. But when she arrived, she didn't even bother looking over the place as she had last time and headed straight to his office. She passed through the office doors and stopped. Everything looked completely different. The shape of the room was the same, but all the furniture was different, arranged in a different way, and the receptionist was different. Amy walked over and stood at the desk.

"Hello, maybe you can help me."

"Certainly."

"I'd like to see Roger Butler," Amy said.

"Who?"

"Roger Butler. I saw him here yesterday."

"Oh I see. I was on leave yesterday, let me go ask Mr. Stapes." With that the young woman knocked on the office door behind her, and entered. A few minutes later a gentleman in his sixties accompanied her back out.

"Hello, I'm Douglas Stapes," the man said. When Amy did not respond, he continued.

"I'm afraid I can't help you. You see I was approached by a man recently, who paid me a lot of money for the use of my office for one day. I gave Sheryl a day of paid leave, and gave him the keys for the day. Has something happened?"

"No, it's quite alright. Thank you," Amy said before leaving. She had not gotten the answer as she wanted, but in a way she had gotten an answer, and one she feared. A million different thoughts ran through her head, but they all came back to the same point: she had been duped. Whatever she had taken, it had worked. But the problem was that there was no support, and she had no idea when she would be back to normal.

Rushing back to work, Amy managed to push the problem to the back of her head and get on with things. The afternoon went more or less as normal, however she felt a little flat in the afternoon. She went downstairs to get a coffee, and the caffeine buzz on the way back gave her an idea.

"Another coffee today? Aren't you more a one coffee gal?" David said as he passed Amy's desk.

"Yeah usually, but I just needed an extra boost today." David smiled and continued on his way. When five o'clock struck Amy wished everyone a good weekend and headed straight to the Golden Arms. She needed to discuss the events with Samantha and get her help. Amy didn't think she could execute her new plan without assistance.

"I've been dying to talk all day, fill me in," Samantha said as soon as she spotted Amy.

"I need a drink," Amy said.

"Vodka and cranberry?"

"Swap the cranberry with an energy drink."

"Coming right up." Samantha presented the drink, and Amy took a sip. There was an extra bitterness she was not used to, but it had to be done. She told Samantha the whole story of her lunchtime expedition and how Roger Butler was pulling some sort of scam. Samantha was completely shocked.

"It sounded a bit out of left field, but I never imagined it was that dodgy," Samantha said.

"I know, I'm still a bit stunned. I shouldn't be surprised, with the way everything happened. But here we are."

"What are you going to do?"

"I have a plan. What's the longest anyone has stayed awake?"

"I don't know. About a week?"

"Well let's find out, because I'm doing it. As far as I'm concerned one of two things will happen: either the effects of that drug will wear off, or I'll be so exhausted that I'll pass out and not dream."

"How many coffees have you had today?"

"Just the two."

"Hmm that's probably good, you'll need to slowly increase that as you build tolerance."

"So you'll help me?"

"I'm in. But you've got to promise me that you'll listen to me if I think you're endangering yourself."

"Ok that's a deal," Amy said and stuck out her hand. Samantha shook it heartily and laughed a little. If someone had told her that her best friend would have asked for help to stay awake for days on end, she would have never believed it. Yet here they were. Amy went to start reading her romance novel and stopped herself. It would be too relaxing, she needed stimulation instead. She grabbed a local paper and did the crossword. After that she took a break and ate dinner. Then the word jumbles. Then the cryptic crossword. After much swearing under her breath she completed that too and looked around. The bar was almost empty as it was just about closing time.

After watching Samantha lock up, they walked to the nearest convenience store. Amy bought herself another coffee, and a packet of tablets. They were specially formulated to keep truck drivers awake on long haul trips. Samantha and Amy decided against public transport and caught a taxi home. Once they were through the door, Amy looked around, wondering what to do.

"Have you ever watched late night TV?" Samantha said.

"Not really."

"Now's a good time to start." First up was a terrible dating show which seemed like it had been created more to humiliate than to bring people together. Next it was infomercials. Kitchen tools to slice and dice with ease, clean with the power of steam and even the perfect bra were all available.

"Who buys this stuff?"

"People who watch TV after midnight?" Samantha suggested.

"Fair enough." Amy changed the channel and watched a few music clips. That seemed to have the opposite effect though. She got up, took two tablets to perk up and sat down again. Samantha looked like she was fading and might be sleeping soon. Amy changed the channel again and it was a completely different kind of show. It was some kind of phone-in game show, where people had to guess a word on the screen. It was all guys guessing, and there was no real secret as to why that was. The host of the show was an attractive brunette in her young twenties, wearing a tight blouse which showed off an incredible amount of cleavage. Clearly the advertisers knew that as well, since the commercials that played were all about sexy chat lines and eager ladies on the other end of the phone.

Disgusted, Amy changed the channel again. She found a news broadcast. It was about some new developments going up in a historic part of the city. Then they moved on to tiger cubs at the zoo and similar fluff pieces. Fifteen to twenty minutes later the stories seemed to repeat. Only this time they used a new bit of footage, that had the mayor praising the new direction the city was moving in. Becoming bored Amy changed the channel again.

After watching some of a slow moving period movie made at least fifty years ago, Amy flicked around again to find something new. Like clockwork she happened to see the new building site development story again. The company building the development was called Keystone Endeavours. She changed it again. An ultra-violent foreign film. Then soccer.

Hours later she felt a bit drowsy so took more tablets. Samantha had long since fell asleep. Amy started to get jittery. She was changing channels erratically, yet uncannily landing on the news channel each time they were discussing the new city development on a historic site, endorsed by the mayor and being built by Keystone Endeavours. After a while she stopped hearing the words and just focused on the pictures. There was something of interest there, that teased her and then vanished. It didn't make any sense to her though, as the story lacked compelling images. There was some stock footage of the location, and then of the mayor's speech and it was interspersed with reporter commentary and the logo of Keystone Endeavours. The key with the strange markings and shape.

"No way!" Amy shouted and practically jumped to her feet. She ran to her bedroom and fetched her notebooks. She only had to flip past one page. There it was, it wasn't her imagination. She raced back to the lounge room and shook Samantha.

"Samantha!"

"Wha…what time is it?"

"Don't worry about that. Look at this!"

"That's the picture you drew. What about it?"

"It's exactly the same as the logo for Keystone Endeavours."

"Who are they?" Samantha asked, still not completely awake.

"They are a construction company doing the new development over that old historic site."

"Haven't heard about it."

"It's been all over the news."

"Wake me up when something important happens," Samantha said and closed her eyes again. Amy was completely energised, but she didn't know why. But she did know that there were no such things as coincidences. She tuned into the news channel again and watched with renewed interest. Picking up a notebook, she wrote down some key facts that she had gleaned from the news segment. The project had been in the planning stages for ten years. The same company, Keystone Endeavours, was attached to the project for its whole duration. A whole block of the city was being redeveloped. The final stages of public comment were in process.

Amy couldn't understand her exact feelings, but she just knew that this was important. She closed the notebook and thought about what she should do next. It was the early hours of Saturday morning, she couldn't do the kind of research she wanted to do until Monday. Plus there was a chance, this was all due to her altered mental state. So, she just had to deal with the most pressing issue, her dreams and sleep issues. There were still a few hours until sunrise, so she decided to do something constructive and cleaned up the kitchen.

As sunlight peeked through the kitchen windows, Amy was starting to feel sleepy again. She shook herself, both mentally and physically, and threw on some comfortable clothes, grabbed her wallet and left the apartment. She walked a few blocks to her local newsagent. She bought a copy of the Heaton Herald, Saturday edition, and continued on her way. Nearby she found a cafe open and bought herself another cappuccino. Walking back home, she passed the newsagent and had a brain wave. She walked inside, hunted through their stationery section and found herself a large cork board. She bought it, with some pins and twine.

"If I'm going to have this strange idea for an investigation, I may as well have some fun with it," Amy thought to herself. She took her time walking home, struggled through the front door with her purchases and coffee, and dumped everything in the lounge room.

Samantha was still asleep, so Amy leafed through the paper and found the main thing she was looking for: an article about the new development with a photo of the mayor giving his speech. She cut it out of the paper and set it aside. Looking around the apartment, there was only one hanging hook provided and it had a nice land-scape painting hanging on it. Amy took down the painting and hung up the cork board. She pinned the newspaper article to it, and stood back to marvel at her handiwork. She heard a rustling noise and saw Samantha starting to stir.

"Good morning. Want some breakfast?" Amy said.

"Ugh what time is it?"

"Nine."

"Way too early for the weekend. Did you sleep?"

"Nope."

"Ok good. I kinda crashed out there. Did you say breakfast?"

"Yeah how about eggs?"

"Great." Samantha drifted off again and Amy made fried eggs on toast for them both. When she brought it out to the lounge room she saw Samantha was up and looking at the cork board.

"That's my new project," Amy said.

"Well I preferred the painting, but I'll give it a chance." They sat down to eat, took turns showering and getting ready.

"Any plans for today?" Samantha said.

"No, but I'll need some more caffeine in a couple of hours."

"Yeah let's go out. We can get some coffees and I want to test something." Amy nodded in agreement and they left the apartment. They walked to Clarfield Park and sat down at the cafe right on the edge. Amy ordered the largest straight black coffee they had, and Samantha a latte.

"Tell me about your test," Amy said.

"Well you told me about your first dream with the animals. Let's see how much effect it had."

"Sure, but let's not jump straight in and work our way up."

"Absolutely." Amy paid for the coffees and they both set off into the park. At first they saw dogs around, but none were near.

"Feel anything?"

"Not yet." Once they were further into the park, Samantha decided to try something different and they headed off the path. Walking through the grass they saw a lot more dogs being walked. Some got closer but were kept tightly on their leashes.

"How about now?"

"I'm ok but feel a little uneasy."

"That's fine, let's try another area." Samantha led the way to a more open area of the park. The dogs were off the leashes and chasing each other around, playing fetch with their owners and being similarly active. They walked through the middle of the space with dogs paying them little attention. Then a tennis ball landed at their feet. A giant dog bounded at them full speed, but was focused entirely on the ball. Once he had it, he held it in his jaws and looked at Amy.

"He wants you to throw it." Amy understood that but was a little frozen. Woodenly she reached down and carefully placed a few fingers around the ball, where the dog was not biting it. It was slimy and wet. The dog still held the ball, but was waiting patiently.

"Go on," Samantha said. Amy applied a little more pressure, then the dog suddenly released its grip and panted expectantly. His tail thumped the ground a few times. Amy reached back and hurled the ball as far as she could, then started walking in the opposite direction.

"I'm pretty impressed at your composure."

"I'm still not comfortable, and didn't feel great. But I wasn't freaking out too much," Amy said. They both agreed that it was a good outcome and walked out of the park. Amy sat down and felt completely drained. It was a combination of the tension of the dog encounter being released, and also her body wanting to sleep. Samantha fetched an energy drink and returned.

"Look, you did great back there. Would it be so bad to have that reaction to all the little things that you fear?"

"No, but I want to be the one to choose that. I don't want it to be something forced on me."

"Fair enough. Let's get you through this weekend. I've got a house party to go to tonight, come with me."

"Sounds great."

Amy spent the afternoon keeping herself busy and alternating between many different ways to stay awake. She splashed water on her face and wrists, listened to angry music, did push ups and star jumps, played chess and did all the puzzles in the newspaper. She shared a light dinner of salad with Samantha before they headed out. The taxi dropped them off at a moderately sized, but largely uninspiring brick house in the middle of suburbia.

"These are friends of mine that I know through work. They're always inviting me to these things, and I figured this time why not," Samantha explained as they walked in. The house was completely full, and Amy had to push through people just to get to the backyard. There were tables set up with drinks, a barbecue going and loud music pumping through giant speakers.

"Well I don't think it's possible to sleep here. Great job Samantha!" Amy thought to herself. She grabbed a glass off the table that looked like punch and tasted fruity. She tried to mingle, but it was difficult to have any conversations. She didn't get past her job and her name in most instances, and instantly forgot the names of the people she met.

"I know it's not really your scene, but this loud mess is what you need right now," Samantha said into her ear and Amy nodded at her.

Hours passed and the numbers of people slowly filtered down, as they went home or to other parties. Samantha introduced Amy to the host of the party.

"This is Amy and she doesn't want to sleep tonight."

"Hi, I'm Daniel and you've come to the right place."

"You're right there," Amy said.

"A couple of the guys were thinking of going to a local rave tonight, if you're interested."

"We should totally go to that," Samantha said.

"I'm not sure."

"Trust me." Amy didn't have any better ideas so she went along with it. They found the other group, introduced themselves and headed over to the rave. It was held in a dodgy looking warehouse in the middle of a commercial area. At least it was fairly well lit. Amy was pretty nervous, but Samantha squeezed her hand and walked her in. The hypnotic dance music was already pumping and the giant space was full of people in a mix of dancing, jumping and gyrating. The strobe lighting was perfectly in sync with the music and it looked like people were playing a musical version of traffic lights. Whenever the light flashed they were in a new position, with the in-between movements obscured or invisible.

A girl in her late teens offered a bottle of water and some pills to Amy but she politely refused.

"The unknown magical pill I've already taken is plenty for now," Amy thought to herself. Still, she tried to go along with the rest of it. She got herself in sync with the rest and danced on for an unknown time. Suddenly the music stopped and she looked up. The entire crowd was stopping, some visibly drained, others still energised. She walked outside into the early dawn and found Samantha outside.

"I never realised what a fun house mate I have," Samantha said with a smile. Amy just shook her head and laughed. She caught a taxi home with Samantha and made sure that she got into bed. Next Amy walked over to the newsagent, still in her outfit from the previous night.

"I must look like a sight," Amy thought to herself, considering the night she had just had, in combination with the fact that she had not slept since Friday morning. She bought a big book of puzzles with her newspaper and a coffee.

Amy spent the morning between her newspaper and puzzles. When Samantha awoke they went to the local pool for a swim and had a light brunch in a local cafe.

"Are you going to sleep tonight?" Samantha asked.

"No I think I can make it."

"What about work?"

"I'll go in, it'll keep me busy. If I can't function they will send me home sick."

"Are you sure about that?"

"I've got to be sure. Either it's done or I just pass out." Samantha didn't argue with that, seeing the determined look on Amy's face. In the afternoon Amy read through an editorial about the new development by Keystone and cut it out for the board. The new complex would contain a shopping area on the bottom with lots of apartments on top. It would loom over the skyline and had many different people both for it and against it. The paper was siding with the locals who viewed the area as historic and wanted it preserved with something that fit better. However the current situation gave them far less bargaining power. All the buildings that had been on that block were either destroyed or replaced already.

Those siding with the proposal cited the economic benefits as well as the creation of jobs and living areas in a city lacking in residences. The mayor was spearheading that movement, using it as a platform for re-election. The editorial summed up its article by saying that progress was inevitable, but must always be kept in check to make sure that things of importance and value were not being lost in the process. Amy found herself leaning towards those against the development, but couldn't really put her position into words yet.

Samantha was for the proposal, having no real attachment to the old buildings there and the area. She pointed out that she never went there now, and would at least visit the new shopping complex a few times. Amy spent her evening struggling with sleep. She had trouble concentrating on puzzles, the television was not engaging enough and music was only a temporary help. She spent much of the night pacing the room, and committing details of the news articles to memory. She alternated that behaviour with cleaning the house from top to bottom and doing clothes washing. She knew that she just had to keep awake until it was late enough to go into the office.

CHAPTER SIX

CONTINUATION

Amy was extra careful with her makeup, trying to hide the effects of not sleeping. She felt an overwhelming sense of exhaustion which coloured everything she did. Just as well she had started to get ready ridiculously early, because it was taking a lot longer than usual. The morning was already warming up considerably, which meant the sooner she got into the air conditioning of the office the better.

Stepping outside, she felt the still weak morning sun to be blazing and bright. She made it to the shady safety of the bus stop and waited patiently. At the same time, she was planning her next coffee. The bus arrived promptly and it was cool inside. Too cold in fact, but Amy welcomed the chill as it kept her alert. Every bump and jolt from the bus irritated her but again she was thankful for the assistance in staying awake.

The first sip of coffee was wonderful and Amy rode that feeling all the way up to her office floor. She glanced out the giant glass windows, but the view just reminded her of the aborted dream about heights and she moved on. She was in the office a little early, so she used the work computer to look up the company information for Keystone Endeavours and printed herself a copy for later. Then she slowly and methodically started her work. Just when she started to feel drowsy a welcome interruption occurred.

"Good morning Amy, how was your weekend?" David asked.

"Good. Busy. How about you?"

"It was good. I went out, caught up with friends and got lots of sleep."

"I'm envious."

"You already had a coffee today?" David said, spotting the cup on her desk and unsure of what to do with the other coffee in his hand.

"Yeah but I'm due for another, thanks." David handed over the coffee cup and Amy had a sip immediately.

"Are you ok Amy?"

"Yeah, didn't get a good sleep over the weekend. I just need to make it through the day."

"Ah ok well I'll make sure I drop in later to see if you are asleep," David said with a grin and walked off to his desk. Before Amy could get any more work done, she heard more footsteps approaching.

"Hey Amy, I like your strategy," Margaret said, winking.

"What do you mean?"

"David's already getting you coffees, now he's going to check in on you too."

"That's not..."

"Don't be embarrassed, I'm happy for you. A bit of proactive action is good on your part, he had another date on the weekend."

"Ok thanks for the updates," Amy said with clear frustration. Margaret smiled and walked off. Other associates remarked on Amy looking a bit tired, but didn't make any further enquiries. Amy got some work done, and was surprised by Samantha around midday.

"Hey there, got lunch plans?"

"Not really."

"Let's go then!" Samantha said. Over wraps and coffee they chatted about how Amy fared in the morning.

"I have to admit, I'm surprised you're doing so well," Samantha said.

"It's so tough, everything is annoying me and I think I'm going up the wall. I have to check everything I do two to three times to make sure I haven't done something silly. Just as well I don't have a lot of work on right now."

"You'll be fine, you used to do this all the time at university."

"That's true, but it felt different then. More fun."

"When are you going to sleep?"

"I think I've pushed myself enough. Tonight or to-morrow night, depending on when I crash."

"I agree. Wait for me to get home so there's someone around when you crash. I'll look out for you."

"Ha-ha you looking for a career change to nursing?"

"Don't laugh, I need to figure something out. I can't work at bars all my life."

"In that case, I'm happy to be of assistance!" Amy said laughing. The coffee, the food and the laugh boosted her energy levels. She managed better back at work, and was mostly present. It was all comparative though, her reactions and senses were significantly dulled. The office was sympathetic though, and David didn't even mention it when he caught her staring into space with a glazed over look. Margaret was similarly kind, but more direct.

"Sweetie, it's time you went home. It's close to time, and you've done a good effort." Amy couldn't even argue effectively to suggest that she should stay. She did have the presence of mind to take the documents home she had printed in the morning.

On the way home she almost caught the wrong bus twice. Once she was on the right one, she missed her stop and had to walk back. As soon as she arrived home, she felt idiotic.

"I should have met Samantha at her work," Amy thought to herself. But she was home now, so she settled in and busied herself. She made the rather sensible decision that tonight she had to sleep, it was just time. So her first jobs were to set up her bedroom and change the sheets. She loved the feeling of freshly washed sheets and wanted to have the best sleep possible. When she felt drowsy she went outside and walked around the block. That didn't quite do the trick, so she did five star jumps. Anyone watching would have burst out in laughter, since she was almost asleep with each one.

"Stay awake Amy," she said out loud and went straight to the bathroom and splashed water on her face. Then she smacked herself on the side of the face.

"Ouch!" Amy cried out, looking at herself in surprise. She attempted to do more word jumbles but couldn't concentrate. Then she wandered through the house, starting jobs and then wandering off to do others. She stared at her new cork board, and looked over the articles she had pinned to it.

"Scissors, ostriches, underwear, neutral, dog, rabbit, elongated…dial!" she shouted out, pointing at the photo of the mayor. With a satisfied look on her face she collapsed on the floor, asleep.

Samantha arrived home just after midnight. It was strange that she couldn't see any lights on in the apartment. She unlocked the door, turned on the lounge room light and saw Amy lying on the floor. With a gasp she rushed over and checked her breathing and pulse. Everything was normal, she was asleep. Breathing a sigh of relief, she went back through the front door and knocked on the door of their neighbour. A few seconds later, a bearded man in his late twenties opened the door.

"Hey John, I'm sorry but I need your help for a minute."

"Ok give me a minute," John said and closed the door. He reappeared out in the corridor a minute later. Samantha led him into the apartment and pointed at Amy.

"She totally crashed, she's fine just exhausted. Can you help me get her into bed?"

"Sure." John positioned himself carefully and began to lift Amy from under her arms. Samantha grabbed the feet and they slowly walked Amy into her bedroom and placed her on the bed.

"Thanks again, I'll take it from here," Samantha said.

"No problem I was up anyway. Take care," John said, then left. Samantha stripped Amy down and pulled the covers over her. She gave Amy a kiss on the cheek and tousled her hair lightly.

"You look so peaceful, I hope you're ok in there," Samantha said softly then partially closed the bedroom door.

CHAPTER SEVEN

DREAM TWO PART TWO

I was back on the cold and windy rooftop. I was tired, and sick of being tired. I looked around at the great heights surrounding me, the lack of barriers and the endless drops. I just didn't care. It didn't seem important. I sat down and tried to think about why I was there. I knew that it was because of a former misstep. But I couldn't remember why. I looked over at the roof opposite and the doorway there. That was clearly the way to go, but it didn't seem like much of an obstacle.

At the same time I felt no urgency. Distant storms with brilliant lightning and crashing thunder created some anxiety, but there was just too much noise. Storms and heights and whatever else, I couldn't pay proper attention to it. My arms and legs were lethargic, and I had no motivation to do anything. I felt like there should have been, but it was all fine. But something was not quite right. I could not rest. I needed to rest. I looked over to the doorway and it was inviting. It was shimmering white and contained an inner glow.

I heaved myself up from the seated position with a lot of effort. My whole body was lead and trying to fall through the floor. I turned and paced over to the opposite edge. I didn't bother looking, I knew what was there. I spun once more and looked over at my objective. It looked like it was a long way away.

"Here we go," I said. Then I pushed myself forward and gained momentum. I got faster and faster and my limbs felt lighter and lighter. Then I jumped. I soared over the world and had the foolishness to look down. I panicked momentarily but had no time for it as I saw my destination looming. Only it was at the wrong height, I wasn't going to make it. I strained forward with my hands and caught the edge, bracing myself with my feet against the tower.

"Fine," I said with a mixture of tiredness and determination. I pretended that I was at the edge of a swimming pool and getting out. In the one movement I pushed down on my hands and moved the rest of my body up. I managed to get a knee on the edge and awkwardly levered myself on to the roof. I stood, a bit wobbly, and turned to look behind me. A huge chasm separated the two towers and roofs.

"At least there's no doing that again," I thought to myself. I walked up to the doorway and tried to peer through it. All I could see was white. I could feel the warmth from it, and as I got closer to absorb as much as I could I accidentally stepped through.

CHAPTER EIGHT

STAGE FOUR

The afternoon sun gently warmed Amy's face, and initially she could not distinguish it from the warmth she felt in her dream. Gradually though, she noticed it was different. She awoke, found her notebook and wrote in a fast yet calm manner. Next she grabbed the art notebook and finished the image she had started drawing before. Looking at it, she saw that her drawing was a gold bar.

"That's interesting," she thought to herself, but not thinking too deeply. She walked out to the lounge room and saw Samantha seated on the couch, reading a newspaper.

"Hey you're up!"

"Yeah, what's the time?"

"One-thirty."

"Oh no work..."

"It's fine, I gave them a call and they expected it after your performance yesterday."

"It's a bit hazy, what did I do?"

"Nothing crazy, you were just exhausted."

"Good," Amy said and sat down with a sigh.

"How do you feel?" Samantha asked. Amy thought for a second before replying.

"I'm pretty good. Still feel a little drained."

"How's things on the dream front?"

"Oh still the same, but I made it through."

"Really? Oh well we will think of something. Are you hungry?"

"Ravenous."

"I bought some stuff earlier, I'll make you some sandwiches."

"Thanks!" Amy called out as Samantha left for the kitchen. Amy looked around the room, unsure of what to do. She spotted the papers she had taken from work and flipped through them. It was a registry listing for the company formation of Keystone Endeavours. One name in particular stood out.

"Walter Goldberg," Amy said. Samantha didn't hear. Where had Amy heard that before? Not heard, but seen. She darted back to her room and found her notebook. The last drawing she had done was of a gold bar. There was a symbol of some kind pressed into the gold as well. She took the paper and the notebook out to show Samantha.

"Check this out," she said, showing Samantha the drawing first.

"Looks like a bar of gold."

"Now look at this."

"You mean the guy called Goldberg?"

"Yeah isn't that a bit of a coincidence?"

"Are you still going on about this?"

"My first drawing was the emblem of their company."

"Yeah it's strange, but there's no connection."

"If you say so, but I think there is," Amy said. She took the list of directors and pinned it up on her cork board, then wrote the words 'Gold Bars' on the paper.

"Hey, don't you have your appointment with Dr. Nelson this afternoon?"

"Yeah, I'm a bit apprehensive about it," Amy said.

"Are you going to tell him?"

"No."

"But he's your therapist, you've been seeing him for years."

"I know, but look how much that helped me. I'm not really fond of my current situation, but I feel like I've achieved more in the last few days than in my entire time with Dr. Nelson."

"I totally agree, just thought you would feel different since you've seen him every week or two."

"It would be logical to tell him something, but I just don't feel that it's right. Let's see how we go," Amy said. Samantha shrugged and walked off to her room. Amy spent the afternoon worrying about whether she had made the right decision. Either way, she knew that being cautious was the right approach.

Amy arrived at three forty-eight and waited at the reception desk. A young blonde woman with glasses walked over and smiled.

"Hi again Amy, how are you doing?"

"I'm good thanks. How are you?"

"Fantastic! Please take a seat I'll let you know when Dr. Nelson is ready."

"Thanks," Amy said and made her way to the couches. Rifling through the available magazines, she found a trashy celebrity mag and picked it out. She flipped through the pages without paying much attention. It was an older issue, and all of the gossip had either been forgotten or proved fictitious. Thankfully she did not have to wait long.

"The doctor will see you now." Amy nodded and rose from her seat. She took the practised walk down the hallway and into the last door on the left. Dr. Nelson was seated in the room, wearing his usual attire: a neatly pressed white shirt, blue and black chequered tie and dark navy trousers with brown leather shoes. His grey hair was combed back and he looked at her from behind his tortoise shell framed glasses. He had his legs crossed and was in the ready position with a notepad and pen.

"Hello Amy."

"Hi Dr. Nelson."

"Again as always - please call me Richard," he said. Amy nodded and lay down on the long couch provided.

"How was your week?" Dr. Nelson began.

"The usual."

"Work going well?"

"Yeah."

"How did you feel? Did you have any anxiety?"

"Nothing out of the ordinary."

"Now that is out of the ordinary. Every single time you come here and tell me about every single little thing that happened. Why the change?"

"How long have I been coming here?"

"Over three years."

"How often do I come in?"

"Three times a month."

"So that's over one hundred visits?"

"Correct."

"Over one hundred visits of me telling you all the silly little things that caused me anxiety, and yet strangely no change in my behaviour or any improvement. Isn't that telling?"

"Aha I see you are experiencing some disillusionment. That is perfectly natural, these processes take time and progress is not linear."

"Zero progress is also not linear."

"I've explained this to you before, we continue to work until we hit a breakthrough. You do remember agreeing to these sessions as a treatment in lieu of any medication correct?"

"I do."

"So what's this all about?" Dr Nelson asked. Amy felt his intense gaze on her, and wondered the same thing. She hadn't come along to start an argument. A part of her felt angry though, and unsatisfied. She deserved better than this, talking to this man over and over with no change. The feeling built up in intensity. Amy stood up and stared directly at him.

"I've had enough. I'm not going to waste a moment more of my life in this room, telling you about the things I have experienced."

"Fantastic Amy, this is the breakthrough we have been waiting for. Let's call it for today, and reconvene next week to talk about it."

"No. You won't see me in here again!" Amy announced and stormed out. Dr. Nelson watched her go with interest, then picked up the phone to make a call.

Amy felt jubilant as she walked out of the building. She realised that she had her fears, and her problems and whatever else. But it was pointless just complaining about them over and over. It was more important to focus on her life and the things she could do. And the things she could work on. She continued walking on in a joyous manner but her mood didn't last. Ahead of her were suddenly throngs of people, chanting something. Amy walked closer to try and hear what they were saying.

"No to misery. Yes to history!" Amy was annoyed at the commotion they were making, and how crowded the streets had become. She became uneasy, and looked for an alternate route. The main street was completely blocked off, with both sides around it crammed full of people. She had walked for blocks, out of her way, to avoid the whole mess. Part of her wondered if there was a faster way through the crowd, but the risk didn't seem worth the reward.

She spent the rest of the evening both looking forward to, and dreading sleep. She was excited by the potential of what she might accomplish, but also scared of what might happen. She didn't want to fail again. Neither did she want to spend days awake, that experience had not been particularly fun. She hadn't properly recovered from that, and it might take a while. Eventually the debate was ended when she decided that it was important to make it in to work the next day. She prepared for bed as she usually did, and tried to make herself as comfortable as possible.

Sleep did not come as easily as she had hoped, due to her oversleeping earlier in the day. But it did come, and Amy resigned herself to it.

CHAPTER NINE

DREAM THREE

I was walking through a fairground. There were lots of rides, stalls of varying kinds and mini restaurants to eat at. One ride was a rollercoaster so big I couldn't see the top. I wandered close to the stalls and had a look. Some were selling toys, others were skill based games. There were a few people at each stall, evenly distributed. Every time I stopped to look at a stall in more detail, other people seemed to be attracted to it. To avoid a crowd forming, I would move on as soon as I noticed that happening.

I found a man giving away free balloons, with nobody paying him any attention. As soon as I started to walk towards him, masses of people suddenly had the same idea. It was incredibly frustrating. I slipped away from the crowds and found a nice empty space with some grass. I sat down and watched the crowds moving around. After a time I noticed a pattern. Anywhere I focused on and started considering a good place to investigate would attract all the nearby people.

For a time I seemingly controlled the crowds that way, with just my gaze. I hadn't tired of it yet when I heard something above me. It was a low rumbling indicating a storm. I stood up and started to look for a place to take shelter, just in case. Everyone else had the same idea, and any spot with a bit of cover was stuffed full of people. Grumbling to myself, I continued on hoping I got lucky with the weather.

The first few drops on my head, I ignored out of principle. The light rain had me walking faster and the intensity of the rain increased perfectly in step with my transition to full on running. I came to the end of the fairgrounds and had a decision before me. Wait at the edge of a group of people and get a little bit wet, or squeeze through them all to be completely dry, right in the middle of the pack. I opted to get a little bit wet. The wind picked up and made my position all the more uncomfortable but I stuck to it.

A short while later, a thought occurred to me. Since the crowds were completely dependent on my actions, there had to be a reason why. The reason eluded me, but the thought remained. I held on to it, knowing it was important somehow. As the rain started to lessen the crowds started to thin out. I followed one of the larger groups, at a safe distance. It looked like they were leaving the fairground. It felt right so I continued along with them.

At the end of the path were stairs going down. I hesitated and looked back, seeing a large cluster of people advancing. I started down the stairs to try my luck. The stairway went a long way and as far as I could look ahead there were people. But at the same time there were many behind me so the best I could do was keep walking. The people ahead had started to form larger groups, so I guessed that there was some sort of blockage up ahead.

There was definitely something slowing everyone down, but I couldn't see it from where I was. I willed whatever it was to clear, since I didn't want to be sandwiched between masses of people. Slowly people were filtering through and I could get a better picture of what was ahead. It looked like turnstiles, which explained the funnel effect. I pressed on getting closer and closer, slowly but surely. People were packing in a little closer around me, which really elevated my heart rate, but there was enough progress to keep me comparatively happy.

All of a sudden I was at the front, right in front of the turnstiles. I went to walk through and realised I had no ticket to operate it. I panicked, looking around for a way to progress. I saw people next to me walking through by using their hands to press on the gate. I tried doing that and a beep sounded. I quickly pressed forward, glad that the turnstile was not locked and actually turned and continued on my way.

Then it dawned on me, I was in a train station. It was packed full of people, but there were little spots of breathing room here and there. The big room I was in was almost full and there were only two stairwells down to the platform. The sheer volume of people had raised the temperature and the feeling was very stuffy and oppressive. I wanted to move on as soon as possible so I headed for the nearest stairwell.

I had to push through a fair number of people, and dodge plenty of others on my way. It just reinforced so clearly why I hated crowds, and why they freaked me out. The masses of people, their inconsistent behaviour and the lack of personal space was all overwhelming. I carried myself through knowing that I would be out soon.

The platform itself was no better, packed full of sweaty smelly people and robbed of fresh air. The pockets of space were smaller here, and on the whole it was unpleasant. I looked up at the train signal, and saw a list of stations. There were twelve in all, but the station names were hard to read, as if they were scrambled. I was missing something.

A train arrived, and nobody got off, but the hordes of people crammed on. I pushed my way through with them, and found myself about half a meter inside the carriage. There was a pole nearby to hold on to, but I couldn't quite reach it. Stability was not an issue however, as when the train pulled away I noticed that it was so packed I could not move. The train crawled by at what felt like a minimal pace and after it hit its top speed it started to slow almost immediately.

When the train stopped, a few people around me left and I could breathe again, if only briefly. Those on the platform, wishing to get on, looked at me strangely. I think they were waiting to see if I wanted to get off the train. I looked back at them, shook my head and they slowly filled the empty spaces.

This same ritual continued for the next few stops. However each time the distance between stations doubled. The smells and stuffy air and unpleasantness of the situation also continued to escalate. At the fourth stop when the people on the platform looked at me expectantly, I almost leapt off the train in my hurry to sample the improved air quality. The platform I was on seemed very similar to the first one with the same distribution of people.

I waited on the platform for a time, and it wasn't pleasant. There was no doubt it was better than being on the train though. Each time a train arrived it was as crazily packed as the one I had left, if not more. The niggling thought from before returned, that the patterns and behaviours around me were to achieve a single purpose. I thought upon that for a moment.

Time and time again I was being directed to be amongst crowds, something I both feared and hated. The train was the worst, but I was given an opportunity to get off it whenever I wanted to. Suddenly I had a brain wave.

"It's not about forcing me into a situation, it's about forcing me into a decision," I thought to myself. I had to choose the icky crowds if I wanted to progress. I was aware in the back of my mind about a similar situation, but I couldn't bring up the details.

With that new line of thinking my perception changed. I looked up at the station guide and the last station name unscrambled itself. It said 'White Door'. I knew that was my destination, and that I had to get there. So when the next train arrived I took a deep breath, steeled myself and stepped inside. The train ride was as before, but with a few twists. The platforms we arrived at were less and less packed. Some even wafted a sweet perfume, trying to tempt me off the train. The last stop before my destination was completely empty, well lit with lounge chairs and fruit bowls. I saw it for the trap that it was, although I almost unconsciously stepped out. That's how much I wanted out, my body was trying to go of its own accord.

Midway to the last station the train broke down. The tunnel around us was well lit and some people were walking around outside. The tunnel was more and more full of people and only those in my carriage were still on the train.

"Typical," I thought to myself. I moved to get out and the sardine tin of people followed me in unison. Once outside, the people ahead had helpfully stopped moving. I had to push through them all one at a time, brush past embarrassingly and feel their sweat as I passed by.

The occasional person was also moving, so I had to watch and anticipate their movements as well. I just felt like screaming. Any time I started to gain some momentum someone large would be planted right in front of me and I'd have to change tack. The promise of the platform was always around the next corner. Suddenly it was there, and in the middle of the platform a giant white doorway. It looked good. However I couldn't access any stairs to get up on the platform. I pushed through crowds all along the length of it, trying to see.

I found a small gap I could climb into, but I would have to keep low. I pushed myself up and was cramped up on all fours on the grimy platform. There was no room to stand up, so I did the only thing that seemed logical: I crawled. On my hands and knees I crawled, threading my way through the people. I paused occasionally to gauge my position then continued. When I spotted a sign of light I forced myself upright.

There was a large man, sweat dripping off him profusely, sitting cross legged in front of the doorway. I asked him to move, but he didn't seem to notice. I gingerly brushed past and awkwardly stepped over him and then basically fell into the warm light. What a relief.

CHAPTER TEN

REM

Amy awoke and continued the ritual of note taking. Her alarm sounded, but she didn't respond and continued writing. Samantha stumbled into the room sleepily and turned the alarm off. She sat down on the bed and watched Amy. Amy was deep in concentration, drawing something. It was an ornate old style clock face, with all the hands pointing at twelve.

"How are you?" Samantha asked.

"I'm pretty good. Skimming through this, I did well last night."

"What did you draw?" Amy showed her the drawing.

"That looks familiar, I've definitely seen it before."

"I don't know it, let me know if you remember," Amy said. Samantha gave her a quick hug then shuffled off to her room and back to bed. Amy prepared for work and began her normal commute. It was peak hour in the city and full of people. She still felt her discomfort and anxiety around the crowds, but it was muted somewhat so she just ignored it. Similarly the dizzying heights and glass displays after leaving the elevator didn't register the same way they usually did.

Her main concern was getting in to the office and catching up on her work. She felt incredibly embarrassed at all the time she was having off.

"At least I made it in on time," she thought to herself. Amy sat down at her desk and busied herself. Hearing someone approach, she looked up.

"Good morning Amy, good to see you in today," David said, smiling. He handed her a coffee.

"Thanks David. Yeah sometimes you just need to let your body catch up."

"Of course. Is everything ok?"

"Yeah it's all fine."

"I'm glad. Remember that I'm here if you ever need someone to talk to."

"Sure, thanks."

"I'll see you later."

"Bye David," Amy said and looked around for Margaret. Like clockwork she appeared out of nowhere, as if by coincidence.

"Hello Amy, good to see you back in the office."

"Good morning Margaret."

"David doesn't seem too enthusiastic about this girl he's dating, I reckon he'll call it off soon before it becomes more serious."

"Thanks for the update," Amy said with some tired-ness and sarcasm.

"I'm just looking out for you."

"I know. Look he's nice, but I would die if I went out on a limb and he said no to me. I wouldn't be able to show myself here again."

"Well for starters he wouldn't say no, and things would be fine here if that did happen. You'll see."

"Thank-you and good-bye," Amy said emphatically and Margaret smiled and returned to her office.

Amy went out to lunch and grabbed herself some su-shi rolls so that she could do more work on her lunch break. She had only been gone for ten minutes when she returned to find an unmarked envelope on her desk. Be-fore opening the letter, she asked around the office and nobody had seen who had left it. She carefully looked over the envelope, and saw no markings on either side. She opened it and found a newspaper clip inside. It was dated from a few years ago, and told the story of how an old clock was restored and donated to the museum. It had come from an old theatre that had burned down. The most intriguing part was the photo of the clock. The face looked exactly the same as her drawing, right down to the details and the position of the hands.

She felt an intense dread for a moment, worried that someone was following her progress. Her anxiety in-creased exponentially and many crazy scenarios went through her head. Then a rather logical one did: Saman-tha. They had discussed the clock in the morning, it made sense that she would drop by an article that she remembered. Samantha was also quirky enough to just leave it without any message for fun. Amy drew a deep breath and relaxed. She reminded herself to not freak out over ordinary things.

With that crisis averted, she thought over what the clue meant. She broke it down to two potential things: either the clock itself was a clue, or the location it had come from. She could investigate both those options by visiting the museum. A quick call to the museum revealed that their closing time was seven o'clock. That would leave her plenty of time to go there after work. Until then she put the thought from her mind.

Amy left the office at exactly five, having caught up on her work and feeling good about completing a full day.

"Let's see if I can work a whole week," she thought to herself. Her life had been turned upside down so much in the last week that she looked forward to a sense of normality. Although the more she thought about it, normality was overrated. She had put up with so much in her normal life, things she shouldn't have to. The fears, the therapy, the loneliness and lack of career progress. It was a holding pattern while she chose not to move on in her life. No more!

She arrived at the Municipal Museum, and visited the free exhibit titled 'Our Local History'. She browsed through a collection of photographs, important documents and small items of note. The next room had larger things, such as artefacts rescued from old buildings or donated from generous benefactors. Onward she continued, until she reached the last room. It was much larger and housed more substantial relics. The centrepiece was the clock face. Just looking at it formed a detailed mental picture, the one she had drawn from.

Amy walked closer and inspected the clock. It was too large for a display case, and had a red velvet rope around it. The face was an off white, with roman numerals for the numbers. The backing was some kind of metal, and looked like it had attachments for a much bigger mechanism. She read the plaque below, skimming through the details. It was originally installed in the old town hall. Then it was moved to the Orphello Theatre. There it remained, even when the theatre was repurposed twenty years ago as a movie theatre. Three years ago, when the Orphello Theatre was destroyed by a fire, the clock was salvaged and brought to the museum for preservation.

Amy took notes of the names and dates of where it had been, and had one last walk around the clock. She noticed a cavity in the back of the clock and peered closer.

"Quite interesting isn't it?" an older woman said as she approached. She was very neatly dressed, with pearl earrings and reading glasses hanging from her neck.

"Yes, I'm trying to work it out," Amy said.

"You can see here where it was originally attached to another mechanism. The compartment here was used to store tools, springs and such for maintenance."

"I see, that's quite clever."

"Indeed. Originally the cavity was designed to keep important historical documents, before it was re-purposed."

"I like it. It has so many stories to tell."

"Yes, it's a fantastic piece. As you can see from its placement, it is the crown amongst our many treasures."

"Definitely. Thanks for your insights," Amy said and then finalised her notes. She placed them back in her bag and left the museum. As she walked she thought over what she had seen. The clock no longer had anything of value in it, if it once had. Her only remaining clue then was to have a look at where it had come from. She had a street name for where the theatre was, and she had a fairly good idea of the area.

In the end it was quite easy to find, the whole area had been cordoned off for the upcoming construction. Standing nearby wasn't really helping her, she needed a better look. Even then she wasn't sure what she would find. However the light was fading, so she made a mental note to return later and investigate further.

On her way home she stopped by the Golden Arms and looked in. The place was jam packed and Samantha looked incredibly busy. Amy got Samantha's attention, waved, and then continued home. Amy thought again about her strange, impromptu investigations. She wondered what the link was to her dreams. What she did know though was that she had to move forward and keep doing whatever felt natural.

When she arrived home, Amy pinned the newspaper article about the clock to her board. Then she tore off the page with her notes and attached that too. She decided to wait up until Samantha got home and thank her for the information and show her progress. Amy drifted off, not quite asleep but not quite awake. The noise of the door opening and closing woke her up. She waved at Samantha, and pointed to the board. Samantha walked closer and had a look.

"Oh wow, great work. How did you find it? That's exactly the clock I was thinking of," Samantha said. Amy instantly became more alert.

"What do you mean, didn't you drop the clipping by my work today?"

"No, I was lounging around here all day."
"Then who left this for me?" Samantha shrugged, but shared Amy's apprehension. Amy took a long time to get to sleep, and eventually crashed with her bedroom light on.

DREAM FOUR

I was in a well-lit street around dusk. Within moments my perception changed, and I had awareness. I was in a dream, and there was something for me to confront. The dream reconfigured itself around me, the swirling and changing made me feel a little sick. I looked ahead and watched the transformations take place.

The street extended further and further. It was like I was travelling with it, even though I remained in the same spot. I could see how it stretched and what popped up on either side of the street. I started to notice something happening to the street. The further it went the dimmer the lights became, until the lights were out completely. Beyond that I could see no further, it was a vast expanse of blackness. Somewhere in there was my goal.

I clenched my fists and started to walk. The fact that it was a dream made it a little easier, but I also worried more. I knew that it wasn't real, but also knew that because of that anything could happen. I had progressed a few blocks when I noticed that the lights had dimmed quite a bit. There was still ample light, but it wasn't the comforting glow that I had experienced at the start. I paused for a moment to compose myself. Things were going well, so I urged myself forward.

In the next section, the light didn't diminish much, but something else changed. I started to notice things in my peripheral vision, only when I turned to look there was nothing there. It was like they were creeping shadows, but there couldn't be any shadow where it was completely dark. I tried to dismiss it and continued on. It wasn't long before I stopped again.

I felt a cold shiver run down my back. It stopped as soon as I ceased walking. I looked around and there was nothing. I tried taking a step and it began again. There was no explaining it. What made it worse though, was that I couldn't get used to the feeling. Every single shiver was like it had never happened before. I had to pause several times to allow myself to continue.

To make things more fun, the cold shivers continued with the addition of another element. I saw eyes watching me from the darkness. It was incredibly creepy and made my skin crawl. Each time I tried to get a better look, they weren't there. Or they moved and I could feel them watching me from somewhere else. My foot kicked something and I looked down. It was a flashlight. I picked it up, and was surprised by its weight. It made me feel safe, because I thought it would be useful as a weapon. Not to mention its ability to light up the darkness. But I knew that it was a trick or trap of some kind.

I'm not sure if it was curiosity or the desire for some momentary safety and warmth, but I switched it on briefly. Its light didn't progress any further than a few metres ahead of me, and I felt myself physically pushed back around 100m. It wasn't as though I moved, but that the street moved under me to take away some of my progress. I sighed, and tossed the flashlight away. Then I continued my walk.

The next trial involved sound. At first it was rustling, then it was whispers. Again every time I stopped and tried to listen I was rewarded with either silence or a different sound from somewhere else.

"Just silly little sounds," I thought to myself. Right on cue I heard a blood curdling scream of pain from somewhere. I quickly turned and saw and heard nothing. I started to run forward, without even thinking. I stumbled on a step and fell on my face. There was no real pain, just some stinging and embarrassment. I swore at myself, and tried to pull myself together. The only way I could advance was by moving forward.

The last transition had happened without my knowledge. I couldn't see anything. I waved my hand in front of my face, and had no perception of it. I felt a little disoriented and sick. I took a step and almost fell over. I squatted down and felt the ground with my hands. It was hard and spiky and painful to touch.

"Oh great," I said to myself. I stood up and took another, more careful, step forward. I felt a faint breeze coming from somewhere, then something brushed the back of my leg. I had to exert ridiculous control over myself to not jump. I swung my arms around and felt nothing. I heard footsteps, but as soon as I started to pick up the rough location of them they became silent. I felt an intense heat, which was replaced by a freezing cold thirty seconds later.

"Enough already!" I shouted into the darkness. I heard it echo around several times with no response. I progressed to a gravel covered area, where I kicked many stones away as I moved forward I heard every single one bounce along the ground then become silent. It was as if they were falling into a bottomless pit nearby.

"Stay," a voice whispered behind me, the breath touching my neck. I wheeled around in a panic but nobody was there.

"That was a good one," I said to myself and pushed onward. I made each step more defined, more confident and almost reckless. My pace increased and I tuned everything out.

Suddenly my final test was before me. I could see a glowing white doorway. The light it cast didn't extend to illuminate anything else. A wind picked up and it felt like there was an unseen chasm separating me from the light. I thought of jumping but stopped myself.

"I have to do this properly," I said to myself as encouragement. I closed my eyes and took a step. I landed on something, but felt like it was only a thin bridge with nothing either side. I put the image out of my head and took another step. I found ground once again. I surrendered to the darkness around me and continued to walk, one step at a time. It was a pleasant surprise when I felt myself enveloped by warmth and light.

CHAPTER TWELVE

PREPARATIONS

A man awoke, much earlier than normal. Everything he had worked on for the last few days, hinged on today. He had checked and rechecked his calculations, and tried to give himself more time. But it was now or never. His whole day was planned out as not a single minute could be wasted. He made himself some boiled eggs and drank orange juice while he ran over the plan again. He took out his business cards, today he was Roger Butler.

The man, known today as Roger, made a few phone calls after breakfast to ensure that both his assistant and his furniture deliveries were properly arranged. Next he walked downstairs to his makeshift lab, and ran one more test. The sample proved positive, and contained no impurities. He reviewed the case notes from his six successful test subjects but the data was unchanged. He had no excuse to delay, nor to abort. He sighed and did a final check of his things before he left. Everything was in order, so he closed the door behind him and walked down the street.

First he tried her regular lunch spot and saw her there. He carefully assessed her behaviour before determining that he wouldn't get the right opening. He had only one chance to approach her, so he had to maximise his likelihood of success. So he waited, and saw her leave her office building shortly after five. He tailed her at a safe distance, and watched her closely. She behaved as expected, but he made sure to note exactly how she reacted. He couldn't afford to get complacent and use behaviour examples that she hadn't displayed today. When she entered the Golden Arms he waited across the road, keeping an eye on the entrance. By her routine if she stayed longer than fifteen minutes, she should be staying for a while.

He waited longer than necessary, not wanting to run into her by mistake. When he thought it was the best time, he procrastinated a further five minutes. But he had to make a move, otherwise all his preparations would be wasted. So he walked over to the pub entrance and rehearsed his lines one more time.

He left the bar shortly after, letting out a huge sigh of relief. He had done it exactly as required, and he had noticed the interested glimmer in her eye. But she would need a push. The humidity outside was starting to become oppressive and he hoped the forecast would result in the promised storms. That might do the trick. He rushed home as soon as possible to avoid any part of the approaching weather. Once he was in the door, he prepared her pack. Then rechecked it three times. There were no margins for error. It had to be perfect. Only when he was satisfied that he had done everything, did he allow himself to relax. But he only afforded himself a few moments of relaxation. Next was sleep, and another day of absolute precision.

He arrived at his temporary office and supervised the furniture delivery. He welcomed his day secretary and informed her that they had an important client coming today. He stipulated that there were to be no breaks because they did not know when she was to arrive. The secretary agreed, reminding him of their previous discussion about the terms, and sat down to make herself comfortable. From there it was a waiting game.

"Please don't go to work Amy," the man said to himself as he watched the time slowly tick away. Later that day he heard some commotion and voices in the other room. He mentally prepared himself and when the secretary came in to fetch him, he was ready.

When Amy walked in he could see that she had had a bad night. She was definitely in the right state to accept his offer. He talked her through the basic theory, but not the reason. It was too early to reveal to her why she had been chosen. Not just chosen, but targeted as the single end goal for his research. Things were progressing well, she accepted the pack and left.

Roger waved goodbye at Amy. He knew from his test participants what she would be going through. It would be hard with no support, especially when she returned to his office to find it gone. But it had to be this way, if he had learned one thing it was that the mind had to believe there was no turning back.

He paid the secretary, called the removalists and co-ordinated a complete return to the original look of the office. Now, for a short time, he could rest. He would need his energy for the next stage. However when he got home, he was already distracted and instead spent his time reading through the notebooks he had collected try-ing to imagine what would happen next. He fell asleep in his chair with a book in his lap.

An alarm woke him suddenly, and he rushed into his bedroom to silence it. After a moment, he remembered what was happening. He had to be up and go observe Amy. He quickly showered then headed into the city. Her phobias were generally quite visible on her walk through the city to her work. He had her route memo-rised, so he started near where her bus arrived. After five to ten minutes, he spotted her. She looked better than the day before.

He watched her movements, her crowd reaction was the same. Next were some animals, dogs walking with their owners.

"Oh my god," he said to himself. Amy's reaction to the animals was 100% better. She still looked uncom-fortable, but the reaction was almost nothing. He made a few notes in a small pad from his pocket.

"This might actually work," he thought, hope creeping into his mind. He had seen enough for the day, so he returned home. He put a line through animals on his list of Amy's phobias. From that point on he had to assume that things were going according to the plan, so he decided to return at the same time to see her progress the next day. It was still too early to progress the plan to its next stage.

He assumed the same position, and watched for Amy to get off the bus. He checked his watch, she was late. He continued watching and waiting. Finally she emerged, and looked worse for wear.

"She failed," he thought instantly. Amy certainly had the look of someone who had failed. He felt bad for her, wished that he could comfort her and reassure her. But he could not. One thing he knew though, was that she would definitely go to see him today. He felt a pit in his stomach, knowing what was ahead of her.

He followed her to work, but didn't see anything else of note. On a hunch, he waited for her to go up and then took the elevator himself. He surveyed the entry to her work. He noted the lovely view of the city which could trigger her fear of heights. He also sneaked a peek at the layout of the office. Not wanting to push his luck, he took the elevator down and then returned home. He thought over what had occurred. The plan could not progress until she was back on the program, making her own progress. He always knew that this might happen. The next step was to get her back into a positive state.

The man, formerly known as Roger, tailed Amy from her work to The Golden Arms. He saw her have a discussion with her house-mate and settle in for the night. He had his suspicions about Amy's behaviour, but decided to wait and see. When they both left the pub at closing and headed to a convenience store he knew what was up. When Amy returned with a large coffee it confirmed his suspicions. She had decided to avoid sleeping as a solution.

"It's ok she has a friend to look over her," he thought to himself and returned home. He planned a quick sleep and then an early start to keep an eye on Amy's progress. If at any point he thought she was in danger of harming herself, then he would step in and abort the plan. He tracked her for most of the weekend. He made a few notes about what he saw:

Bought a cork board
Played catch with a dog!
Attended a rave
No sleep for entire weekend

It was a very strange list of things to do. But he knew the effects of sleep deprivation on the mind, so would puzzle them out later. He was incredibly impressed at her playing with a dog though. That was real progress. He made sure he was available again to watch her walk to work on Monday morning. She was a little early, and still had not slept.

"Tonight she has to," he thought to himself. He waited until the evening and then drove his car to Amy's apartment, parking nearby. He could see all the lights on for most of the night. After Samantha returned home, most of them were off.

"Sleep well Amy," he said softly. The morning sun woke him up in his car, and he became instantly alert. He watched the apartment until nine o'clock and neither Amy nor Samantha left.

"If she's still asleep, then things went well," he thought to himself. He drove home to make a few preparations for his regular work, which he would have to resume soon.

He popped out to observe Amy attending her therapy session. She looked well as she entered the building, so he felt his chest relax. He hadn't realised how worried he had been. He almost missed her leaving the session though. It was well short of her one hour time slot, and her face was beaming.

"What just happened?" he thought. The smile on her face made him worried. Any deviation from her normal behaviour with Dr. Nelson was likely to set things in motion. The plan might need to move ahead, whether she was ready or not.

The next morning he was prepared. Today was the beginning of the next phase. He had to kick start her development and thinking. He watched her walk to work and noted her distinct lack of crowd avoidance. To the untrained eye it would have been subtle, but he was not only trained, he had also watched her many times.

"Thank god, I can move things forward today," he thought to himself. He spent the morning loitering near the office, waiting for lunch time. When he saw Amy leave the office and turn right, he knew she was going to her sushi place. He didn't have much time, she would probably be eating at her desk.

He dashed over to her building and frantically pressed the elevator call button. When it arrived he pressed the level eleven button and then the close door button immediately. Once he was on her floor, he strode into the office as if he belonged there. Most of the staff were eating in the kitchen or otherwise not at their desks. He prepared his cover story in case he was challenged, and then dropped the letter on Amy's desk. He turned and walked straight out. His only worry now was getting spotted by her on his way out.

He decided on a risky move. He would keep pressing the call button to keep one of the elevators at this level, and when another elevator arrived he would take his one down. He checked his watch, it was about the right time for Amy to return. He heard the ding of another elevator arriving, so he stepped into his elevator and looked out. He could see Amy heading for her office as the doors of his elevator were slowly closing.

"Don't look back," he said to himself, and luckily she didn't. As he left the elevator, the release in tension was so intense that he almost stumbled. He felt himself winding down as he returned home. His life would mainly return to normalcy tomorrow. He prepared himself for work, as he usually did.

The last thing he did was empty out his jacket pockets. He found more Roger Butler business cards, and threw them all in the bin. It was a relief to be himself again. He grabbed his regular business cards and looked them over carefully.

Dr. Gary Featherby
Psychologist
Head Researcher - University of Technology

He slept peacefully without apprehension. Things were progressing as they should be. Although he wasn't looking forward to his next meeting with Amy, whenever it was.

CHAPTER THIRTEEN

REACTION

Amy went through the motions again, writing notes and drawing a picture. This time it was a large and detailed feather. She looked at it, puzzled. But she didn't dwell on it too much, the other drawings had been similarly odd, yet each one had provided a useful explanation so far. What concerned her as she prepared for work was the article that had been left for her. It was no accident that she had been provided with that article, with that image on it. Had someone been in the house? She had left her notebooks at home yesterday. She walked around to all the windows, and examined the door closely. She was no expert, but there didn't seem to be any signs of forced entry.

She reviewed her conversations, and she had only spoken about it to Samantha that morning. She tried to analyse the situation and came up with two possible explanations. The first, as she had already started to explore, was that someone had accessed her apartment and looked at her notebooks. The second, was that someone had noticed her investigations and was giving her the next piece. Either way, she could not deny that there was someone out there watching her. The thought made her skin crawl. There was only one thing to do, find this person.

She did her usual commute to work, but glanced around a lot to see if anyone was following her. All that rewarded her with, was a feeling of paranoia. When she arrived at the office, she put it out of her mind for a while. Right on cue, David arrived with a coffee.

"Good morning Amy. Everything back to normal eh?" he said.

"Yes, my good old routines are back."

"Good to hear that. Well how about a break to that routine? A bunch of us are having a few drinks tonight if you would like to come."

"I'm not sure what I'm doing."

"That's fine. If you are free come to the Blue Room tonight at seven. Hope to see you there!"

"Sure, I'll see how I go," Amy said. Part of her was shy about going, the other part of her was apprehensive about her stranger following her around. She looked around for the inevitable pep talk from Margaret, but none came. Feeling slightly disappointed, she continued on with her work.

When lunch time came around, she decided to do a test. She went down towards her favourite sushi place, then immediately headed back to the office as if she had forgotten something. All the while she was on the lookout for suspicious people. However she didn't recognise anyone and there was nothing left on her desk. Feeling a little foolish, she returned and actually bought some sushi to eat at her desk. She didn't usually eat the same thing two days in a row, but she had already wasted enough time with her lunch time ruse.

Over lunch she started brainstorming ideas that could involve the feather image she had drawn. She started by thinking back over what the previous drawings had meant. The first one was a company logo, another a man's name, and the other a landmark item. The company logo was an interesting one, she could find out what companies were working with Keystone Endeavours and see if any had a feather logo. Similarly she could find out if any of the other directors had the word feather in their name. In terms of landmarks or items of significance though, she didn't think it was worth pursuing.

That afternoon, she printed out reports on the companies that were partnered with Keystone on the restoration project, their list of directors and examples of their letterheads. She didn't notice anything strange while compiling the information, but she wasn't looking too closely. She decided to limit her time at work spent on her investigation. She spent the rest of the afternoon being productive, and was preparing to leave around five pm. That was when Margaret pounced.

"Hi Amy, got plans tonight?" she said.

"Kinda."

"Well a little birdie told me that David is having drinks and invited you."

"You have a talking bird? That's amazing!"

"Your sarcasm is just a defence mechanism. Are you going?"

"Maybe, I'll see how I go."

"Just go, I want a full report tomorrow."

"No promises."

"Full. Report. Have a fun night see you tomorrow."

"Bye," Amy said and she waved. She should have known better than to think she would get out of the office without a comment from Margaret. She knew the woman meant well, but it was frustrating at times. Amy decided to go catch up with Samantha. She left the office, and kept an eye out for any odd people on her walk. However the city was so busy, that she arrived at The Golden Arms with nothing but a foolish feeling.

She saw Samantha at the bar, ordered a drink and sat nearby slowly sipping it and watching the crowd. She had two issues to resolve: the meaning of her dreams, and the person or persons following her. The more she thought about it though, she was missing something. A key detail, or connection. All the other drawings had such obvious links to the events she was piecing togeth-er. After a while she went back to the bar and patiently waited to flag Samantha's attention. Once Samantha came over, Amy ordered another drink. Samantha stopped what she was doing, and looked at her suspiciously.

"Hang on a minute, I've seen this behaviour before. You have nothing to do, nurse your drink for ages and then come over to buy another one to help kill time."

"What are you talking about?"

"C'mon I wasn't born yesterday, you're avoiding something. You always have something to do next, even when you're hanging out here. What are you doing Amy? Spill it."

"There's nothing."

"I'm not buying it."

"Ok fine, David is having drinks with friends tonight and I was invited." Samantha chuckled at Amy's response.

"Now it all makes sense. Let me guess, you're wasting time here so that you 'accidentally' miss drinks?"

"It's not that simple."

"Yes it is, what time are they meeting?"

"Seven."

"Where?"

"The Blue Room."

"If you leave now, you'll be fashionably late."

"Maybe."

"If you don't leave now, I'll get the bouncers to escort you out." Amy started to gather her things reluctantly.

"That's better. Have a good time!"

"Bye," Amy said and sighed. She left, and walked the fifteen minutes over to the Blue Room. She quickly scanned the room, and couldn't see David. A sense of relief washed over her, and she turned to leave.

"Amy! Over here!" a voice shouted out. Instinctively Amy looked over, and saw David sitting at a table. Their eyes made contact, and there was no backing out. She took her time walking over, trying to assess who else was there. David was sitting with one other person, with two empty chairs across from them.

"Hi Amy, glad you could make it. This is Adam, he's an engineer by day and a wanna-be writer by night. The other two guys ditched us after one drink to play the pokies."

"Hi, nice to meet you Adam," Amy said and sat down in one of the empty chairs.

"You two work together?" Adam asked.

"Yeah," Amy said.

"So you're a lawyer then?"

"No I'm a legal secretary."

"But she's actually got a law degree, she can practice whenever she wants," David said, interjecting.

"So you want to be a writer?" Amy said.

"Yeah, I've got something I'm working on. It's hard though, I think it has gotten away from me a bit."

"What do you mean?"

"I had an idea and started writing. At the beginning I had no formal training, and I still don't really know what I'm doing. The story has had some cool things happen, but I'm struggling with the characters. It's almost like they're doing their own thing and causing me headaches."

"Ha-ha sounds like fun. At least you'll end up with an interesting book."

"If I ever finish it. So why aren't you a lawyer?"

"I went through a very traumatic period right around the time I got my law degree. I guess I just haven't worked up to it yet."

"It's a waste, you're so switched on Amy and you know it all backwards. You'd make a fine lawyer," David said. Adam got up to go to the bar, and left them alone for a minute.

"It's good to see you out, you never go to the work functions," David said.

"Yeah, well I guess they're not really my thing."

"If you don't mind me asking, what's still keeping you a secretary?"

"I don't know."

"You have my support, when you want to take that step. I'm serious, I'm not just being nice."

"Thanks, I'll let you know."

"Is anything else going on? You've been a bit funny lately."

"Nah just slept poorly with that crazy storm, and it snowballed a bit."

"Ok, well again if there's anything I can help with just ask."

"That's sweet, I'll keep it in mind." Adam returned with a round of shots. Amy tried to refuse, but the other two were so insistent that she went along with it. She managed to dodge the rest of the drinks, while Adam and David kept going. David's two other friends never reappeared.

"You know, I think I might go back to university in a few years," David said.

"You didn't spend enough time there doing law?" Adam joked.

"Clearly I've drunk too much and forgotten those years."

"What would you do?" Amy asked.

"I'm considering doing teaching. It would be a nice change of pace, and something for me to fall back on later if I want to. What about..." David said before being interrupted.

"Hey can I join you?" a young woman asked. She was in her mid-twenties, with brown hair and glasses. She was well dressed and wearing heels. She touched David on the shoulder as she spoke. He looked over at her and smiled.

"Sure. This is Melissa. Meet Amy and Adam," David said.

"Nice to meet you both," Melissa said, before sitting down next to Amy.

"I wonder who she is. She is probably the girl David's dating. She's really pretty." Amy thought to herself.

"As I was saying, maybe teaching for me. What would you go back to university for Amy?" David said.

"I don't know, maybe journalism." Amy said.

"Writing too eh? I already went back to university for that," Adam said.

"Yeah what are you doing?" Amy asked.

"Creative writing, of course! It's actually very interesting, with a mixture of rule based structural things and more out there stuff."

"Like what?"

"Well this semester I'm doing a psychology class. It's a real psychology class too, run by the head of research at the university, a Dr. Gary Featherby."

"That's such a professor's name," David said. But Amy didn't really hear him.

"Dr. Gary Featherby, at what university?" she asked.

"The University of Technology." Amy pulled out a small notepad and wrote down the details. Her mind was racing like crazy.

"You also interested?" Adam asked.

"Sure. Hey I better be going, thanks for the invitation." Amy said hurriedly. She grabbed her things, waved to everyone and almost ran out.

"There are no coincidences," she said to herself. She then hailed the nearest taxi.

"University of Technology please," Amy said to the taxi driver.

"Sure, isn't it a bit late?"

"I'm meeting a friend after night classes." The driver said nothing further and fifteen minutes later they had arrived. Amy paid the driver and hurried to the main building. There was a map showing the different faculties and she found the Humanities wing. The buildings were still open, there must have been classes or events on late. She wandered the halls, until she stumbled upon the Psychology department. Apart from a few rooms there was only a relatively small noticeboard. She skimmed over semester dates, important events and notes. One of the notes was about Dr. Featherby returning from leave. She kept looking and found a piece of paper with contact details for the faculty and office hours. Next to each entry was a small photograph. She found the entry for Gary Featherby and looked at the photo.

"Roger Butler. No way," Amy said under her breath. There was no denying it, as strange as it sounded. She turned and slowly walked out, trying to wrap her head around the revelation. In a purely logical way, it made sense that a research psychologist would run some sort of fly by night operation to test something new. But why on her? She took out her notepad and wrote down his office hours before leaving the university.

In the taxi home her thinking went in another direction. What were her drawings trying to tell her? It seemed odd that now she would discover the identity of Roger Butler, not before when she was looking for him.

"Unless this is the man following me," Amy thought to herself, in wonder and then horror. She wasn't sure if it felt better that her stalker was someone she had already met. It explained how he had been spot on with her behaviours, that maybe he was following her longer than he let on that day. But it didn't explain why he had left her the newspaper article.

Unless he was controlling the images that she drew, if that were even possible. Once she was home, she sat up thinking of all the possibilities, and put up a new note on her board aligning Roger Butler to Gary Featherby and linking him to the newspaper article. She couldn't sleep yet, so waited for Samantha to come home.

"Hey you're still up. Got some exciting news for me?" Samantha said.

"Yes, I couldn't sleep."

"So, tell me all about it. How was David? Did he make a move?"

"What? No. I'm pretty sure his new girlfriend showed up at the end. Anyway you know how I've been drawing things?"

"Oh Amy, I'm so sorry to hear that. That must have been so awkward."

"Well the last thing I drew was a feather, and David's friend Adam mentioned his professor at university was a Gary Featherby."

"Is David's friend single? That could be something."

"No, he was wearing a wedding ring. Samantha listen to me! I went to the university and found a photo of

Gary Featherby and he looks exactly like Roger Butler," Amy said, exasperated. Samantha immediately took notice and processed the news for a few seconds.

"So you've tracked down Roger Butler?"

"Yeah."

"Because you hung out with David?"

"Yes," Amy said tiredly, expecting a very specific phrase from Samantha.

"See aren't you glad I made you go?" Samantha said and Amy groaned inwardly.

"Yes. Look this is totally crazy, I dreamed up the clue to who this guy is, and David's friend told me the name. What's happening?"

"Don't ask me, ask this Featherby guy."

"I plan to. He's got a lot to answer for." Amy sat up for a while longer, wondering about what she would do or say in a confrontation with him. At the same time, she dreaded sleeping. It was a bit of a mental hurdle, knowing that you had work to do in your sleep and it wasn't just a refuge for rest. Eventually though, she did sleep.

CHAPTER FOURTEEN

DREAM FIVE

I was standing in a giant warehouse. It had giant triangular windows near the similarly shaped roof. The windows were so dark, that I couldn't really see out of them. However periodically they lit up with some light from outside. I walked across the echoing concrete floor to the end of the warehouse and slowly opened the huge door. I could see a storm in the distance. Flashes of lightning had been showing through the windows.

"Here we go," I said to myself. I had an idea of what would be happening next, and that made it worse. The anticipation was terrible, and my mind raced through a lot of worst case scenarios. Many of which no doubt would occur, only because I thought them up. I resigned myself to whatever fate was before me and took a step forward.

Light rain fell on me and I could hear a low rumbling in the distance. I didn't mind the rain and the thunder sounded distant enough to not worry me. I was walking down what looked like a city block, so there was some shelter around. I didn't bother stepping under them though, knowing that they would just delay me without gain in the best case, and make things harder in the worst case.

As the rain intensified the cover became available less and less. The surrounding buildings slowly shrank in size, until I was in a suburban street. I was closer to the storm now. The flashes of lightning were more visible, and the thunder closely following. I remember reading that the closer the lightning was followed by the thunder, the closer it was to you. The sky was darkening considerably, and soon I found it hard to see without the flashes of light that started occurring more and more frequently.

The boom of the thunder made me jump, but it was also followed by another loud sound that I couldn't place. I looked over my left shoulder and saw a tree falling right on me. I dived forward just in time to escape, hearing the shuddering thud as it hit the ground. I picked myself up and looked back, the tree had just toppled in one piece. I wasn't sure what would have happened if it hit me, but I wasn't curious either.

The wind picked up and I felt like at any moment I could be picked up and swept away. I wasn't sure what was louder, the thunder or the wind. Trees were bending over at odd angles, everything on the street that wasn't part of a foundation was flapping madly. I couldn't hear my footsteps anymore. Something tapped my shoulder so I turned and saw nothing. It was then I noticed small pieces of ice on the ground. It wasn't ice though, but hail. That pushed me a bit far, I covered my head with my hands and dashed into the nearest yard, finding a shed. The door wasn't locked so I let myself in and breathed the awful smelling air in deeply.

The hail intensified and the whipping wind scattered it in all directions. I thought I was ok with the storm, just slowly adjusting to the crazy sounds and lights. But the physicality of it, I couldn't handle it. The cold was also starting to affect me. My teeth were chattering of their own accord. Unfortunately I knew that the storm would not get better, and in all likelihood would just continue to escalate while I waited. I closed my eyes and urged myself forward.

I tried to ignore my water logged feet, the odd piece of hail hitting me on the head and the horrible mix of whistling and roaring from the weather. I took step after step forward. I was almost frozen, both physically and mentally, but I continued on. I just knew that I had to, even though my whole body was crying out. At least it would end eventually.

I looked up and saw that the buildings were becoming less frequent and ahead of me was a giant paddock. It extended as far as the eye could see, and had really tall grass. I felt some relief at arriving. There was no shelter, but also no trees or objects to fly at me. The hail stopped too, so I just had the rest of the storm to deal with.

Lightning flashed right in front of me and I jumped back. There was even a smouldering patch of grass just metres in front of where I had stood. I saw some sort of structure in the paddock, and walked toward it.

I felt very exposed right out in the middle of the paddock, but I had to find a way forward otherwise I would be trapped in the storm. I tramped on, the grass slowing me down. As I neared the weird structure I saw that it was a small platform with something on it. It was a metal stand with a large metal sword on it.

"That looks very unsafe in these conditions," I said to myself. I stepped closer and looked at the sword more closely. It didn't seem sharp, but there was writing inscribed along the blade. It said 'lightning rod'.

"Typical," I said under my breath. I picked up the sword and held it as low to the ground as possible. Nothing happened. I lifted it higher to place it back in its stand and then something caught my eye. A glowing white doorway was visible in the distance. Feeling relief, and renewed hope I put the sword back. Only the doorway was gone. I screamed out in frustration and fury. The storm echoed my feeling and surged even more.

"Fine, have it your way!" I shouted back at the storm. I picked up the sword and held it aloft enough so that I could see the doorway and marched towards it with purpose. Within 30 seconds lightning struck nearby and I dropped the sword in fright. Cursing at myself, I picked it back up and continued. The sword felt slippery with the rain, and so heavy. Not to mention the possibility of attracting lightning. Yet I continued to hold it and forge ahead.

A few more close calls happened with the lightning, but I reasoned that they were just tests and I was safe.

"It's all a show," I said to myself. I took another step forward and suddenly flew back and crashed hard. My whole world turned white and I couldn't see or hear anything. I stood up gingerly, unable to feel anything properly. My clothes were torn and scorched in even proportions. The ground was blackened where I had been standing, and the sword was nearby. It looked unaffected though.

"Did I just get hit by lightning?" I thought to myself. But everything was hazy, so I just picked up the sword and the glowing door came back into view. It was so close now. Step by step I closed in, and the storm started to clear. As I reached the door, the sword disappeared and my pain started to recede. The strength from my legs failed me and I fell into the glowing warmth.

CHAPTER FIFTEEN

PROACTIVE

Amy rose, wrote in her notebook and drew a detailed drawing of an old chair. She didn't read over her dream, as she remembered most of it. The drawing only got a casual glance, as she didn't think it was important yet. She didn't need a direction, there was still something important to follow up. Dr. Gary Featherby would be getting a visit today.

Amy checked the notes she had made the previous night and saw that today Dr. Featherby was in his office until 6:30pm. She had plenty of time to get there after work. That was her mission for the day, to confront him and get some answers. It was only when she was arriving at work that she remembered about David. She had left so suddenly and so awkwardly.

"He's going to think I'm a mental case," Amy said to herself. But strangely she didn't feel too bad about that. It was a problem for another day. She was thankful for having something else to focus on. She had completely forgotten about it until David arrived, and handed her a coffee.

"Good morning Amy, how are you today?"

"I'm good, can't complain. How about you?"

"I'm great. You left rather abruptly last night. I know I had a few drinks, did I say anything offensive?"

"No, not at all. I don't usually do shots, it must have gone to my head a bit."

"Fair enough. Adam said if you're still interested in meeting his professor, to let him know. Adam will be visiting Dr. Featherby this afternoon," David said. Amy thought hard about it. She had planned to go anyway, but it might be strange if she did so and knocked back Adam's offer. Especially if he saw her there.

"Sure, but I don't want to impose. Maybe if he just directs me to the right office?"

"I'll have a chat with him today. I'll give you an update later."

"Thanks, see you later," Amy said. She cringed inwardly, she had probably sounded so weird. David was so nice too, what was the deal there? Oh well at least one way or another she was seeing the professor today. How strange and intertwined her life had become lately. She returned to thinking of the present, and dreaded the inevitable Margaret visit. So she stood up and walked over to Margaret's office to get it over with.

"Oh good morning Amy. So nice to see you in my neck of the woods. What can I help you with today?"

"I just thought I'd give you an update about last night."

"Oh, about what exactly?" Margaret said, playing coy.

"Oh you know, my drinks with David and his friends."

"Ah yes, do tell."

"Well nothing much happened, we all had a chat about general things, and then David's girlfriend showed up."

"Oh is that all? I had a chat with David this morning. He was suggesting that we start your preparations for transition to an attorney. That certainly sounds like something happened."

"Oh well, that is nice of him."

"I thought so, but also very practical. Now since you saved me the effort of popping over to your desk, we would like you to fly out to an important client to get a full deposition. David would be supervising of course, but it's a good start to put you to use."

"Oh wow, that's fantastic. But I really would prefer not to fly, if at all possible."

"It's too far to drive, that would be incredibly wasteful. Think it over, if you can't fly we'll just send David."

"Sure. Thanks for the offer."

"Think it over carefully. You shouldn't let these things get in your way, you have a bright future here." Amy nodded and returned to her desk. She had gone to get a difficult conversation out of the way, but had landed in a worse one. She could still remember vividly the last time she had flown. The anxiety and tension that she held, and the way she had thrown up. The fact that she felt worse after throwing up, not better as was always the case otherwise. The looks the other passengers had given her. She was almost sick just from the memory. But at the same time Margaret was right. If Amy wanted to move on with her career, she had to move past these fears.

But then she reminded herself of the progress she had already made. She had played catch with a dog, handled crowds and not freaked out when looking out of her building. They were important steps, important building blocks. She hadn't tested her handling of the dark, or of storms yet, but felt that she was better, at least in some way. A confidence from within her spread.

"Maybe I'll dream about flying tonight," Amy thought to herself. That would be convenient, and resolve her problem. She was feeling stronger overall, but she didn't want to have to fly without any help.

Amy caught herself looking for odd people while she was out at lunch, even though it seemed silly. It was almost confirmed that Dr. Featherby had been following her and since he was back at work and had office hours today he couldn't be following her. There was still some unease in her though, since she hadn't confronted him yet. To change things up, she ate away from her desk. It was nice to be out and amongst people in the sun. She pondered whether her feelings about crowds had changed enough to make her lunch more enjoyable. However she concluded that the density of the lunch tables she was sitting at would not have been a problem previously either.

Early in the afternoon David popped by her desk to update her. He mentioned that Adam would wait at the university entrance after his appointment with Dr. Featherby for Amy and then direct her. She thanked David and decided that it was a good outcome. She didn't offend anyone, or raise suspicions and she would have less difficulty finding the right office. The afternoon passed incredibly slowly and Amy found herself constantly watching the clock. She was both excited and anxious to get to the University but at the same time unable to make a decision about the flight. She thought about what Samantha would say.

"Take the flight and get some quality alone time with David," Amy thought to herself in a perfect imitation of Samantha's voice. But in her mind, it wasn't that simple.

When 5pm struck, Amy bounced out of her chair and left the office with surprising speed. She power-walked to the bus stop and just made it in time. She had to stand up, but didn't care. However her speed and great timing worked against her. She arrived ten minutes early and had to wait at the University gates for Adam. Again time crawled by at a ridiculously slow pace. When Adam finally arrived, he was five minutes late. Amy pushed her annoyance away and smiled.

"Hi Amy, nice to see you again," Adam said.

"Hi Adam, thanks for the kind offer."

"No problem, you seemed really excited last night and I was already here today meeting him to discuss my paper."

"Well, still thanks for your time. Do I need an appointment?"

"Generally no, although there can be a wait sometimes. However I told him I had a friend that wanted to talk to him about his course and he's happy to see you."

"Did you introduce me at all?" Amy said, hiding her worry. If Adam had mentioned her name, she would lose the element of surprise. Or not be able to see the professor at all.

"No, should I have?"

"No no no, I was just curious." She asked Adam a few polite questions about how his coursework was going, and how he was doing fitting it in with his regular job. Within a few minutes they had arrived at the door. There was a sign clearly displaying the name 'Dr. Gary Featherby'.

"Thanks for your help, I'll buy you a drink next time."

"No problem, I hope you have a good discussion," Adam replied with a smile and then left. Amy stared at the door, took a deep breath, and then entered. The man she wanted to find, was sitting at his desk looking over some papers. She said nothing as she walked in and sat down in the chair opposite.

"Just a minute, I'm finishing something off," he said without looking up. Amy appeared to be the picture of patience, but her head was running through different scenarios. She wondered what to say first. She had so many questions, and all seemed to be equally important. Dr. Featherby started to speak as he put his papers away.

"Now what can I..." he said, before trailing off mid-sentence. His face was frozen in shock. He spoke again before Amy could reply.

"No, it's too soon. You shouldn't be here."

"You owe me some answers."

"In time, yes. Not now. You can't be seen here."

"You're not making any sense. Have you been following me?"

"Not like them. You have to go," he said, his panic levels rising constantly. He rustled through his drawer and took out a small box, placing it on the desk.

"If they come for you, take this," he said then stood up and went to leave. Amy grabbed his arm, to stop him.

"Don't stop me. There's too much that you don't understand yet. It's vital that you don't seek me out until the final hour," Dr. Featherby said, shrugging off Amy's grasp as he left. She wanted to chase after him, but she was just confused. She had imagined many things, varying from outright denial to full disclosure. But not this, it was completely unexpected. He didn't seem that bad, but it was hard to judge from their conversation. She put the small box in her pocket, wandered out of his office and looked for him, but he had already disappeared. There was definitely something odd happening, but she was missing something. He was right when he said that there was too much she didn't understand yet. It annoyed her though, that he had just fobbed her off and ran away.

Amy left the university, feeling more confused and in the dark than she had been when she arrived. She hadn't been with Dr. Featherby long, but Adam had already left. It was probably better that way, she didn't have to fabricate a response if he asked her about her chat. She crossed the road, and started heading for the bus stop. There was a very long queue of students ahead of her. When a taxi sidled up near the bus stop she broke from the line and got in the back seat. She told the driver her street and then zoned out a little.

Fifteen minutes later she was snapped back into reality, when she noticed the way the driver was going.

"You took the wrong turn, you need to change lanes and take the next left," Amy said.

"No this way is better."

"No, I'm the passenger you have to go the way I say."

"This is the only way."

"No, I've gone the other way every time. Take the next left turn," Amy said, exasperated. The driver stopped responding. She repeated her instructions several times and he ignored her.

"Ok fine stop the car," Amy said. The driver responded by locking all the doors. The 'phunt' sound of the latches closing sounded incredibly ominous. When the taxi stopped at the next set of lights, Amy tested her door. Even when unlocking it, it didn't open.

"I said let me out." There was no reply.

"What are you trying to pull? If you continue to say nothing I'm just going to assume that you're kidnapping me." His silence said it all. Despite putting on a brave face and acting unconcerned, Amy was starting to panic. She was trapped in a taxi and didn't know where she was being taken. Ordinarily it would be cause for concern, but after her meeting with Dr. Featherby he had already suggested that something similar might happen.

She took a deep breath and assessed the vehicle. The driver was in a completely enclosed section, so she couldn't get to him.

"What about my safety," she said under her breath. The rest of the taxi seemed like a normal vehicle, although she didn't think that total door security from the driver's seat was a standard feature. She tried to wind the window down, but the switch was unresponsive. Next she banged on the window. Her hope was to get attention, and maybe force the window somehow. All she achieved was making the driver speed up. The streets they travelled on became less and less populated. She went from having some idea of the area, to knowing nothing. The dusk and then darkness didn't help.

She thought back on her brief encounter with Dr. Featherby. He had been strange, and acted totally differently than before. But underneath it all, there was a genuineness to him. Which didn't make any sense, because he had gone to a lot of trouble to disguise himself and leave no trace for her to track him down. Then she remembered about the box he had given her. Unless this was some sort of prank, he had been right. She retrieved the box from her bag and opened it. Inside was a small sheet, and inside that a single pill. It was quite small, thankfully. That meant it would be easier to swallow, as she had no water, and it should be absorbed quicker.

The question was whether she trusted Dr. Featherby. It could all be a setup, he could have signalled the taxi driver and arranged this to ensure she took the pill. She didn't even know what it was, at least last time she had some kind of idea. But he had seemed genuinely panicked, and not that organised.

"Well I'm being kidnapped, what else could this pill even do anyway?" she thought to herself. When the driver's attention was focused elsewhere she quickly popped the pill and swallowed hard. It stuck to her throat a little and she momentarily panicked. However it went down and she masked the whole thing as a cough. With that done, she started to imagine the possible effects of the pill. Not only that, but also the fact that he had the pill ready, even though he wasn't expecting her. Her train of thought was interrupted by the taxi stopping.

Amy prepared herself, this was her last chance to get away. She looked outside and saw that they were inside a large warehouse. She hadn't noticed when they entered, but then as she thought back she had a realisation. There hadn't been any street lights for a while. Even the warehouse was poorly lit, most likely on purpose. She heard the driver leave and footsteps circle the car. This is it, she thought. She tensed herself and waited for the door to open. When it did, she didn't leave immediately, pausing a moment to assess. The driver was standing there looking at her. She quickly formed a plan in her head.

Amy slowly stepped out of the vehicle, then quickly rushed at the driver to kick him in the groin. However something stopped her. She felt something hurt, and she fell slowly and didn't know why. She was out before her head reached the ground.

CHAPTER SIXTEEN

CAPTIVE

Amy came to in a seated but slightly reclined position. She moved her arms, but they didn't move. As her consciousness and vision improved she noticed that her arms were strapped to the chair she was in. Only it wasn't like a normal chair. It was an old style chair, like the one that a dentist would have used before the modern era. Her left arm felt cool, so she looked at it. There was a needle in it, connected to a drip. The fluid was half empty. Amy struggled for a few moments, then tried to relax.

"Ok look for something useful," she said to herself. The room she was in was completely featureless, just plain white walls. There was nothing else in it except for her chair and the drip. She looked down at her feet and saw that they were also strapped into footholds at the base of the chair. She looked back at the drip, scared of what it might contain.

She felt very strange. A mix of drowsy and restless. A door opened and a woman entered the room. She was dressed all in blue, with a hair net and face mask. She looked like a surgeon. She said nothing, just came and looked at Amy's drip. She pressed a few buttons on it, and then made some notes on a piece of paper. Without giving Amy another look she left the room. Amy tried to call out, but she felt too tired. Amy blinked, and then the strange silent woman was back. Feeling confused, Amy looked at her drip and it was empty.

"How much time passed?" she thought to herself. The woman acted as before, only this time she replaced the empty bag with another one. She left without saying a word and Amy was alone again.

She slept for small spurts, but didn't dream. The extent of her consciousness was to notice somebody entering the room occasionally. Suddenly she opened her eyes, and felt more awake. The room was entirely dark, which wasn't affecting her yet. It was a curiosity. Then she felt her pulse quicken. Strange sounds started to come from the room. Whispers, and whistling were the first. Next were animal sounds and strange echoes. Her anxiety rose and she felt a mild panic set in.

"But I've dealt with this," she thought to herself. And then it changed. The darkness remained, but she became aware of the walls of the room. Every ten heartbeats the walls moved closer. The air felt stuffier. As much as she looked around, she couldn't see the walls. But she could still feel them moving closer. Soon she felt the very walls touching her arms and pressing down on her head. She felt like she couldn't breathe. Her darkness enclosed her completely and she lost consciousness.

Amy opened her eyes and found herself still in the chair. However the room looked different. There were other chairs around, but they were different. Then her brain clicked and she recognised them as airplane seats.

"Oh we're on a plane now," she thought to herself. She felt the room rumble and then start to move. Slow at first with a few turns.

"We're taxiing," she thought. Suddenly the room started to accelerate rapidly and the speed increased.

"No here it comes," she said. The room started to angle upwards and her stomach leapt. The moment of take-off was at hand. But unlike usual, it didn't transition into flying. It remained, and she felt more and more uncomfortable. She felt nauseous and sick and frightened. She was stuck between the ground and the air, in limbo.

Like that, the transition ended and she felt the room flying. It was smooth sailing to begin with, then a bit of turbulence hit. It increased in severity and Amy was rocking around like crazy. She heard the roar of a storm outside. The room shook more and more, with deafening thunder resounding everywhere around her. Flashes of light that had to be lightning blinded her. It was an assault on her senses, from every conceivable direction. Then a flash of light was accompanied by a huge crash and a long metallic groan. The room started to tilt down and its speed increased. She heard the loud wail and failing engines and freefall as she plunged down. Her chest seized up as she waited for the impact. But it didn't come, she was just falling. When she couldn't take it anymore, she felt a crash and blacked out.

Amy opened her eyes to what looked like a bar. There were lots of people there, but she couldn't see the details of their faces. She was still in her chair, which seemed out of place. She turned and saw David sitting next to her. She tried to ask him for help, but said something else entirely.

"Will you go out with me?" she asked him.

"Never."

"Do you want to have a drink sometime, just the two of us?"

"No why would I do that?"

"Would you have dinner with me?"

"No."

"Would you like to have lunch at work one day?"

"No."

"Can we have a more serious talk?"

"No. In fact I can't believe I'm letting myself be seen with you. You disgust me," he said, before storming off. Amy felt like her heart had been ripped out and then turned into dust. She closed her eyes to try and block out the pain. When she opened them again she was at work. She had a cake with her, and offered some to David.

"Did you make it?"

"Yes, it's fantastic!"

"I'm sick at just the thought of eating it. Take it away."

"Why?" Amy thought to herself. As she stood there David spat on her cake and she dropped the plate in surprise and it fell in slow motion, shattering into many pieces. She felt something in herself breaking at the same time.

Amy awoke again, and the room felt more real. The light was back on in the room, and she was still strapped into the chair. The same nurse-like woman from before came in, unlocked Amy's straps and helped her up. She struggled to walk and leaned on the nurse. Amy was shown to the bathroom and left alone. She thought in the back of her mind that she should be doing something else, looking for something. But her mind wasn't clear. It was like her brain was stuffed with a fluffy blanket, separating the parts that should be working together. She was walked into a much bigger room. It was full of lights, and there was an upper level with a separate room overlooking the space. At one end of the room were armed guards dressed in black, and at the other end were white doors that were closed.

"Hello Amy," a giant voice boomed from somewhere. It was changed somehow though, and wasn't recognisable. It didn't even sound human, more robotic. The voice continued without her response.

"You are free to go, if you can." The white doors opened and beyond them was blackness. Complete and utter darkness. Amy was confused, she knew it was a test of sorts, but in a way that didn't matter. Beyond that darkness, was something better. So she didn't think twice, and starting walking towards it. Nobody moved to stop her. She reached the edge of the room, and saw the blackness. She couldn't see anything there, but took a step forward anyway.

Amy was pushed back. Two guards emerged from the shadow as the loud voice let forth a cackling laugh.

"You chose differently last time, how interesting. I'm sorry, but we aren't quite done with you yet." Amy didn't fully understand but she was carried off by the two guards to another room. She was strapped to a different chair, and a woman came by with a metal tray on wheels. There were a series of needles lined up on the top.

"Be still, we have a few to get through," she said to Amy. Amy swallowed hard and braced herself for what was to come.

Daylight warmed Amy's face and she relished the feeling. She eventually opened her eyes and took in her surroundings. She was on the curb in a small lane-way. Her back was against a building and she was wearing different clothes. They were rough, dirty and ripped. It didn't feel right, but she couldn't remember what she should have been wearing. Everything was muffled, hazy and difficult. She found a piece of paper in her clothes with an address. That was easy, she could do that.

She walked down the street, oblivious to the strange looks she was getting. She saw a man with glasses waiting for a bus and stopped next to him.

"Excuse me," she said, the words hard to form and coming out slurred. The man turned to face her, and a look of disgust on his face quickly showed then was replaced by sympathy.

"I need to go here. Am I going the right way?" He looked at the note and thought for a moment.

"Yes. Just make sure you turn left at the next traffic lights."

"Thank you," she said and walked off. She couldn't think about anything, so she just walked. After waiting at the lights for a time, she remembered his directions and turned left instead of crossing. She took the paper out and looked at it again. She was closer. She decided to hold it out in front of her for easy reference. After a few blocks she thought that she was almost there. She turned to look at the other side of the street and felt a tug. Her paper was gone, someone had snatched it from her.

"Noooo," she said to herself, she had no other ideas on where to go. She walked on, then stopped suddenly. She recognised the building, and on instinct walked in like she belonged there. She pressed the elevator button for up and then the eleventh floor. She walked through the entry of an office and sat down at a desk. A man walked past, saw her and ran over with concern on his face.

"Amy! What's going on?"

"Who?" she said.

"I'll get Samantha to come and get you," the man said, then walked off. Amy sat there, wondering at the man's panic. He returned to keep an eye on her, but said no more. Then a woman arrived, and Amy overhead them talking.

"Thanks for the call David. Has she said anything else?"

"No, I'm not sure she knows where she is or what's happening."

"It's ok I'll take her to the doctor." The woman walked over and looked at Amy.

"Hey Amy it's Samantha. Let's go." Amy nodded and walked with her. They walked to a bus stop, then caught the bus to a small doctor's clinic. The waiting room was full of kids with the sniffles. However when the doctor came out to get the next patient, he saw Amy and brought her in immediately.

Amy had trouble answering his questions and had to undergo many different tests. She waited outside while the doctor spoke to Samantha.

"I'll rush the test results through and we should get a picture tomorrow. However just from an examination I can see that she's had a cocktail of just about every illicit drug we know about. That combined with her regular medication would explain most of this, but there's something else. There's something else at work here." Samantha nodded and listened carefully. She thought about the dream altering pill that Amy had taken, but didn't want to mention it to the doctor.

"Will she recover normally from this?" Samantha asked.

"I'd say she should recover her faculties when the drugs completely leave her system. But I can't predict what lasting damage there may be. It could be nothing, it could be something. There are a lot of unknowns."

"Ok, now between us. Is this something she could have done to herself?"

"If it were just the crazy drug cocktail, it's possible although unlikely. But this combination of things is not something anyone would do to themselves. How would you even get all the different drugs?"

"Thanks Dr. Edwards. How long do you think she'll need?"

"A week."

"I'll look after her. Thanks again."

"I'll call when I have the results," Dr. Edwards said and Samantha left his office. She rescued Amy from the sneezing kids and they walked home. Samantha convinced Amy to lie on the couch, and soon after she was asleep. Samantha decided to do some catching up, so she went in Amy's room and grabbed the notebooks. She read through the stories of Amy's dreams. She was completely moved by the things that Amy had gone through already. As strong as Samantha felt, she knew that she'd never really confronted her fears. In a way she thought that Amy was stronger.

Next she looked over the drawings and viewed them in conjunction with Amy's clue board. She had been all too happy to dismiss Amy's ideas as a bit paranoid and silly. Coincidental. Looking at Amy now, and reviewing her research it became clear to Samantha that something was going on.

"What happened to you?" Samantha said softly. She had never really thought her friend crazy, but always let the possibility linger in her mind. But now her mind was changed. Amy was many things, but not crazy.

Samantha had only met Amy by chance, a few years ago. Samantha had been living in a share house, and it was lots of fun. But between her work and the parties at the house she never got time to unwind. She was stuck in a life without having the space to move forward. So she started looking for somewhere else to live. She saw the ad to live with a quiet female in a nice apartment in a quiet neighbourhood and leapt at it.

She remembered how Amy looked at the interview. She seemed quite shy and withdrawn. Amy had explained that she now wanted someone to live in her spare room to help out with the rent. But Samantha saw through that, she saw the request for another presence in the flat, a friend. It was just the thing Samantha wanted, so she gave Amy a warm smile and the rest was history. They had become good friends over the last few years, and the living arrangements suited them both perfectly. It was a quiet place, and their work was at different hours so they weren't always in each other's hair, but there was still someone around. Samantha called up her work and told them she would be out for a few days and then busied herself, waiting while Amy rested.

The next morning Amy awoke on the couch, feeling groggy. She walked around the apartment, and checked in on Samantha. She was asleep, but when Amy called out she opened her eyes immediately.

"Good morning. Hungry?" Samantha said.

"Yeah, I hadn't realised."

"Ok I'll make us something." Samantha looked through the cupboards and realised they didn't have much, so she served up cereal with milk. Amy wolfed it down hungrily.

"How do you feel?"

"Better. I'm almost myself, but there's gaps. And all of the last day is pretty hazy."

"Well while you slept I looked through your notebook, I hope you don't mind." Amy was at first shocked, but then nodded.

"It's alright, I just was a bit surprised."

"Yeah, well you went through some crazy things in your dreams. But that's not the important bit. I've looked at your board of clues, and I think you're on to something. I'm sorry that I doubted you before."

"It's fine, I was a sleep deprived mess when I started to piece it together so I know how it sounded. What do you think we should do?"

"Did you dream last night?"

"No, nothing."

"Well, we should work on that last clue you drew. I'm not sure where you are getting them from, but following them is the way forward," Samantha said. She handed the graphical notebook to Amy who opened the first page.

"Ok so this is the Keystone Endeavour logo. They're doing the redevelopment of the historic area and are about to break ground," Amy explained. Samantha nodded and Amy continued.

"Next we have the some gold bar. One of the founders of the Keystone company is a man named Goldberg. It's a bit of a tenuous link, but highly coincidental." Samantha nodded.

"Then it was the clock, which you recognised. But it was the newspaper clue I got which made it solid."

"I didn't give you that."

"I know, I have my suspicions where it came from. Anyway I investigated it, and discovered that the clock had come from the old theatre that's in the historic area."

"So that's another tie to the development project?"

"Yeah," Amy said, turning the page again.

"This is the feather, which seems to be referring to a man named Dr. Gary Featherby."

"That's the last thing you told me before you disappeared."

"Yeah, let me think. I met him, and something happened after. But it's not clear."

"What's the next clue then?" Samantha asked. Amy turned the page and then dropped the book. Samantha picked it up and looked at the picture. It was an old style doctor's or dentist's chair. She looked over at Amy, who was staring at nothing, her mouth slightly open.

"Amy what's wrong?"

"They strapped me in that chair."

"Who did?"

"Roger Butler is Dr. Gary Featherby."

"He did this?"

"No, they did," Amy said, then went quiet. Samantha waited a minute, and then went to speak, but Amy started up again.

"He gave me something to take in case they came. It was a taxi."

"He gave you a taxi?"

"No I took it in the taxi. The driver wouldn't let me out."

"Who gave it to you?" Samantha asked patiently.

"Dr. Featherby."

"Where did the taxi take you?"

"The pill did something, it helped."

"Helped with what?"

"The things they did. It stopped the old dreams, just new dreams. But bad ones."

"The doctor said they gave you a lot of drugs."

"Yeah, but the pill helped. That's not important, this is," Amy said, pointing at the drawing of the old chair. Samantha was about to ask her something else, when she heard a knock at the door. Cautiously Samantha stood up and crept up to the door. She peered through the peep hole and saw an ordinary looking man in his thirties standing there. She opened the door a fraction to see what he wanted.

"Hello," the man said cheerfully.

"Hello."

"Does an Amy Dantes live here?"

"Yes, why?"

"I found this bag on the corner of Market and Firth sticking out of a rubbish bin. It seemed like a nice bag so I investigated." Samantha sized the man up, he looked and sounded genuine.

"Oh wow thank you. Let me take your number so she can thank you herself," Samantha said.

"No that's fine, glad to see it returned. Take care," the man said then left. Samantha took the bag inside and noticed that Amy had fallen asleep. Samantha took the bag and emptied it out on the dining table. She checked the inside of the bag for any hidden electronics or strange objects.

"Now who is paranoid?" she thought to herself. She didn't find anything unusual and then emptied Amy's wallet. There was nothing added to it, and even the money was still there.

"Very strange," Samantha said softly. She put everything back in the bag and waited for Amy to wake up.

She didn't have to wait long. Amy gasped and suddenly opened her eyes.

"Another dream?" Samantha asked.

"No. No dreams, just nothing."

"How are you feeling?"

"Better. Sorry about before, that memory triggered something. I think I had some sort of drug fuelled episode while I was gone."

"Well the last thing you talked about was that Dr. Featherby. Let's start there."

"No, I remember his reaction. He was freaking out, I think he was scared that I tracked him down. But he wasn't scared of me, there must be some link between me being taken and my visiting him. I don't want that to happen again."

"Yeah I can understand that. Hey just before some guy dropped off your bag. He said he found it at the corner of Market and Firth."

"That's a block away from my work. Did I go into work before?"

"Yeah dressed like a hobo. They were kind of freaked out."

"Oh no."

"It'll be fine. The doctor said you should take a week off so I called both our works and sorted it out."

"Oh well, I guess there's more serious problems than my colleagues thinking I'm crazy." Amy walked over to the table and picked up her bag. She was about to empty it when Samantha stopped her.

"I already did that." Samantha said. Amy laughed.

"Great minds eh?"

"You mentioned that the last drawing is important." Amy picked up the notebook again and looked at the drawing of the old chair.

"Yeah, I'm not going to pretend that I can remember all of what happened, but I was in this exact chair. If we can find it, we can find where I was. Hopefully that leads us to the people that Dr. Featherby is scared of."

"I don't like this Amy. It was better when it was a crazy theory you had."

"Yeah I know, but I need to get to the bottom of this. There's something else going on that we're missing. And I can't just resume my life knowing that these things could just happen to me."

"Yeah we have to do something, but I still don't like it."

CHAPTER SEVENTEEN

DETECTIVE

Amy rose the next day with a single purpose: to discover the origins of the chair she drew. She knew that would lead her to her next clue. She woke Samantha and they had breakfast together.

"Any more dreams?" Samantha said.

"No."

"Well we don't know how this works. It could be that you need to track down this clue first, it could be that the drugs in your system are blocking it."

"Yeah, it's odd. I wanted the dreams to stop, but now I think they could be useful."

"You could always ask?"

"No, it is more important to find what I'm up against."

"Well let's start with an antique dealer then?"

"Sure," Amy said, and put the graphic notebook in her bag. They got into Amy's car, a stock white sedan, and Samantha gave directions. They found a park opposite the road from 'Archie's Antiques'.

"Doesn't look like much," Amy said dubiously.

"Don't judge, Archie is super knowledgeable," Samantha said. They crossed the road carefully and entered the shop. There was a wide array of antiques from furniture to clocks and jewellery. There were even old signs. Amy looked through the shop, and didn't spot anything like the chair. She was about to leave when Samantha stopped her.

"Just hold on a minute, give me the notebook." Samantha walked up to the sales counter and Amy followed. The man standing behind it was in his sixties, and wearing dusty overalls.

"Hey Archie how are you going?" Samantha said.

"Just swell, thanks for asking. It's been ages, how are you?"

"Oh I'm good. We have a special request today, wondering if you can help us."

"Sure, what can I do for you today?"

"We're looking for something exactly like this chair," Samantha said, offering Archie the book. He put on the glasses hanging around his neck and examined it closely.

"I'd say that's a William's doctor chair, close to one hundred years old. They're a specialty item, I don't really get them."

"Oh well thanks for your help."

"Don't thank me yet, now I know an old codger who is batty about these things. Only deals in old medical furniture. Let me find his details," Archie said. He proceeded to rummage through all his papers and notebooks.

"Aha. This is him I'll write this a bit neater for you," he said, carefully writing some information on a square of paper.

"Good luck and take care," Archie said with a smile.

"Thanks so much."

"Thank you," Amy said and the two of them left the shop.

"How do you know him?" Amy asked.

"Well I was really into antiques when I was younger. Would be hanging around his store all the time. But when I grew up a little I put the idea on hold until I got my own house."

"I had no idea."

"Ha-ha yeah, well one day this party girl has gotta settle down," Samantha laughed. Once they were in the car, Samantha scrutinised the address.

"I've got a fair idea of where this is, let's got check it out."

"Definitely," Amy said. She pulled out and drove carefully, taking heed of Samantha's directions. Ten minutes later, Amy spoke up suddenly.

"Hey see that black car, I think it might be following us."

"Usually I'd laugh it off as silly, but those days are over. Turn right here, it's a small lane that nobody ever uses." Amy turned and drove at the same speed, as if the route had been planned all along. She slowed as she reached a T junction and kept an eye on the rear mirror.

"Well that's mighty suspicious," Amy said as she saw the black car turn into the lane.

"Look it could be a coincidence, but let's have some fun with it anyway," Samantha said.

"Turn right so he sees it, then left and then left again." After Amy made the turns Samantha directed her to speed up a little.

"Now we're doubling back to the lane we came from, and we've left plenty of possible turns behind us." Amy turned back into the original lane and sped along it to rejoin the main road. The whole time Amy kept an eye on the rear mirror and saw no sign of the black car.

"After this expedition, let's get super paranoid," Samantha said.

"What do you mean?"

"I'll explain later."

"Ok," Amy said, confused. They drove for a further ten minutes and parked.

"The place we want should be a few blocks down this street."

"I could have parked closer," Amy said.

"Super paranoid remember? Let's assume the car is bugged or tracked."

"I like your style."

"Also, I know this guy who is a bit of an electronics guru. We can get him to check it out."

"Sure. Well the thing is, I haven't driven the car since all this started happening, so there has been ample opportunity for someone to do something."

"Now there's the paranoia I was looking for. You're way too normal at the moment," Samantha said, laughing. Amy just shook her head and continued to walk. After walking three blocks they saw the store.

"Johnson's Medical Antiquities," Amy said, reading out the sign.

"So we want to track down this chair right?" Samantha said.

"Yeah, so let's see where he gets them from, where he sells to. We have no idea how far this trail stretches."

"Got it. Leave this one to me, I'll get us something," Samantha said with a wink and a smile. They walked into the store and saw that they were definitely in the right place.

"Archie you're a legend," Samantha said to herself. There were chairs of all types, old medical tools, bags and much more. Amy browsed while Samantha went straight to the man at the back. He was wearing pants and shirt with suspenders. His white hair was neatly combed back.

"Hello, I'm hoping you're the man that can help me," Samantha said.

"Hello to you, here's hoping. What do you need help with?"

"We are desperately looking for one of these chairs. My friend did a sketch of it for me." Samantha handed him the notebook and he pondered it for a minute.

"That's a William's classic 12a, very hard to come by. I'm afraid I don't have any in the shop right now."

"Really? Do you expect some to come in soon?"

"No, that's not the kind of thing that just walks in from a dealer. I'm afraid you need to luck into one. If you'd like I can add you to the waiting list."

"Waiting list?"

"Yes, I have a list of interested people waiting for these kinds of chairs."

"Collectors?"

"Yes, mainly collectors."

"So they might even have one like it already."

"Yes, I'd say so. Many of these collectors are keen on restoring and are always looking for new chairs to achieve a perfectly restored one."

"I've an idea then. Could I have a copy of that list, and try and buy a chair from one of them directly? It would work for you, since they'd be even more in the market for another one if you got one in."

"I'm afraid I can't do that, it's a breach of privacy," the dealer said. Samantha sidled up to him and placed her hand on his shoulder.

"Mr. Johnson is it?" she said. He nodded.

"This is a special favour for a friend, can't I just glance at the list with you? If any of the names are local and have a shop front then that's not a breach of privacy is it? I would really appreciate it." Samantha was quite friendly and suggestive with her tone of voice and body language, but at the same time a picture of class and promising nothing. Mr. Johnson blushed a little and shuffled back. He cleared his voice and then spoke.

"Well, I suppose that would be fine, since the list would stay here and you wouldn't be knocking on the door at folks' homes."

"Thank you so much," she said. Mr. Johnson went out the back, and returned with an old ledger. He flipped through the pages and found the right page. He motioned for Samantha to come closer. She did so and tried to focus on two things: an entry that looked suspicious and an entry that looked like a dealer so she could pretend that it was her choice.

"This one wheels and deals a bit," Mr, Johnson said pointing at an entry. It perfectly fulfilled what Samantha had asked for, but she hadn't found a suspicious entry yet.

"It's not that close is it?" she commented while continuing to look at the list. She pretended to look for a better one and completed her scanning.

"I think that's your best chance," he said.

"You're exactly right, and I wouldn't feel bad about contacting him or saying that you referred me," Samantha said. She copied down the address and phone number for the shop.

"You've been a fantastic help, thank you so much," she said.

"You are welcome, good luck with your search," he replied and waved goodbye. Samantha found Amy and handed her the paper as they left the shop.

"What's this?" Amy asked.

"Plan B. If my memory is good, then we just hit pay dirt."

"What did you find?"

"On the waiting list for those chairs is a certain Dr. Richard Nelson."

"My therapist? It's just a waiting list, it's nothing concrete."

"But it's also highly coincidental. The expert said that most of the people on his waiting list are collectors who already have one of these chairs."

"I totally agree. But I just don't want to think that my therapist, although he's a bit weird, has anything to do with all this."

"There's only one way to find out."

"I know. I'll do it. But first, let's find your electronics friend."

"I was going to suggest the same thing," Samantha said. They returned to the car and drove to a large house out in the suburbs.

"Is he a family man?" Amy said when they arrived.

"Nah, he just needs a lot of space. You'll see." Samantha said. They walked up to the front door and knocked. It looked like all the rest, nicely maintained garden and freshly painted exterior. After a minute, a dishevelled looking man with a curly beard opened the door.

"Hey Sam," Samantha said.

"Hey Sam," he replied with a grin.

"Can we come in?" Samantha said.

"Sure. Just mind your feet." He opened the door further and Amy's jaw dropped. There were cables everywhere and each room she passed was full of gear stashed on every surface. They stopped at the rear of the house in the relatively clear kitchen. Sam sat down at the table and they sat down opposite him.

"Pretty cool huh?" Sam said.

"I had no idea, it's full on. The front yard looks perfect," Amy said.

"Yeah I get a landscaper in, I don't want any nosing around from my neighbours. They probably know that I kind of run a business here and it's techy, but the neat yard reassures them."

"The place looks exactly as I remember it," Samantha said.

"Nah c'mon you haven't noticed all my cable management? It's heaps better now."

"Sorry, it's just a sea of cables to me. I'm still impressed though."

"So, what brings you here today?"

"My friend Amy here, has had an interesting week. I won't go into details, but we think someone's following her. Can you check out her car?"

"That's an odd one. Look it's going to be a time intensive job, you sure about this?"

"Yeah I know it sounds a bit paranoid."

"Oh no it's not paranoid, it's just being careful. I just want to make sure you're serious."

"We are," Amy said.

"Ok well leave the car with me. It'll take a day or two to give it a proper look over. I might need to throw something together to help me scan it."

"What do I owe you?" Amy asked.

"If there's nothing there, buy me a case of beer for my time. If I find something, you've got bigger problems and I'm glad I helped you out."

"Are you sure?"

"100%, a friend of a fellow Sam is a friend of me. Besides I've gotta pay her back for all the free drinks."

"You're a life saver Sam. Here's our home number, I'm hoping we have to buy you a case of beer."

"Me too."

"Here's the car keys. Thanks again," Amy said and left the keys on the table.

"I'll be in touch," Sam said and walked them to the front door. Samantha and Amy walked to the main road and waited for either a taxi or bus. A bus arrived first and they hopped on travelling back into the city and then following their usual route home.

It was after 5pm when they arrived home and there was a message on the answering machine.

"You don't think he found anything yet?" Amy said.

"I'd be surprised." Samantha pressed the play button. The message was from Dr. Edwards, he had the test results and he provided a contact number.

"I'll call him tomorrow morning," Amy said.

"How are you doing?" Samantha said.

"I'm pretty drained. There's so much going on, I'm having trouble processing it all. I don't feel good about this Dr. Nelson thing."

"Yeah, it could be nothing. But what if it's not?"

"That's the thing. Don't worry about me, I'm going to do what's necessary. I'll have to find a way."

"Don't forget you have me too."

"Yeah, I appreciate it. But I won't have you doing things I should do myself," Amy said. With that said, she called up and ordered Thai food for dinner. They enjoyed the food and didn't discuss the events of the day any further. Amy went to bed, hopeful and also nervous. She was on the edge of something, and didn't know where it would take her.

The next morning she called the doctor back. She was put on hold briefly, and then the doctor answered.

"Hello Amy, how are you feeling today?"

"Better. More stable. However I can feel the gaps in my memory, and they don't feel good."

"That's fine. I have the results of your blood work. As I suggested you tested positive for all the usual suspects."

"Like a spiked drink?"

"No, these concentrations are impossible for that. Someone systemically pumped you full of drugs. I would say the benefit here, is that you wouldn't have developed a dependency or addiction for any of them."

"What else?"

"Well, on a hunch I did one more test. You were administered an unusually high dosage of a psychoactive drug. It is generally used by psychologists for the treatment of anxiety, but in incorrect doses can bring about confusion, amnesia, delirium and increased emotional state."

"Thank you for the information."

"Do I need to refer this matter to the police?"

"No, I think I know what happened. Thanks again Dr. Edwards."

"Take care, please keep in touch." Amy hung up the phone and almost collapsed onto the couch.

"What did he say?"

"Well apart from the cocktail of recreational drugs, I was given an overdose of a psychoactive drug usually used by psychologists to treat anxiety."

"Holy shit."

"Yeah. The coincidences keep piling up. I'm actually scared to go back to his office."

"Do you want me to go?"

"No, if he's the one he'll expect me to go back for therapy. I'll have to use that opportunity to scope out his office for the chair."

"Well, what if there's no chair?"

"We check his house."

"And if there's no chair there?"

"Then we keep looking. And if there's no chair, then he might be legitimately wanting one."

"And if he has a chair?"

"Then he doesn't need another one, unless he's a collector. So he's probably got a spare one somewhere, with straps."

"That seems fair. Either way, we're going to have to investigate him closely. There's just too much evidence that points in his direction."

"Yeah in a way I've changed my mind. I hope it's him, because if it isn't we're out of luck."

"So when are you going to go?"

"Today, I don't want it hanging over me."

"What do you want me to do?" Samantha said.

"Stay home in case Sam calls. I'll meet you back here when I'm done and we'll work out the next move."

"Sure." Amy prepared herself and then went to leave.

"Good luck, you'll be fine. Just pretend it's like normal," Samantha said, giving Amy a quick hug.

"Thanks, I'll see you soon." Amy walked out the door and out to the bus, acting like she was going to see Dr. Nelson as usual. However it was anything but normal. She suspected him of doing horrible things and was returning to try to find evidence. Did he do this to all his patients? Amy quelled the thought, she was getting ahead of herself. She had a simple task, see if Dr. Nelson's office had a William's classic 12a chair. It wasn't conclusive by itself, but suggested a lot. Plus the chair had to be significant, it was in one of her dream drawings.

She arrived, and paused before going in.

"Just be normal," she said to herself and then opened the door. The waiting area was exactly as she remembered it. There was someone else waiting already, which worked in her favour. She approached the receptionist.

"Hi, I don't have an appointment today, I was wondering if there were any openings?"

"Hi Amy. Let me see here. Well there's no availabilities, but I think I could probably squeeze you in after this next person."

"Great, what would the wait be?"

"Between 30-60 minutes."

"Ok, hey do you have a bathroom here?"

"Of course, down the hall and second door on your right." Amy thanked her and walked off towards the bathroom. The last door on the left was Dr. Nelson's consultation office. She had been there many times, and not see the chair. There were three doors on the right, the middle one being the bathroom. She tried the first door, saw it was just a filing room.

"Next one," she heard the receptionist call out. Amy shuffled along to the next door, but knowing it was the bathroom kept going. She didn't know what the last room was. She slowly turned the handle and discovered that it wasn't locked. Just as she was about to enter she heard voices coming from the opposite room.

"They must be leaving," she thought to herself and abandoned her attempt at the mystery room. She quietly rushed over to the bathroom and entered, locking the door. She huddled just inside, listening carefully. There were voices and footsteps. She waited for them to fade, and then return and fade again. She flushed the toilet, washed her hands and carefully closed the door. She was trying to minimise noise to not draw any attention from the receptionist.

Thinking it safe, she crept back up to the mystery room. She paused and listened, and heard nothing. Using this opportunity she quickly entered the room as quietly as possible. Once inside she turned and looked at what was there. It was a memorabilia room, with trophies, medals, certificates and more littered all around the room. The centrepiece was a beautifully restored William's classic 12a. Just seeing it gave Amy the chills. It wasn't just what the idea of the chair meant, it was the look of it too. It brought back the feelings of her capture.

"Leave," she told herself, knowing that she was done. She left the room and ensured the door was closed behind her. As she returned to the waiting area she had an idea. She clutched her stomach and put a pained look on her face.

"Hi, sorry I'm really not feeling well. I better go home," she said to the receptionist.

"Oh, no problem. I hope you feel better. Do you want to make another appointment?"

"I really can't," Amy said, wincing. She sold it perfectly, the receptionist was empathetic and said goodbye. Amy continued her act all the way out of the building and a block down the street. Then she moved into a faster walk.

She thought about what the chair meant. It meant that Dr. Nelson loved those chairs, since he had one in his trophy room and was on the waiting list for more. It didn't mean that he had another one for other purposes, but the imagery was just too suggestive. It was way too coincidental. She couldn't shake the feeling that it was him, and now she had to prove it. Amy arrived home to find things just as she'd left them.

"No phone calls. How did you go?" Samantha said.

"He had a bloody pristine showroom quality exact same model of that chair."

"Oh sweetie, how do you feel?"

"Angry, confused and confident that he's bad. But without any proof."

"Ok well let's find some. Where do we start?"

"This place I was taken, it was way out in the sticks. On the outskirts of the city."

"That's a good start."

"So we attack it from two angles. We can do title checks and see if Dr. Nelson is connected to any properties there. Also we can use the chair as a way to narrow it down. What if there's an abandoned lot or antique warehouse or something that might just have the chair naturally," Amy said defiantly. She was focused entirely on the problem. Samantha agreed with her ideas and they brainstormed some options. Samantha was going to call any antique or second hand dealers in the area Amy suggested and ask them about abandoned lots or places to get old furniture. Amy was going to go into work and do some research on Dr. Nelson. She could find out what companies he was involved in, and what properties he had an interest in. Chances were with their information combined they could select some potential locations to visit.

Amy chose midday as the best time to visit her work. That way most people would be either at lunch or busy doing things before lunch. She didn't want to attract much attention, just to get what she needed and get out. She also didn't want to explain what she was doing to anyone. She arrived at her building and took the lift up. On a whim she walked over to the windows and looked out at the city. She felt a bit apprehensive, but the dominant feeling was one of wonder. The busy, thriving city was fascinating. She never really looked at it this way. Not wishing to waste too much time she hurried over to her desk.

She began by doing a directory search on Dr. Richard Nelson. Thankfully there was only one. She only found two entries, one for his practice and the other called 'Inspired Planning'. She printed out a list of directors for 'Inspired Planning' and the place of business. She skimmed through the print out looking for anything of interest. The place of business was only a PO Box.

"That's odd, I thought it needed to be a street address," she said to herself. There were five listed directors, Dr. Nelson being one. Another one caught her eye though.

"Walter Goldberg, we meet again," Amy said softly. She thought it was very interesting that he was a director of this strange company linked to Dr. Nelson, and also Keystone Endeavours. Amy changed her approach, and instead did a search on Walter Goldberg. She found a list of six companies. She printed all the details. Amy checked her watch, it was approaching one o'clock. Most of her colleagues would be back in the office soon.

She limited her investigation to one more thing. She searched for any property linked to Inspired Planning. She found three results and printed them all out. She collated all her data in a file and put it in her bag. Not a moment too soon, as she heard someone approaching.

"Oh hey Amy! What are you doing here? Feeling better?" David said. Amy had to scramble for a proper response.

"Hi David. Yeah getting there, but I just had to come in. There was a little thing on my mind that I couldn't forget about."

"I know the feeling. What are your plans for the rest of the day?"

"Oh I think I'll go home and rest. This was my expedition."

"Well take care of yourself, see you soon," David said with a smile and continued on to his desk. Amy felt a surge of relief then left immediately to avoid any other difficult conversations.

She grabbed some sushi on the way home, but didn't want to look at her documents yet. She found Samantha sitting at the kitchen table with pages of notes and the phone within arm's reach.

"Any luck?"

"Yeah, I think so. What about you?"

"Bits and pieces. The most promising lead is a company that both Dr. Nelson and Walter Goldberg are directors in. The company is linked to three properties."

"Wow, that's weird. Worth investigating," Samantha said. Before she could continue the phone rang and she answered it. Amy opened her file and looked over the printed documents.

The addresses she had didn't give anything away.

"Well there's good news and bad news," Samantha said after she hung up the phone.

"Who was it?"

"That was Sam. The good news is that there's no audio recording devices in the car."

"And the bad news?"

"There's a location tracker. It's only medium range so anyone monitoring it has to be in the general area."

"Well at least I'm not paranoid without cause. Did Sam take it out?"

"No he said it was up to us," Samantha said. Amy thought for a minute. It wasn't completely unexpected, but it was also crazy. A tracking device on her car? But there was only one way forward.

"We have to leave it. If we take it out they'll know that I'm on to them, and I don't know how they will react. They may even just replace it and then we will think we're safe when we're not."

"Yeah to be honest, I was thinking the same thing. We'll have to be careful in how we use the car from now on."

"Yeah. There might even be an opportunity later on for some misdirection."

"Ha-ha honey you are wasted on the legal profession."

"Maybe. Let's look at these locations," Amy said. They dragged out a street directory and looked at all the addresses that they had noted down. They eliminated the addresses Samantha had that were too far from the business addresses.

"So here's our shortlist," Samantha said.

"Yeah. An abandoned hospital, an old medical supplies factory and the three business addresses."

"At least it won't take long to scope them out, but it's a long way to get over to that neck of the woods."

"Yeah we need a car."

"Let's visit Sam and see what he says." Amy put the shortlist of addresses and the street directory into her bag and they left. Two buses later they were back at Sam's house.

"Welcome back," he said as he opened the door.

"So how bad is it in your expert opinion?" Amy asked.

"It's a tough one," Sam explained as they walked through the house, "I don't often get a look at this kind of stuff. It is quite sophisticated but like I mentioned on the phone still needs manual tracking within a certain radius."

"How far?"

"A couple of kilometres."

"How accurate is the positioning?"

"I can only guess. At worst probably the block your car is on."

"That sounds like something we can work around most of the time. Can we borrow your car tonight?"

"Tonight?" Samantha said, confused.

"We can't sneak around in broad daylight."

"Hey fine by me, I'm just looking out for you."

"I'll manage," Amy said defiantly.

"For tonight only," Sam said.

"Thanks again. We owe you one," Samantha said. Amy took both sets of car keys and worked out a plan. She drove her car home and Samantha followed. Once they were home, they left Amy's car and Samantha drove Sam's car. It took them two hours to drive out to the region they wanted to investigate, called 'Bilford'. The streets were large suburban blocks. Then they suddenly changed to industrial lots.

"Not much interesting development here, it's nothing or warehouses," Amy said. Samantha agreed. Amy directed them to the first business address on their list. It was easy to find. They didn't even need to stop when they found it, as it was just a large empty lot.

"That's one down," Samantha said. Amy crossed it off the list. The next address was more promising when they drove up. It was a large warehouse. They parked the car and walked over near it. Dusk was falling but it wasn't completely dark yet.

"So who's going to check it out?" Samantha asked.

"Scissors, paper, rock?"

"You're on." Samantha played rock and Amy paper.

"You're lookout then."

"Sure, be careful," Amy said. She loitered on the street near the gate, occasionally peering in at Samantha. After entering the gates, Samantha had walked up to the warehouse doors and discovered that they were locked. There were some garbage bins and smaller sheds on the side so she approached those. Looking up, she saw that by standing on one of the sheds she could look in and see inside the warehouse. She clambered up the giant dumpsters and onto a big box and then onto the shed roof. Pausing for a moment to catch her breath, she inched over to the edge of the shed and peered into the warehouse. The whole place was full of construction supplies. Bags of materials, planks of wood and other beams. Samantha carefully climbed down, dusted off her hands and jogged back to Amy.

"Full of construction supplies," Samantha said.

"Definitely not it then," Amy said and crossed it off her list. She just had the one more address for Inspired Planning. A mixture of disappointment and relief hit her when they arrived. It was a tiny hole in the wall business premises. The front doors were glass, so they could look in. There were only some lounges, a few desks and a tiny office up the back.

"Might be worth a look later, but not what we are after," Samantha said.

"Yeah. Well maybe it was a stretch expecting them to do dodgy things from registered addresses," Amy said. Next on their list was the abandoned hospital.

"I really don't like the idea of this."

"Don't worry, we'll both go in," Samantha said. It was dark by the time they found it, and the building was very old. It looked unsafe, and there wasn't much street lighting giving it a very ominous look. Shivers were going down Amy's spine as they snuck in through the old, poorly secured gates. A light wind whistled around the empty buildings, putting them both on edge. As they approached the main doors, Amy shook her head, and they continued around the perimeter. After five minutes of walking they found another large building around the back of the lot.

"I don't think this is it, I think we drove right in," Amy said.

"There's a small lane behind here, let's look closer," Samantha said. It was just as she said, with a driveway providing access to a rear door. There were no lights or any hint of activity inside. Samantha started to lift up the roller door and Amy assisted her. The building looked largely empty but was too dark to tell. Amy inspected either side of the doors, looking for lights. She flicked a switch but nothing happened. Samantha found a flash light. She banged it a few times and flicked it on and off and it finally turned on, giving off a weak light. Old rotting furniture was strewn haphazardly around the area, with the centre of the space mostly empty. There was another smaller door at the back that they headed towards. The door was slightly ajar, so Amy carefully pushed it open trying to see what was within. She could see a large shape in the middle of the room.

Samantha stepped closer and shone a light onto the object. It was a chair, very similar to the one they had been looking for. Amy jumped a bit. However after the initial shock she stepped closer and inspected it. The chair was rusted through and broken.

"I'm not sure what this means," she said.

"What's important is that it says that this isn't the place," Samantha said. Instead of returning the way they came, they exited to the lane and walked around the block. Samantha's light died and she tossed it away. Once it was gone they realised just how dark it was out. There were barely any street lights. Amy was incredibly relieved when they made it back to the car.

"I have a feeling that we're close," she said.

"Well there's just one more place to look at," Samantha said. They got back into the car with relish and drove in silence to the last location. Amy could feel something in the pit of her stomach. It was as if she knew something was about to happen. She didn't want to speak up, lest the fear she felt was obvious in the cracking of her voice. They were a long way from home, with no means of protection and traipsing around in the dark looking for the warehouse where she was held captive. It was not a good situation to be in, and a week earlier she would not have imagined it possible. But events were in motion, and she had to move with them.

Within minutes they arrived at the last location on their list. It was a very large nondescript warehouse with tightly locked gates. Amy and Samantha had to check the address a few times and drive around the block to make sure they had the right one.

"I'd hate to break into the wrong place," Samantha said. Once they were satisfied they parked and stood out the front. The street was very poorly lit, and it was very hard to see anything in the distance.

"Well it looks dark enough," Amy said.

"Yes, but can we find a way in?" Samantha countered.

"There will be a way." Amy walked ahead and Samantha followed. After completing a lap of the building they investigated a small passage between the building and its neighbour. There was a section of wall that was a flat rectangle on the top, possibly due to a small garage or shed against the wall. That inviting wall platform was very close to the adjoining building.

"If we could get up there, that's a way in," Amy said. Samantha wasn't too keen, but they went over for a closer look. There was a ladder leading to a fire escape on the other side.

"Let's try it."

"Are you sure?" Samantha said. Amy nodded and started climbing up the ladder. The first landing of the fire escape was the right height. They stopped there and looked over. Amy looked down at the ground and reckoned that she was about five metres up. The edge of the fire escape was so close that she could almost touch the wall. So she took a deep breath and hauled herself up so that she was sitting on the thin edge of the fire escape railing. From that position she could touch her feet on the wall, but moving over would not be easy.

"I really hope I don't regret this," Amy said as she grasped the railing and twisted herself so that she was facing the fire escape and her feet were unsteadily placed on the wall. By stretching out she stepped back on the wall section and then pushed against the fire escape. She maintained her weight backwards, teetered and fell down on her bottom. But she was safely on the wall platform.

"You ok?" Samantha called out, as quietly as possible.

"Yes. Come over." Amy steadied herself and looked around for a way down. There were some large open bins full of cardboard. Amy jumped down to that, and then climbed out of the bin onto the ground. She dusted off her hands, happy with her achievement. She heard Samantha following soon after.

"How did you go?" Amy said.

"Not bad, it helps being a bit taller," Samantha said. There were no lights and noises coming from the building. They quietly and carefully walked around to the front doors. They were hefty and metal, but not locked. Amy ignored the butterflies in her stomach and her increased heart rate. She started to pull the door open and Samantha pitched in to help. They slowly swung it open and the door complied without a sound. That in itself was promising, because it suggested that the door was in regular use. The inadequate street lighting did nothing to illuminate the inside of the warehouse. It was a giant black cavity, threatening to swallow them both whole.

"This is full on," Samantha said quietly. Amy took Samantha's hand, then took a step inside. As their eyes adjusted to the dark, there still wasn't much to go on. Amy could see what looked like the walls of the warehouse, so she opted to make her way around the perimeter. With Samantha in tow they steadily crept around the edge of the warehouse. Every five or ten metres they would stop and look around, a futile effort to see something.

Towards the back of the space, Amy spotted what looked like a door set into the wall. She stopped and pointed it out to Samantha, who stared blankly for a moment, then nodded. Amy found the cool metal door knob and slowly turned it. The door opened easily into a smaller room. It was dark or darker than the warehouse space. Amy instinctively felt around for a switch near the door and found one.

"Close your eyes," she whispered. She closed her eyes and flicked the switch. Blinding brightness assaulted her, burning through her eyelids. She covered her eyes further and tried to readjust to the light.

Amy opened her eyes a little, and was thrown off by the brightness of the room. Then she recognised it as being all white. There was an object in the middle of the room but she couldn't quite see it properly. Then all of a sudden it came into perfect focus, filling her vision. Her legs failed beneath her and she collapsed onto the ground, but unable to look away from the object. Samantha quickly helped, not knowing the source of the problem. Once she had ensured Amy was alright, she took a proper look at the room. It was a perfectly white room, with a rough but serviceable antique doctor's chair in the middle. It looked like the one they were after, only it had been fitted with straps to restrain the patient.

"I'm so sorry Amy," she said. She sunk down and held Amy, while looking at the chair. How horrible it was, to see the instrument that had held Amy through her captivity. Amy sobbed, then sighed deeply.

"I shouldn't be upset, this is what we came to find," she said. Her voice was still thick with emotion.

"Yeah, let's find a clue," Samantha said. She helped Amy up and they had a closer look at the room. It was empty except for the chair. They inspected the chair, and it looked as they expected.

"There has to be something about this chair," Amy said and she examined it again. She looked for anything special, anything that could link it to its owner.

"Maybe there's no link, maybe it was just left here?" Samantha said. Amy ignored her and kept looking. She heaved the chair over angrily and inspected it from the bottom.

"Hey, can you write something down. There's stuff in my bag," Amy said.

"Sure." Samantha found the pen and notepad and prepared herself.

"Curler's Cove Feb 090620," Amy said. Samantha jotted down the words and number.

"Do you think it's a serial number?"

"Must be. Could be worth checking." Amy rose and collected her things. She wedged the door open as wide as possible and left the light. She peered out into the rest of the warehouse.

"That helps a bit. Let's see what else we can find." Samantha followed her out and they continued going around the edge of the space, this time with better vision. They came to another door, but this one had no handle. Amy carefully pushed on the door and stepped inside the room. She flicked a light switch and braced herself for the shock. She heard the hum and buzz of fluorescents and felt the light slowly increase in intensity. She opened her eyes and took in the room. It was a bathroom, with two basins and two stalls. They took a stall each and looked around for any clues. Their search turned up nothing. At best they could say that the bathroom had been maintained recently.

"Let's keep looking," Amy said. They left the bathroom and continued. After the back wall they found a staircase which went up to an area above the warehouse space. The metal stairs made a 'tink' sound as Amy walked up, with Samantha behind her and slightly out of sync.

The door was ajar, so Amy opened it the rest of the way and entered the room. She felt carpet beneath her feet and bumped into a table. There was an old lamp on the table, so Amy switched it on. One wall of the room was entirely glass, looking out at the warehouse. The rest of the room was soundproofed, but otherwise empty.

"Someone was very thorough," Samantha said.

"Yeah, odd that they left the chair though," Amy said. Samantha shrugged her shoulders. Amy switched off the lamp, and they backtracked the way they came switching off the lights as they went. Just before they reached the front door they heard something on the roof.

"Stop. Listen," Amy said. The sound increased in intensity then settled into a pattern. The moisture in the air told the rest of the story.

"Just rain," Samantha said. They waited at the open door for five minutes, watching the rain. When it looked entrenched they ran to the front gate and had a look.

There was no way to circumvent the lock. With some effort they clambered up the now slippery bins and shed.

Bridging the gap to the adjacent fire escape was harder in reverse, with the rain also increasing the difficulty. Samantha boosted Amy and supported her to get a decent hold. After she hauled herself across she helped Samantha. Once they reached the ground they were already so soaked that they just walked to the car at a leisurely pace.

They got lost three times, trying to retrace their route. It took hours to finally arrive home, and once they did Samantha parked the car a few blocks away and they walked to the apartment in the rain. After showers and baked beans they sat on the couch and discussed next moves.

"We have a clue from the chair. I'll go and ask the expert about it tomorrow."

"I'll return Sam's car then," Samantha said. Amy nodded and dragged herself off to bed before she fell asleep where she sat.

"I have a lead. Let's see where it takes me," she thought to herself before welcoming sleep.

CHAPTER EIGHTEEN

FOLLOW UP

Amy awoke late the next morning, feeling well rested. She still hadn't dreamed though. Samantha told her not to worry and they reconfirmed their plans for the day. They agreed to meet back at the house in the afternoon. Amy walked up to her car and a twinge of sadness passed through her. It was the fact that her car had been compromised, and for the time she had to just accept it. She turned on the engine and let it run for a minute. Then she headed for Johnson's Medical Antiques.

The weather was overcast, but not raining. The roads were still a little slippery from the rain so Amy drove carefully. She parked a few blocks away from the shop as before. She felt a light sprinkling as she walked but ignored it. The coolness was actually welcome. She located the antiques shop and walked in. She spotted the owner talking to a customer so browsed through the collection. She couldn't deny the quality of a lot of the pieces but she just felt like it was all a bit creepy.

"Hello again," a voice said behind her. She turned and saw the owner standing right there.

"Oh hello Mr. Johnson, we came in the other day asking about Williams chairs," Amy said.

"Of course. How did you go?"

"Thanks to your information we found a chair in reasonable condition. I came today to ask you a question about it."

"Sure, I can answer almost any question about them."

"Well, we looked over the chair and found this information carved in on the underside of the chair," Amy said then showed him the paper. He looked carefully and then commented.

"Yes this is the serial information which identifies the chair. I'm guessing you didn't find a name plate?"

"No."

"Well that same information is also inscribed on a gold name plate on the back of the chair. The plates are one of the hallmarks of the chair, so most often are the pieces taken from the chair to be resold or transplanted to another chair to improve the resale."

"Oh so there's a chance that another chair out there will have the name plate with these details stamped onto it?"

"Sure. A collector would generally do that when restoring chairs from the best parts they can find."

"Thanks again, you have been a great help."

"Come back any time," he said. Amy walked quickly out of the store, her mind bristling with possibilities. One was first and foremost though.

"Dr. Nelson's chair is immaculate, it probably has a name plate. If the name plate matches the serial number from the chair I found, that's the link," she thought to herself. However it would mean going back to his office once more, and getting a look at the chair. She drove home, contemplating how she should gain access to the trophy room again. She didn't want to repeat her last performance.

"You have something on your mind," Samantha said as Amy entered the lounge room.

"Yeah, the dealer said something interesting. Basically that serial information is usually stamped on a gold name plate on the back of the chair."

"We didn't see one. You think Dr. Nelson has that name plate on his chair?"

"Exactly. Which means going back again to his office. Which would be a second time after deciding I never wanted to return there."

"I'll go, or take me with you. It'll be easier with two of us."

"Are you sure?"

"Of course, it'll be fun," Samantha said and grinned.

"I'm not so sure of this," Amy said, but she was glad for the company. They took the car and parked it around the corner from Dr. Nelson's practice.

"So how are we going to play this? Am I the distraction?" Samantha said.

"How about you're my crazy friend that I'm bringing in for a consultation? You can wander off and do the investigation."

"Ok I'm game."

"There's a corridor behind reception. On the right you have the office, bathroom and trophy room in that order. On the left you have the consultation room."

"Got it. I'll get in to the trophy room and compare the name plate details to the ones you wrote down."

"Yes. Here's a copy of that information," Amy said and handed Samantha a slip of paper.

"Ready or not here we come," Samantha said and they walked in. The waiting room was quite full, with only two seats left. However if all went according to plan they would not need the seats. As soon as they stepped into the practice Samantha's entire demeanour changed. She had a slight slump to her walk and her gaze was off into the far off distance. She would alternate between staring at something intently and looking around aimlessly.

"Hi Amy," the receptionist said.

"Hi, it looks a bit busy today."

"Yes we're a bit behind and it was already a rather optimistic schedule."

"Well I won't try and squeeze in today, I was here to enquire about my friend. Oh she's wandered off," Amy said, gesturing at where Samantha had been. The receptionist looked at her with sympathy.

Samantha was headed down the corridor with purpose, although exerting all her effort to appear otherwise. She even hovered around the bathroom for a time before continuing. She could hear Amy talking in the distance. She had an appreciation for Amy's bravery when following in her footsteps. The trophy room was right opposite the consultation room, so Dr. Nelson could almost walk out at any time if luck was against you. She opened the trophy room door and entered carefully. Instead of closing the door fully she left it slightly ajar. Should she be discovered, it would be less suspicious. The room was full of shiny things but Samantha only had time for the chair. She walked straight over to it. Amy had been right about how well restored the chair was, it looked amazing. But it was also creepy, as it reminded her of that horrible old relic that they had found at the warehouse.

"Just how naughty are you Dr. Nelson," she said under her breath as she looked behind the chair. On the back was a gold name plate as big as her palm. She read the model number of the chair first, then the manufacturing details and serial number.

"Curler's Cove Feb 090620. You bastard," Samantha said softly. She had confirmation. She just had to return undetected.

Amy was busy explaining about her friend to the receptionist. Her years of therapy had given her plenty of different words to use.

"So I really thought Dr. Nelson could help," Amy said.

"It's so heart-warming to hear that Amy," a smooth deep voice said. Amy turned suddenly and saw Dr. Nelson standing next to her.

"Linda, I'm sure we can squeeze Amy in immediately," Dr. Nelson said. Amy froze in terror. She didn't know if he was the one, but even still the idea of spending more time with him was horrible. She had no proof, but in her mind he was guilty. She couldn't look at him without feeling disgust.

"WOOOOOOOOOOOOOOOOOOOOO!" Samantha yelled out as she jogged past. Amy regained her faculties and thought on her feet.

"Sorry, that's my friend I better chase after her," Amy said and ran out in pursuit. Dr. Nelson watched her leave with interest.

Out on the street, Samantha stopped and resumed a normal walk. Amy caught up and walked alongside.

"I thought you needed rescuing," Samantha said.

"Yeah, I was speechless and frozen."

"I totally understand, that man's a monster." Amy stopped immediately and turned to look at Samantha.

"Then you mean?"

"Yes, the name plate matches the chair we found. I don't think we'll find anything as direct unless we get a confession."

"I knew it. I just had this feeling. The more information we found the more it resonated with this feeling. Somewhere deep down I think I knew."

"Let's go home," Samantha said. They drove home in silence. Amy was thinking about what they had discovered. It was a victory in a way, but didn't feel like a revelation. Once they were back in the apartment she spoke.

"I'm not sure what to do next," Amy said.

"What do you mean?"

"Well, we got proof that Dr. Nelson is either the person who drugged me, or is linked to that person. What does that tell us?"

"That he's the lowest form of scum."

"True, but what's the significance of that?"

"I don't know. Maybe you are supposed to expose him."

"There has to be more to it. He's been seeing me for a few years now, and when I show some progress and cut off my sessions he kidnaps and drugs me? Why?"

"Yeah he can't be that worried about repeat business. You said that you found this other guy before you were taken?"

"Yes, Dr. Featherby."

"Well, maybe he didn't want you being in contact with Featherby. Didn't you say Featherby panicked when he saw you?"

"That's right. Plus I'm confident that Featherby was the one that left me that note. You think that Featherby is helping me in some way, and Dr. Nelson wants to stop it?"

"Well Featherby did go to a lot of trouble to anonymously give you that pill, and I've seen firsthand how it has helped."

"Again, why is Dr. Nelson so keen on not seeing me improve?" Amy asked. Samantha paused for a moment to think about something, and then replied.

"Forgive me for asking, but you started therapy because of something traumatic right?"

"Yes."

"Do you remember it?"

"Not clearly, just a vague feeling."

"Maybe there's something in your history, either related to that event or before. Dr. Nelson is trying to keep you down. Maybe he's also trying to keep something under wraps."

"Maybe. There has to be some connection to all these things I'm dreaming. I'm just missing a lot of information though."

"Yeah. Well the chair gave us Dr. Nelson. There has to be more to him that we don't know."

"Agreed. More research is required. Not just on him, but on another."

"Who?"

"Walter Goldberg. He's connected to Dr. Nelson somehow."

"Great. We got two dodgy fellows, one we know and one we don't. That's a start," Samantha said.

"How about we tackle one each? I'll take Goldberg and you can take Dr. Nelson," Amy said.

"Sure. I think you've dealt enough with the crazy doctor. Where do we start though?"

"Historical searches. Newspapers, academic journals, and similar things. Let's establish a history and see what connections come up."

"I can do that. You gave me the easy one too, I'm not sure what you'll do with that Goldberg guy."

"Something will come up," Amy said.

CHAPTER NINETEEN

MISDIRECTION

The next morning, Amy and Samantha discussed their movements over breakfast.

"Ok so I think we should split up, so we can research both targets at the same time," Samantha said.

"Agreed."

"Plus I think I should take the car, that way if it is tracked they will be watching me not you." Amy pondered the idea for a moment.

"It's a good idea, but I'm not that comfortable with you taking that much risk for me."

"Don't worry, they haven't been in close proximity to us lately, and as soon as they see it's me they'll back off."

"I hope you're right," Amy said. She wished Samantha good luck and they went their separate ways. Amy began to head into work, to try and do more research on Walter Goldberg, when she had a different idea. Why not investigate that office they spotted the other night. It was linked to the company that both Goldberg and Nelson were partners in.

Once in the city, Amy caught another bus to check up on her hunch. She tried to come up with a plan on the way, but her mind drew blanks. She just had no idea what to expect, or how she should approach the situation. From the name she guessed it was a construction or development company of some kind. Which made sense if it was somehow connected to Keystone. She thought back and remembered that the buildings they investigated were an empty lot and a warehouse full of construction materials. All that remained was to see what was in their office. She got off the bus and walked the last two blocks. The area was much nicer during the day. It was peaceful with not a lot of traffic.

Amy spotted the small office and kept it in her vision as she approached. She continued walking past, glancing in as she did. The office looked as it had before, only now it was staffed by a man behind the main desk. She turned the corner and stopped, thinking over her strategy. She could pretend to be a secretary sent to fetch something, and see what she could get away with. She didn't think that going in as a clueless punter would work. Amy returned to the front of the office and entered the door.

"Good morning," the man said.

"Good morning, I'm Doris," Amy said with a smile.

"Daniel. Take a seat."

"Thanks. My boss is a contractor, he sent me here to pick up some documents for him."

"What's his name?"

"Roger."

"Roger," Daniel said and flicked through a list on his desk.

"I don't have a Roger here."

"Really? He said he was asked to quote, by a man named Goldberg," Amy said. She could see Daniel's expression change at the mention of the name.

"Well, in that case let me see here. I've only got the architectural drawings here right now. The detailed specifications won't be in until the next few days,"

"That's fine, can I take a copy of the drawings? It would be better to have something to take back."

"I'm sorry, those are confidential."

"Really?"

"Yes, I'm afraid until the bidding process is completed we are keeping the locations secret. They're rather sensitive."

"Oh wow, well I wouldn't want to get you in trouble."

"Thanks for your understanding. You can call back in a few days, here's the number," Daniel said and handed Amy a card.

"Thank you for your time, you have been very helpful," Amy said then left. She was shaking from the tension. She had pulled it off, found out something, but needed a rest after that. But she wasn't done yet. She needed those plans, but how to get them?

Amy loitered around the office, watching Daniel's movements. He left at lunch time, but locked the doors when he went out. When he returned he stayed in the office until 5pm and then locked up and went home. Amy had hoped to find an opportunity during the day, but she had a 'Plan B' just in case. She walked around the corner and found a phone box. Inside was a phone directory. She looked up a local locksmith and dialled the number.

"Hello I'm Mr. Locksmith, but you can call me Alex," the voice said on the other end of the phone.

"Hello Mr. Locksmith, I'm Amy and I'm locked out of my office. Can you help me out?"

"Sure what's the address?"

"118 Mint Rd."

"That'll be $50. I'll be by in 15 minutes."

"Thanks, I'll be waiting out front." Amy hung up the pay phone, waited for five minutes then walked over to the office. She stood in front and waited. Five minutes later a van parked out front and a man in his forties with a large tool belt stepped out of the vehicle and approached her.

"Amy is it?" he said.

"Yes. Mr. Locksmith?"

"Yep, but call me Alex. Sorry to ask, but do you have some sort of identification?"

"Sure, but I'm just a secretary here. Hmm let's see, I've got my boss's business card if that helps?" Amy handed over the card she had gotten from Daniel. Alex looked at it questioningly.

"Please help me out, I'm desperate. If he finds out I locked my keys inside I'll never hear the end of it!"

"Alright. I can sympathise, I had a horrible boss. That's why I'm working for myself these days," Alex said and walked over to the door. He took out some thin wire, jiggled it in the lock and pushed open the door. It took all of 20 seconds. Amy handed over the money, amazed.

"There you go. Have a good night," Alex said and tipped his hat.

"You too, thanks again," Amy said and walked into the office and closed the door. She sat down at the desk, frantically searching for keys. After Alex drove away she dropped the pantomime and switched over to looking for architectural plans. She assumed that they would be big, so she looked around the room, trying to judge their location based on size. The cupboard at the rear had to be it, in the little office nook. She found some big rolls of paper, and unfurled them. They were plans.

Amy didn't want to take the plans, so she looked around and spotted a large photocopier. She couldn't fit the entire sheets on there, so she ensured that she copied the section that had the table of information. There were five to copy, and she did them all as fast as possible without trying to read any of the details. Every time a car drove by her heart stopped, but it was never someone stopping. As she finished the final one, a car stopped and parked out front. Amy froze in fear, then ducked down below the desk. She waited, and remembered that the door wasn't locked. If anyone entered they would know something was wrong. But she heard nothing. She popped up and looked out, seeing nothing. She stashed her copies in her bag and left, locking the door behind her.

"I hope these were worth the effort," she thought to herself as walked away from the office of Inspired Planning. She found a taxi rank populated with people, and thought it would be safe enough. She told the taxi driver her address, and he took her home without incident. Samantha wasn't home, so Amy ordered Thai food but included an extra dish just in case. Then while she ate she pored over the plans she had obtained.

One of the locations was the empty lot they had spotted before. Amy noted it as odd, and looked at the rest. They were all near each other. She checked the addresses with her street directory and noticed something interesting. She quickly left the apartment and bought a city map from the local convenience store. She brought it home and marked up the locations on the map. It was as she had thought, the addresses filled a large city block. Not just any block, but the historical district. The one under development by Keystone Endeavours. The same development that had opposition by large sections of the community and the Mayor James Freeman was trying to push through.

Amy looked through the plans again, and noticed the dates. Most of them were three years old, but one was ten years old. She checked the oldest one with curiosity.

"Why was this one drawn up so much earlier?" Amy said to herself. She checked the address and position and realised that it was the Orphello Theatre. The one that burned down three years earlier, quite close to the dates on the other drawn plans. Plans stored at Inspired Planning, which had Dr. Nelson and Walter Goldberg as directors. The same Walter Goldberg who was a director in Keystone Endeavours.

"Dr. Nelson is linked to the developments. The development was originally planned for the theatre, but the others were drawn up after the theatre burned down. What if the theatre fire wasn't an accident?" Amy thought out loud. It was a powerful thought, one that resonated with her. She had intended to investigate Walter Goldberg, and in a way she had. But this was an important lead. She had to investigate the theatre fire and find out how it started.

Amy posted her map to the cork board, and attached some notes with dates. She rearranged the notes and linked the articles where appropriate. At the top she had Walter Goldberg and a note saying 'Was Orphello Theatre purposefully destroyed?'. Happy with her progress, Amy prepared for bed. She worried a little about where Samantha was, but knew that it wasn't uncommon for her to be out all night.

DREAM SIX

I was sitting on the grass watching planes take off. It was a beautiful day with perfectly clear skies. Looking at them made me feel a little uneasy, as it got me thinking about being on a plane. Knowing it might be unwise, I turned away and watched the clear sky opposite. There were birds gliding through the air easily. I felt at peace again. A loud rumbling noise got my attention. It was followed by what started as a low pitched groan and rose to a whine. I could see before me a giant plane, its engines on fire as it plummeted down at great speed. I couldn't look away.

The plane started to crumple as it impacted with the ground, creating a gigantic boom. It slid along for a distance before colliding with a building and exploding into a massive fireball. I turned away and looked at the planes taking off. They continued to do so, continually, without any pause. It was as if they didn't care that one had crashed. I knew what I had to do, but I didn't like it. I walked over to the airport. I tried to delay things by buying a ticket, but they rushed me through the security and got me on to the tarmac. I was shown to what looked like a medium size plane. I walked up the stairs and was directed to my seat, by the window. The regular anxiety set in.

What made it worse, was that I was aware enough to know that bad things were coming. The plane filled up, and taxied around for a while. Then it accelerated incredibly quickly. My stomach lurched while I felt the g-forces. We continued to climb, but didn't quite level out. I heard an announcement over the intercom.

"G'day this is the captain speaking. We've hit a spot of bother and we'll have to make a water landing. It should be fine, I don't think anyone will die," the voice said. I felt the panic set in, and braced myself for the impact. I could feel the plane dropping, combined with the groan and whine I had heard before. It conjured up the image of the giant plane explosion, even though I knew it was a water landing.

A wave of force hit us, and I heard an accompanying splash. Our momentum slowed and then with a shudder we stopped. I was wet with sweat. Then I was wet with water. Water was seeping into the cabin. I grabbed my life jacket from below the seat and put it on. I followed the crowd out the emergency exit and rode the slide down into the water. I inflated my life jacket and bobbed around in the water. I was frozen from the cold. I was shaking from a mixture of adrenaline and chill. Eventually a small boat came and collected me, dropping me off at a small wharf.

As soon as I placed my feet on dry land I felt much better. My clothes dried instantly and my life jacket vanished. I sat down on a nearby bench and let all the tension leave my body. I turned and saw a giant sign directing people to the airport.

"I know, I know," I said with a sigh. I picked myself up and started to walk back to the airport. The sky started to darken gradually. It was so slight at first that I didn't notice. But by the time I reached the airport a good old storm was brewing. The small, logical and optimistic part of my brain thought that the storm would save me from flying. I even pointed to the storm when a flight steward came to hurry me on, and she just smiled and shrugged her shoulders.

Thunder and lightning made my jog along the tarmac more exciting. I appreciated the relative comfort of the interior of the plane, but my stomach knew that worse was coming. It was already churning like crazy. This time there was no prelude, we just accelerated really fast and took off. And as soon as we started to climb, we started to drop. Then climb again. The lurching made me feel so ill, I had to grab the nearest sickness bag. But it filled up and I had to grab another. I heaved stomach contents that I didn't know I had. When the plane levelled out an attendant came over and offered me an anti-sickness pill. I so desperately wanted it, but I knew that it was a step backwards. I had to conquer my anxiety.

I was sick once more then the plane settled down. But I felt dread. I knew that more was on its way. Looking outside just confirmed it. The skies were black and lightning was in the distance. The plane started to rock from side to side. It was shoved up and down roughly and I was gripping my seat. I closed my eyes and everything became still. When I opened them again, it started again, but even more violently. I just had to grin and bear it. A giant shock hit the plane and emergency oxygen masks dropped from the ceiling. I put mine on and waited anxiously.

After several panicked minutes the assistant pilot came up to me. He asked me whether to keep flying or turn around. My whole mind and body was screaming at me to end the flight. But it wasn't to be. I had to move forward. I told him to keep flying, and was rewarded by a thunderous boom. The plane rocked but continued flying. It was followed up by something that I didn't anticipate. I guessed lightning hit the plane. All I knew was that the power was completely drained and it started to lose altitude. People were rushing around in a panic, reflecting how I felt. The staff started handing out parachutes and then I really started to panic. The emergency door was open and air whistled through the cabin. One by one they jumped out of the plane with their parachutes. It was just me left on the plane. There was no parachute for me. I struggled over to the emergency exit and stared out. There was a glowing white door, just beyond it. It stood out amongst the blackened and storming sky.

"No way," I said. But there it was. I knew that if I didn't take the chance, then my ordeal would repeat. I let go and dived out of the plane. I fell into a warm glow.

CHAPTER TWENTY-ONE

DECEPTION

Amy awoke and wrote in her notebook. Next she drew another picture, this time of a special seal. She couldn't quite place what it was from, but decided to take it with her when she left. She was quietly happy that her dreams had returned. She checked in on Samantha, and then made herself eggs on toast. Her goal for the day was to investigate the Orphello Theatre fire. The records for the investigation would be at the main Metro Police Station. She couldn't just walk in off the street, but she had an idea of how to get in.

Amy finished her preparations and went in to work. She went straight to her desk and started looking through the active cases on file. She hadn't been there long when she was surprised by a visitor.

"Well hello Amy, how are you doing?" Margaret said.

"I'm good. Enjoying my leave, just popping in to look over a few things."

"Great timing. Did you hear the news?"

"No I didn't."

"David's girlfriend is travelling for a few weeks. Not a good sign for such a new romance."

"Oh ok. That's interesting," Amy said with curiosity.

"I know, I can picture David now. He's probably imagining life with someone else," Margaret said, winking at Amy.

"Actually, I have a quick question about our current cases."

"Anything you can ask me, you can ask David," Margaret said and disappeared. Amy sighed and walked over to David's desk. He was on the phone, but smiled and waved when he saw her. Amy waited, not knowing where to look and trying not to overhear the conversation. She was about to walk away when David waved her closer and ended the call.

"Sorry about that. Hey Amy how are you?" he said with a smile.

"Yeah pretty good. How are you?"

"Very busy. What brings you into the office? Aren't you still on leave?"

"Yeah, I actually had a question. Do we have any active cases that have reports from the Metro Police Station?"

"I think so. Why?"

"Well since I missed out on that field trip to get a deposition, I thought I could go look at records or something like that. Something small."

"Good idea, that's proactive. You wouldn't normally have time to do that with your regular work load," David said. While he was flipping through files Amy spoke again.

"If possible, something requiring discovery from a few years ago, so I get to do a bit of digging around."

"I think this will work. It's an insurance case from four years back. They made an appeal and it's been reopened," David said. He handed Amy a one page summary with some photocopied reports.

"What do I do?"

"I'll call ahead to let them know you're coming. Find the original police reports and make sure there's nothing missing from our records."

"Sounds great. Thanks for your help."

"Any time. Have fun." David waved at Amy as she left then picked up the phone to make the promised call.

Amy left the building, confident that she had what she needed. It wasn't that far so she walked to the Metro Police Station. It was an old sandstone building which stood out in the middle of skyscrapers. Inside the station was a mix of old and new. She walked up to the main desk and waited patiently.

"How can I help you?" the officer said.

"I'm looking for records."

"Go right, turn left and it's at the end of the corridor."

"Thanks," Amy said and followed his instructions. There were a lot of people going in and out of the station. As she progressed down the corridor she spotted the 'Records' sign above a window at the end. It was manned by a woman in her fifties with glasses and a kindly smile.

"Hello, what can I get for you today?" the woman asked.

"Hello. I'm Amy here to review some records."

"Ah yes, your colleague called ahead. Do you have some identification with you?" Amy took her driver's licence out of her wallet and handed it to the woman.

"Nice to meet you Amy, I'm Anne. Come through," Anne said as she handed back the licence. She unlocked the door alongside her window and Amy walked through. They passed through the small cubicle where Anne was seated into a much larger room full of filing cabinets.

"Lovely isn't it," Anne said. Amy was amazed. They wound their way through the stacks and rows to the back.

"These two cabinets have arson case files. They're arranged by case number and date where possible. Those cabinets date back about five years so you'll be fine."

"Thanks that's great."

"Normally I'd retrieve things for you, but I understand there's some fact checking to be done so it's better you do it yourself. You can't take anything out of here, but you can make copies and I'll sign them off for you,"

Anne said. Amy nodded and Anne walked out of the room back to her post. Amy got straight to work. She went for the case that David had supplied her first. She had the feeling that Anne might be checking up on her, so she wanted to have something to show just in case.

As it so happened, it proved to be a useful approach. Because she had a case number and date to search for, it made it easier to locate the files she wanted. Which would enable her to find the Orphello file easier. She found the two files she had been sent for within minutes. They were both together. To buy herself time Amy took one of the files and stuffed it somewhere else in the cabinet, out of place. Then she went over and photocopied the first file and put it in a folder. She resumed her rummaging in the cabinet. As she expected Anne came over.

"How are you going?"

"I found one, now looking for the other. Going to see if I can finish the work here too."

"Ok great. Please call if you have any trouble." Amy watched Anne walk back then resumed her search. She went through the section where it should have been based on the date, but it wasn't there. So Amy went through the rest of that cabinet. It wasn't there. She tried the one below and eventually found it stashed right at the back. Amy grabbed the file, and the others that she was supposed to find, and took them to the photocopier. When Anne returned she had all the documents laid out on the little table next to the copier.

"Found them but having some difficulty piecing it all together," Amy said.

"So you copied them for later?"

"Exactly. I'm just compiling them now I'll bring it all over in a minute."

"Sure." Amy quickly assembled the files and checked her work. She had stashed the Orphello photocopies amongst her work provided copies. Her hands trembled as she hid them. With any luck she could get the Orphello copies out as well. Amy returned all the files back to where she found them, even the wrong spot for the Orphello file. Gathering all her copies she took them up to be viewed by Anne.

"Here's the two photocopied files I'm taking with me," Amy said showing off her neatly stapled files. Anne checked over the page and case numbers.

"That's all fine I'll initial here and sign there. What's that you have with you?" she said, pointing at Amy's other file.

"Oh it's my copies from work, for comparison," she said offering the file. Her heart leapt into her throat, hoping that she wouldn't be discovered. Anne glanced at the first few pages and handed it back.

"Well I think we're all done here. I hope you got what you wanted."

"Me too. Thanks for your help," Amy said, smiled at Anne and turned to leave. But she had an idea, requiring another question, so pushed her luck.

"Maybe you could help me with something else," she said.

"What is it?"

"We have a document with this seal, and we're trying to track it down." Amy showed her the drawing of the seal. Anne looked at it carefully, pondered for a minute then offered an answer.

"Well it signifies a sealed document. As you would know sometimes files are sealed for sensitivity or due to the age of the suspects."

Amy nodded. Anne continued.

"I'd say this one is around 20-30 years old correct?"

"Yes," Amy said, playing along.

"Based off the writing and layout, I'd put it down as a Shine County seal. If you're really keen go talk to Gladys down there and tell her I sent you. She'll help you out."

"I can't thank you enough, take care," Amy said. She played it cool, but internally she was frantic. Each step of the way out of the station she expected Anne to come running after her with handcuffs. Amy's load lightened considerably when she took those first few steps outside the police station. Each step that took her back to the office also helped. However she wasn't done yet. When she returned to the office she went straight to the bathroom. Inside she rearranged her documents and separated out the Orphello pages. With that sorted she returned to David's desk.

"I found the two files they have and copied them. Do you mind if I do the analysis later?"

"Sure that's fine. Just leave them on your desk in case I need them earlier."

"Thanks. See you later."

"Bye Amy. Take care," David said. Amy smiled and left. She had done it, she had the file and a lead on the drawing she did.

"Go Amy," she said to herself. She celebrated with a late sushi lunch then headed home. Samantha was home, and in the lounge room looking through some notes.

"I hope you've got something, because I have nothing to share," Samantha said.

"Well I have the police file on the Orphello Theatre fire and a lead from a dream I had."

"Wow, you'll have to talk me through it."

"I discovered plans for the Orphello Theatre and the other redevelopments by Keystone Endeavours at Inspired Planning."

"How'd you get in?"

"A locksmith let me in," Amy said. Samantha laughed and looked at her friend incredulously.

"Then I looked at the dates and surmised that the Orphello Theatre may have been an arson, so I used work to get me into the Metro Police Records and copied the Orphello file."

"And the dream lead?" Samantha asked. Amy showed her the drawing.

"The records keeper at the Police Station said it looked like it was from a sealed document and I should check with Gladys at Shine County."

"You've got a lot on your plate. Shine County? Are you going to go, you'd have to fly right?" Samantha said. Amy nodded.

"If necessary."

"You've become quite the detective. I never thought you'd be this resourceful."

"Yeah, I seem to have a knack for following leads. But at the same time, these could all be dead ends," Amy said.

"Like mine. I could tell you when and where Dr. Nelson got his degree, and all his awards and commendations since, but nothing useful. So tell me, why do you think the Orphello was arson?"

"It's just a hunch. Seriously though, the plans were drawn up years before the fire, and the other plans for the surrounding buildings were drawn up after the fire. It just seems a bit suspicious. Not to mention that these plans are stored in the office of a small company that's not Keystone, and has Dr. Nelson on its board of directors."

"Yeah it's all a bit fishy. Let's take a look at that police report," Samantha said. Amy sat down at the table with her, and they pulled it apart. Amy read the summary first, while Samantha looked over the statements and notes.

"The summary says that it was most likely an accidental blaze. Likely scenario a cigarette," Amy said. Samantha didn't respond, concentrating on the details. Amy took a few pages of the support notes and read along herself. After a few minutes they swapped pages.

"What do you think?" Amy said.

"I'm not sure, I don't know enough about fires. But it doesn't seem as simple as the summary."

"Yeah, it's a bit inconsistent. To begin with, the fire started in a store room underneath the theatre. There's no ventilation there, not a good place to smoke and get away with it."

"And the statements from the employees say that none of them on shift that night smoked."

"Which they could be lying about. But their statements also suggest that they were busy at the time the fire started and can vouch for each other."

"Yeah but if one of them accidentally started it, I'd believe that they would cover each other."

"How about this: 'Scorch marks on the floor suggest lubricant oil based accelerant' but the room was filled with cooking oil, which was been referenced as the accelerant."

"Interesting. I also read there that it says the scorch marks suggest the fire started on the opposite side of the room to the oil drums."

"Which is more likely in arson, and less likely in an accidental fire," Amy said. They let that statement hang in the air for a minute.

"If we're not experts, and this seems so dodgy, then why did the experts not address these things?" Samantha said.

"It could be a cover up. This is a big development, and has been in the planning stages for a while."

"Yeah, but we're in the same position again. A lot of suggestion and links, but nobody's been caught red handed."

"We just need to keep digging," Amy said.

"Does that mean you've got a flight to book?"

"Yeah." After dinner Amy called and booked a flight for the next morning. She planned to stay overnight and fly back the following day.

"Two flights, I hope I'm better," Amy thought to herself. With all that done, she updated her detective board with notes about their arson theory. Then she called it a night and tried to get herself a good night's rest.

CHAPTER TWENTY-TWO

TRAVEL

Amy awoke the next morning, noting the lack of dreams. Since her captivity, she didn't know what rules they went by.

"Well I have this clue to chase up anyway," she thought to herself. She packed her small case with a change of clothes and called a taxi. She said goodbye to Samantha, who managed to wish her good luck and instantly return to sleep. She waited by the door for fifteen minutes and then heard the beep of a taxi. She walked down with her suitcase and approached the driver's side.

"Amy, going to the Domestic Airport right?" the female taxi driver said.

"Yes that's right," Amy said and wheeled her little bag around to the boot. The driver opened the boot for her then returned to the wheel.

"When's your flight love?" the driver said.

"11:45."

"Yeah, we got plenty of time." The driver said no more and turned up the radio. Amy listened to the radio and tried to tune out. She didn't want to think too much about the impending flight. The taxi trip was over before she knew it, and she stepped out to look at the airport. It reminded her of her recent dream, the images of plane disaster all too fresh in her mind. Amy dismissed them and walked inside. She queued up and checked in without incident.

While waiting she bought a coffee and drank it slowly. At first it relaxed her, as a reminder of her routine. But the fact that she was in an airport didn't change. She bought a paper and read it. Thankfully there were no articles about plane disasters. After she finished the paper, she still had an hour to go. So she proceeded through the security check. She felt unnecessarily nervous while they x-rayed her bag although there was nothing dangerous in it. But she considered those documents with her stolen.

After more waiting at the gate, they finally called her flight. She thought she would be relieved that the wait was over, but she wasn't. Amy forced herself to stand up and walk over with the other passengers. They formed an orderly line and she moved closer and closer, one step at a time. She showed her boarding pass and walked through the tunnel down to the tarmac. She had to walk outside and board her plane from a set of stairs. She forced away the comparisons to her dream.

"Window seat, on the right," the attendant said when she entered the aircraft.

"Typical, I should have asked for an aisle seat," Amy thought to herself. She stowed her bag in the locker above and took her seat. She fastened her seatbelt and settled herself. She looked out her window and watched the rest of the passengers filter through to the plane.

Her anxiety was there, but not too unsettling. She took deep breaths and focused. After an eternity the passengers were all seated and the plane started taxiing. Amy watched the safety video with interest, although she felt like she already had experience with all the apparatus. As the plane started to accelerate, it felt scarily familiar. Her stomach lurched but she remained in control. In that moment between the ground and being airborne she thought she might be sick, but she got through it. Once the plane reached its cruising altitude she relaxed.

"I did it," Amy thought to herself and she beamed a huge smile.

"Nervous flyer?" a voice said next to her. Amy turned and saw an elderly man with thick bushy eyebrows and thick rimmed glasses.

"Yeah, but I'm alright today."

"Indeed, I wouldn't have noticed if I wasn't feeling the same way. It all started oh I'd say thirty or forty years ago. I was on a flight and we had to make a sudden adjustment to avoid an oncoming plane."

"Oh wow, that's crazy!"

"Isn't it just. But don't you worry, these days they have much better flight control." The man gave Amy a reassuring smile and she returned one, as best she could. The plane suddenly rocked side to side and the man instinctively stuck out his hand. Amy held on to it hard. She braced herself for the inevitable horror, but the situation never escalated further. It was a tense hour though, as the plane alternated between calm flying and rough turbulence. Each time it restarted just when she thought it might finally be over.

With shaky legs she disembarked from the plane and waved goodbye to her fellow nervous passenger. Her nerves were tested, but intact. Looking over the airport didn't inspire confidence. What looked like a small shack seemed to be the main building. However each step she took towards it on solid ground calmed her, and gave her more strength. Her legs felt more solid by the time she had reached the main, and only, building. After a moment of indecision she walked over to the single car rental kiosk. She chose a red compact car and took time carefully checking its condition. Once she was satisfied she drove out of the lot, heading for the town centre.

Shine County was living up to its name, with the beaming sunshine reflecting off the polished and well maintained buildings. Lawns were neatly mowed, picket fences duly painted and a perfect white. All of it exerted a soothing aura. Amy slowed as she reached the main strip, looking for accommodation. She noticed a decorative sign on a street corner directing her to "Mama K's

B&B". Amy followed the sign and pulled into a nicely paved driveway leading up to a large house. She parked and walked around to the front.

Stepping through the front door, the first thing she noticed was the cool. It was a refreshing change from the steadily increasing heat outside. Amy glanced around and saw that the premises were originally a large house. There was a small table in front of her, labelled 'Reception' without anyone attending. Amy walked up to it and rang the bell once.

"One minute!" a female voice called out from another room. Amy waited with patience. Within a minute or two a kindly lady rushed over, dressed in an apron and clearly perspiring.

"Sorry I'm just baking something. How can I help you?" the lady asked.

"Hello, I'd just like a room for the night."

"Of course, here are our rates. I'm Kate, the owner."

"Thanks, I'm Amy. Hmm, well I'll take the Queen room."

"Great, please just fill out this form and I'll hand over your key," Kate said and then looked through her keys. Amy filled out the form, signed at the bottom and then collected her key. She sought out her room, which was at the back of the building.

Opening the door revealed an immaculately clean room with few but luxurious furnishings. Amy was satisfied, so she put down her overnight bag and took out the seal she wanted to investigate. Her next stop was the primary reason for her visit. She was going to see Gladys, the records keeper, at the local police station. Hopefully her investigation would reveal a new clue.

Amy had no trouble finding the local police station, it was on the main strip. The building was old but in good condition, its bricks clean despite their age. Amy took a deep breath, then entered. The layout seemed familiar, a desk near the front and a few chairs. Then corridors going elsewhere.

"Hi, I'm looking for the records section," Amy said to the officer on duty. She had her explanation ready just in case. He sighed then replied.

"Oh right sure, just continue around to the left."

"Quiet day?"

"Always. Such a sleepy town, nothing ever happens here."

"Isn't that a good thing?"

"I guess so. Hey while you're in town, if you see any criminal activity just think of poor Constable Roberts sitting here. I'll even settle for shoplifting kids!"

"Sure I'll keep it in mind," Amy said half joking and half serious. She found the idea of a bored police officer somewhat reassuring. At the end of the hall she found the records section. Behind the window was a young woman, with perfectly straight long black hair.

"Gladys?" Amy said with confusion as she approached.

"That's my name, how can I help?"

"Anne recommended you, to help me investigate something."

"Anne? She's a darling, such a sweetie. She's a walking encyclopaedia and happy to share it as well. You'd be surprised at how many of our colleagues are information hoarders."

"You know it doesn't sound that surprising."

"Ha-ha yeah goes with the territory I suppose. What did you need?"

"I came across this seal and Gladys said you should be able to help me track down the original documents," Amy said, handing over the seal drawing. Gladys examined it closely then handed it back.

"Yeah that looks like the local seal for protected records. I can't remember it being used in my time however. Let's go on a hunt." Gladys opened the door and beckoned for Amy to go in.

"I'm Amy, and thanks for your help."

"No problem, I'm not busy and owe Anne a few favours. Plus you've intrigued me with this one." She walked confidently through the rows of boxes and filing cabinets, Amy following closely behind. Gladys soon stopped in front of a dusty old mid-height cabinet.

"You're in luck, I recently stumbled across this one. Pretty sure it's all the old and interesting stuff." Gladys unlocked the cabinet and looked at some of the records, interested in the seal.

"Show me yours again," Gladys said. Amy handed it over, wondering what Gladys needed it for. She waited patiently as the record keeper compared the records to the seal.

"It's different, in subtle ways. Take a look," Gladys said. Amy took both the items and looked from one to the other. The central motif was the same, but the text and styling was different. From a distance they would look the same, but close up the difference was noticeable.

"Do you think I have the wrong place?"

"No, it's too similar. That seal you have with you came from here, I wonder though…" Gladys caught a few strands of her hair and played with them as she thought. Suddenly she jerked her hand away and her expression changed completely.

"Come with me," she said. Amy followed, her curiosity building. They wandered further through the records area, stopping at a dusty corner that looked mostly bare. It was below a stairwell and looked recently disturbed.

"This is where I pulled out that cabinet from. I seem to remember there being something else. Excuse me," Gladys said as she squatted down and almost crawled into the available space. Amy watched on in interest and Gladys soon emerged with a dusty old document box.

"Looks like I missed something. Let's take a look," Gladys said. She took the box to a nearby desk and sat down. Amy stood close, looking over. Gladys carefully removed the lid from the box, disturbing even more dust. Inside was a folder with a seal on the front.

"This is it."

"You're right. These are old, my guess about the seal was correct," Gladys said. She flipped through the documents within, looking attentive. Then she stood up and moved away, offering Amy the chair.

"Well that's the exciting bit for me. The documents are old enough that the sealed status no longer has any meaning. Enjoy yourself, just remember that the documents can't leave this room."

"Thanks," Amy said and sat down. She watched Gladys walk off then started with the first page. Since she had no idea on the contents, she decided to start at the beginning and examine each page carefully.

The first page was a police report of a suspiciously burned shed. The summary was that arson could not be proven due to the extremely flammable contents of the shed. Amy didn't analyse the information, just absorbed it and continued on. The next report was suspected arson in the national park. Lighter fluid for camping use was the cause of the blaze. The fires had raged for days and employed the entire fire department to keep under control.

One thing that Amy noticed while reading the reports, was that the nature of the reports was totally different from the one she had read about the theatre fire. The tone, the information and the analysis were of a better standard. There was a certain rigour and deliberateness to these reports that just wasn't present in the theatre fire report. It certainly reinforced her doubts about the conclusions of that document. Completely absorbed, and about to view the next report, Amy felt a tap on the shoulder. She spun suddenly, but was only looking at Gladys.

"Hey there, I need to close up for today. But come back tomorrow and you can read all you want."

"Sure, thanks."

"You have accommodation right?"

"Yeah."

"Great have a good night, see you tomorrow."

"Thanks and bye," Amy said and waved goodbye. She appreciated Gladys's help, but was frustrated at the interruption. Something was in those documents, but she would have to wait to discover what it was. The nature of the documents and how they were stored was also interesting. It definitely felt like they had been buried, and not meant to be discovered.

As Amy left the police station, she noticed two men reading newspapers on a nearby bench. They were dressed in plain suits, and didn't stand out in any way. But they felt wrong, like they didn't fit in. They didn't blend into the peaceful town atmosphere. Amy considered that they might just be travellers, but she couldn't shake the feeling of dread slowly creeping along her spine.

She felt better when arriving back at Mama K's. Amy had planned on just asking about where to eat, but didn't get a chance. A veritable feast was already laid out on the table, and Kate didn't take no for an answer. After eating her fill, Amy thanked Kate and excused herself.

Despite her earlier unease, the meal and company had calmed her down. So it was with enthusiasm that she turned to bed.

But she didn't neglect her routine, and fished through her bags for flight information. She found the itinerary and flipped over to her return journey. She had booked herself on a 2pm flight. It was an odd time, not early but not late. Unfortunately it was the only time available. She had thought there would be plenty of time but now she wasn't so sure. Amy planned to be at the Police Station as early as possible, to ensure that she would get the information in time. Or find a way to take something with her. She set her alarm for six o'clock and snuggled under the blankets. Soon Amy was deep in sleep.

She yawned and felt restless, it felt like she had only been asleep for a few minutes. It was jet black outside, so it was still late. Confused, Amy rolled over to get a better look at the window. She saw a quick flash of light, then darkness. It was like somebody had just exposed a light and then quickly hidden it. Instantly, she awoke and felt a tightness in her chest. Something was definitely wrong, and she was not going to ignore her instincts.

Holding her breath Amy waited cautiously, straining her ears for any sound. She heard a slight scuffling sound outside her window and decided to move. As quickly and quietly as possible she threw on some clothes and grabbed her wallet and the rental car keys. The rest of her luggage was left. As she turned to leave she paused and went back to the bed. She stuffed her pyjamas under the blanket to form a person like shape and then dashed out of the room.

Amy went straight for the front entrance, to get to her car as quickly as possible. She was parked on the street, so access wasn't going to be a problem. A voice in the back of her head started criticising her actions, pointing out her behaviour as paranoid and crazy. But the feeling in her gut was so strong that she just blocked those thoughts and kept riding the adrenalin.

To avoid making any extra noise she used the key to unlock the driver's side door rather than the unlock button. Her hands were so unsteady it took three attempts to get the key into the lock, and she turned it the wrong way on her first attempt. This activity was interrupted by quick glances up to see if anyone was chasing her.

Once in the car she locked the door and put the key in the ignition. Being inside the car calmed her a little, and it only took two tries with the key. Just as she turned the key in the ignition a hand banged the side window right next to her head. She stopped in fright, and looked over at the sound. After a second of confusion she recognised the face: it was one of the men she had spotted after leaving the police station. One of the suited men who had looked so out of place. The realisation galvanised her into action, and she started the car and pulled away as quickly as possible.

Looking through the rear vision mirror she saw another car come to life half a block away, and a man entering it. Her heart raced further and she accelerated faster. She didn't think about where to go, just knew she had to get away. That freed up her thoughts to focus on the car following her, and tracking its progress. She didn't have far to go, but it was gaining on her steadily. She slammed on the brakes without thinking and was shocked into forgetting the car behind. She looked over and saw the police station.

"Of course, the police station. Where else would I go?" she said to herself with encouragement. But her brain skipped ahead and pondered the question and came up with an answer other than the obvious: for the sealed documents.

Amy sprinted across the road, looking over her shoulder to track her pursuers. They had almost caught up, and were slowing. She wasn't sure if the sight of the police station gave them pause, or if they were just preparing to stop and continue the chase on foot. But it didn't matter, she had to get inside the station regardless.

She burst into the police station and looked around. Constable Roberts was still at his post, but he looked up at her. His features were a mix of surprise and readiness.

"Are you alright?" he said, his voice filled with concern.

"Not quite. Two suited men are after me."

"Are they armed?"

"Not sure."

"Go hide in that room over there, if anyone comes in I'll confront them." Amy did as directed and Roberts tensed himself, ready for action.

"Be careful what you wish for," he said to himself under his breath. With any luck though, the woman was just scared and nothing would happen. But somehow it felt real, that something was really wrong. His right hand crept down and he held it on his gun, ready to draw it.

Two suited men walked through the doors, with a casual manner.

"How can I assist you?" Roberts said, surprising himself with the calm in his voice. The older of the two men spoke up.

"A friend of ours ran off tonight. She's, how do I put this, mentally unstable. We want to find her and provide her with some treatment."

Roberts looked over the men carefully. He didn't trust them, but he couldn't deny that the woman they were after was at the station. He would have to try and throw them off the scent.

"Yeah I did have a lady come in moments ago. I directed her to the interview room down the hall. Not really sure what the story is, but you've saved me some trouble I suspect," Roberts said, his hand slowly creeping up along his pistol, preparing to draw it.

"You don't know the half of it," the older man said, then nodded at his colleague. The movement fulfilled two purposes. It signalled to the other man that it was time to fire, and it distracted Roberts just long enough so that he was caught unprepared. He slumped to the floor, still alive, but unsure of where he was hit. Before he made any other moves his training kicked in, telling him to stay put and let the two men believe him dead.

He heard the two men walk off, in the wrong direction. They had swallowed his story so he had bought the woman a few moments of respite. As he strained to hear their progress, he noticed other footsteps approaching.

"Go now, get away," he said.

"I can't, not yet. Do you need help?" Amy said.

"Definitely, but I don't want this to be for nothing. Get going!" Amy looked around, but made no move to leave. She walked around the reception desk, picked up the telephone and placed it on the ground next to Roberts.

"If you don't want this to be for nothing, I have to get what I came here for, what they're trying to stop me finding. I need the key to the records room," Amy said, in a strangely matter-of-fact way. Some other instincts had kicked in, and she was almost on autopilot. Roberts took a deep breath, sighed, and then pointed to the key ring on his belt.

"One of the ones on the green ring. I don't remember which," he grunted with effort. He looked up at Amy and saw the determination on her face. Whatever she was involved in, she wasn't crazy.

"Thanks. Don't die on me, I'll feel terrible," Amy said.

"Don't get caught, I'll feel even worse," Roberts said with a small laugh, which caused a coughing fit. He motioned her away and stretched out his arm to show that he could reach the phone. Amy nodded and stood, peeking around the corner at the long corridor ahead.

She was confident of how to get to the records room, but she also realised that it was the same direction that the two men had gone. She wasn't sure how long she had spent with the policeman, but if the two suits came back this way she would be spotted for sure. Taking a gamble, she guessed that the police station might be methodically laid out. So she tried going the other way, hoping it would loop around. At least it would increase her chances of remaining hidden.

Amy crept along the parallel corridor carefully, taking each opportunity to sneak into a room and look ahead for danger. As she progressed she heard voices in the distance, but they seemed to be stationary. That made her bolder, she moved closer and closer to try and hear what they were saying. As soon as she was within earshot she found a room nearby to hide in and listened.

"She must have heard the gunshot and bolted."

"Well that cop looked mighty suspicious, no matter how hard he tried to hide it."

"You think he gave us a bum steer?"

"Possible, but if he did he's paid for it. She could be hiding somewhere else around here."

"I don't want to stay for too long, if there's a shift change we're in for some complications."

"Yeah you're right, we can always pick her up at the airport."

Amy's heart caught in her throat. She hadn't expected them to be so bold and go after her in broad daylight. If she hadn't listened in on their conversation she would have fallen into their trap. The footsteps sounded louder, which she first thought was her imagination then realised was not. They were walking back a different way, and would be right outside the room she was hiding in soon. She quickly looked around, and noticed a little desk in the corner. She dashed over as quietly as possible, and crawled under. The door to the room was open, she had left it open to listen better, but it was too late to close it. Amy huddled into a ball and tried to be as small and quiet as possible.

The footsteps got louder and louder and then stopped. They changed direction and she heard them enter the room. Her heart thumped away, the fear of being powerless and potentially exposed made her numb. Not being able to see how and where they looked just made it even worse. She was paralysed, if they found her she would be unable to fight back.

And then suddenly the steps started again, but away from her. Slowly her breathing returned to normal and she dared to leave her hiding spot. With care Amy slid out from under the desk, fearful of what might be there. She breathed a huge sigh of relief when the room was empty. But since the immediate danger had passed she quickly focused on the next problem: getting those documents while she still could.

She crept back into the corridor, peering both ways to look for signs of activity. The police station appeared empty. Amy purposefully walked toward where she thought the record room was. It was good to stretch her legs again. As she turned the corner she spotted the room and felt a surge of energy. There was a job left to do.

Despite feeling a bit better her hands still shook like mad, and opening the records room was a lot less stealthy than she had wanted. The jingling keys made a huge racket, and she had to try them all before the door gave way. But as she strode into the room it looked exactly as she remembered. She allowed herself to hope that the dusty box of records was where she had left it. Amy almost jumped for joy when she found the box, and all of its contents intact.

"Thanks Gladys, you are a lifesaver," Amy said to herself. She flipped through the documents to ensure she had the right ones, then took the folder with her.

"Sorry Gladys, no time for copies," Amy said to the room regretfully as she left. The door was much easier to lock, and she hurried to the entrance of the police station.

Voices in the distance made her pause, and she walked the last metres as quietly as possible. She glanced over when it was safe, and saw Roberts on a stretcher with two paramedics attending. He caught her gaze, acknowledged it, and then looked elsewhere.

"He's trying not to alert them," Amy thought to herself. She followed his gaze subconsciously and noticed a side entrance to the police station. That was a much better option. So she waited for them to wheel Roberts out the front, then she dropped his keys behind the reception desk and left via the side entrance.

A collection of emergency vehicles were beginning to accumulate out the front, so Amy didn't consider herself in any danger from the two suits. Nonetheless, she didn't want any unnecessary attention, so she walked the long way around to the car. She unlocked the car, drove a few blocks and then parked it again. She had a decision to make.

The question was: what to do next? She believed the two men, that they would try and seize her at the airport. But would they wait back at the bed and breakfast in case she showed up? She bet that they would, just in case. So where should she go? She had risked a lot for these documents, and a police officer got shot for helping her, so she needed to plumb their secrets. To do that required time and a safe environment. The airline was out, which she did feel a bit of guilty pleasure for. She had flown, with some composure, but still enjoyed the prospect of not having to fly again so soon. Suddenly she had a brainwave: the car.

Amy took a deep breath, then began to plan. She would drive back home, and use time along the way to decipher the documents she had. Then, she would have their information already, and could hide the originals somewhere safe. There would be some sacrifices, like her luggage, but it was worth doing. Amy started the car and headed for the edge of town, looking for a convenience store. She found one, bought some maps and energy drinks, and then prepared herself for the first leg of what would be a long drive.

CHAPTER TWENTY-THREE

ROAD TRIP

The first half an hour was exhilarating, with Amy fuelled by the energy drinks and the leftover adrenaline from her encounter. But then she settled into the drive, the dark bland landscape stealing her enthusiasm. From studying the map she knew that the next town was a few hours away, and she wanted to be there as soon as possible. The two suits would waste time waiting for her at the airport and she would have a good head start, even if they tried to follow.

She thought about Samantha, who would start to worry if Amy didn't call later in the day. Samantha would already be on edge, knowing that Amy was flying. But she had time, she would call Samantha when she could. Work should be fine, they didn't really expect her in. The case files she had borrowed with their assistance were just a side project as far as they were concerned.

Thinking of work brought her around to thinking about David. He was a sweet guy, but she had missed her opportunity with him. Even if she had one, she couldn't shake that feeling that he would say no to her, and she couldn't take the rejection. Any thoughts in that direction would trigger her mind to play over the scenario of him rejecting her, and it made her feel sick.

Feeling sick made her remember the police station, and how close she had come to being captured again. Hiding under that desk had been paralysing. It wasn't just the fear of being discovered, she hated enclosed spaces. She thought that being contorted under that desk had played a part.

"Look at me, I'm still a mess," Amy said to herself. But she managed a laugh afterwards. That made her feel better.

A few dreary hours later Amy started seeing signs of life again. At first it was the odd shack, then petrol stations and convenience stores, and then houses and a shopping strip. The town was called Backett and looked sleepy in the early morning sun. Not much would be open at such an early time, but she kept an eye out for a newsagent. She spotted one on the main strip and parked the car outside.

She wandered through the newsagent, not really sure what she was looking for. When she passed the newspapers she picked one up and looked at the front cover. There was nothing about the incident at the police station, but then she realised that it was too soon to make the papers. It might be in the afternoon edition. She continued walking, passed the magazines and cards and saw a photocopier in the corner. That would be handy.

Amy ducked out to retrieve the folder of documents from the car. She made three copies of each page, stapled them together and then bought a bottle of water. Returning to the car she dropped the papers off into the passenger seat and then consulted her map. She could probably drive the rest of the way home in around twelve hours, but she didn't trust herself to drive that long with no sleep. Plus she needed to give herself time to read through the documents. So she decided to drive to the next town and stay there overnight.

Feeling a little sluggish, Amy put the map and documents away and went for a short walk to explore the town. As soon as she spotted a coffee shop her stomach rumbled, as if it were planned.

"No point fighting it, I need to eat sometime," she said to herself and went inside. There was only an elderly couple sitting up the back, no other patrons. It was probably too early for the normal crowd. Amy sat down and waited for service.

She ordered a cappuccino when the waiter came around and examined the menu with gusto. They had all day breakfast, which made her instantly like the place, although at such an early hour it didn't matter. When her cappuccino arrived she ordered eggs benedict and stared out into space. The smell of the hollandaise sauce snapped her out of the temporary daze and she gobbled up the breakfast with gusto.

Once satisfied, her thoughts turned to the previous night once more. The actions taken against her were extreme, and suggested that whoever was behind things was getting desperate. The question was: were they desperate about her progress in general, or the documents she had come to get? That was something she needed to know. But she didn't feel comfortable enough yet to examine them. She needed more distance between her and the suits, in a place that felt safer.

After a quick stop at a service station, both she and the car were full and ready for the next leg of their journey. Amy took the opportunity to call the car rental place and extend the hire. The last thing she needed was police attention. Soon she had left the small town and was on the open highway. The area she was travelling through was virtually a desert. Apart from dust and low level scrub there was nothing in the distance as far as she could see in any direction.

It was a lonely drive, even other vehicles on the road were few and far between. But that also provided her with some comfort, nobody was here to make her feel threatened. With this frame of mind she decided to stop at a rest area and stretch her legs.

There wasn't much to it, a few tables with benches and a toilet block that she wasn't interested in investigating. There was no real shelter from the elements either. It was relatively free from garbage, but she suspected that was more about how infrequently it was used than good clean up procedures. The peace and quiet made her feel a bit more at ease, so her mind turned to the problem of the documents. She returned to the car and took out one of the photocopied records to read over.

It was a police report, which she was now a bit more familiar with. What interested her immediately, however, was that it was also related to an arson. The equipment shed in a local school had been set fire to. The investigation concluded that someone, most likely a student, had stolen some cooking oil from the cafeteria and used it to start and maintain the blaze.

That sounded awfully familiar to the theatre fire. It was also quite telling that all the records she had found so far in this file were arson police records. They were all quite old as well. There had to be a connection, nothing else made sense. Her dream, the suited men, they all pointed to these records being key for unlocking a secret.

Amy decided to mull that over while she drove, she didn't want to stay too long in the rest area. It was too isolated for her tastes, and not safe. But it had served its purpose. She started working on a theory, and decided that it was likely that the person who started the theatre blaze was the same person responsible for all these old fires. The pattern seemed to fit, and it would explain why someone was going to great lengths to stop her getting the records. If that was the case, she just needed to find a name.

But she didn't remember seeing any suspect names on the files she had already read. That was something to look into further when she was able. The drive continued in its monotony, but after a few hours the landscape started to change. The odd property or shed littered the area. The quality of the road started to improve, and it became less dusty. She started to see some houses, and driveways. Civilisation was slowly emerging, and communicating the presence of a larger town. Midday was approaching and Amy was starting to get hungry again.

A sign soon announced the next town she was approaching - Drafton. It was bigger than Backett, and when she arrived at the town centre it was more than just a single street. There was even a shopping centre, although not that big. The heat and dryness of her drive had sapped her energy a little, so she decided to escape to the air conditioning of the shopping centre.

She parked, then went inside to investigate. She found the food court first, so she started by having a simple lunch of sandwiches. Next she stumbled across a department store and replaced some of the things she had left behind. After dropping her shopping off at the car, she paused for a moment and considered her options. Her curiosity demanded that she examine the rest of the documents, but she didn't feel safe.

It wasn't an unusual feeling for Amy, due to her many phobias, but she couldn't tie the feeling to anything concrete. It just seemed like it wasn't the right time to scrutinise the rest of the documents. So she prepared for the next drive, the last one for the day.

It felt sad, slowly driving out of town into the outskirts, and then the dreary highway. But she was heading in the right direction - toward home and more discoveries. The middle of the day had passed, and the sun slowly sank as she sped along the long road. She saw one or two rest areas, like the one she stopped at before, but felt no need to stop again. She was focused on her destination.

And like that it suddenly appeared before her. A big sign said 'Welcome to Charterville'. As she continued, she felt the familiarity of her surroundings build. She remembered coming here as a kid, to visit family. The long drive, and even longer family visits. The poking, prodding and shallow conversation of older relatives. But looking back with her adult eyes, she realised it wasn't that bad, maybe even nice. They cared, but as a child it was nothing but irritation.

Amy decided that the first motel she saw would get her business. She kept a look out for any, curious what she would find.

"Well, well, looks like it's your lucky day 'The Smart Traveller's Lodge'," Amy said as she pulled into the drive. It looked like your typical motel, rooms aligned in a row on raised structures, like school buildings with parking right out front.

Reception was a tiny box in one end of the building. She rang the bell and waited. A thin man responded promptly. He looked normal enough, so Amy booked a room for the night and walked back to her car. She took her things out, including the documents, and walked over to her room. It was tiny, the furniture was a few decades out of fashion, but it looked clean. The bed looked terribly inviting, despite its odd styling, so she lay down for a quick rest and fell into a deep sleep.

CHAPTER TWENTY-FOUR

DREAM SEVEN

I found myself in a giant room. It was so huge that I was more aware of the walls and ceiling, than being able to see them distinctly. I walked forward, the sounds of my footsteps echoing loudly throughout the space. I was acutely aware that something was reacting to my steps, but I didn't know what it was. So I continued walking, knowing that I would soon find out.

I must have walked for an hour or more with little or no change in my environment. Feeling puzzled, I turned around. There was a smooth white wall less than thirty centimetres from my face. I didn't remember there being anything behind me, and I was incredibly startled. I walked forward three paces and turned again. The wall was the same distance, or maybe slightly closer to me. So it had moved up as I moved.

I tried to ignore the wall closing in behind me and continued walking. Within a few minutes I felt better, effectively forgetting about it since it was behind me. Although I still had this strange feeling in my neck and shoulders. Like something was hovering there. Shortly that feeling spread to the top of my head. That was incredibly confusing. To counter it I tilted my head to look up and demonstrate that there was nothing there.

Only my head hit something and I cried out in shock. Using my right arm I felt around me and confirmed that there was now something right above my head. I ducked down a little so that I could look up and saw a smooth white surface, a ceiling. I had no idea when it had come down so far, but I decided to ignore it and keep going. I straightened myself, well tried to, and then discovered that the ceiling had come down further when I ducked, so I had to walk on hunched over.

Further changes weren't really noticeable, until I stopped and realised that I was almost doubled over. It was at this point I noticed the other walls had also joined their friends. I was boxed in on both sides, behind and above. Only in front of me was open and the way forward.

It was at this point that I started to panic a little. I had been brave, but when the walls quite literally closed in on me I couldn't believe it. My back was in pain, I felt really uncomfortable and my chest felt really tight. But I refused to bow down further.

I'm not sure how long I lasted, but eventually I was crawling along. I was sweating like crazy, and I didn't know what was causing it. I felt so hot and overheated, and the air felt stale and sticky. I kicked out at one of the walls in frustration. My reward was the pain of it connecting, and the wall changing colour. It immediately turned grey, instead of white. But it didn't stay grey, it started changing back to white, and then randomly flashing between the two colours. But the flashes weren't even, the walls ended up looking dark with the occasional bright flash illuminating them.

If the idea was to accentuate a growing darkness and enclosed space, it was working. The floor started sloping up, but the ceiling was not matching the angle, so I was even more cramped. The uphill slant made my progress tougher still, and I felt like I was creating a river of sweat. The change in surface made that impression worse, somehow it became more slippery. No matter how careful I progressed, I would slide into a wall somehow, as if it was a reminder.

Despite the pain, discomfort and building panic, I somehow knew everything would be ok. I started focusing on that feeling, and suddenly I emerged into a large room again. Not as large as before, but I could stand straight and not bump against anything. The air smelled sweeter and I could breathe deeper. After taking a moment, I walked forward to see what else awaited me.

I was staring at a wall. I moved closer and had a better look. There was a thin crack, or gap in the wall exactly my height. But it was so slight, I was confused. But slowly the realisation built, that I was supposed to squeeze through there. It didn't seem possible, but I knew there was no other option. I started taking a deep breath, then thought better of it.

I turned my body sideways, and then my head to make the best of it and minimise my size. I shuffled into the gap and pressed myself inside. My heart rate raised sharply, and I felt like I could dance out of my skin. As I squeezed in I felt all parts of my body under strain. I couldn't even see how far there was to go, it was just blackness.

Progress was extremely slow, as the odd shuffle I could manage barely moved me anywhere. I had to control my breathing carefully because of how enclosed I was. The oppressiveness of it was unbelievable. I had no sense of progress, because I couldn't look back. All I could do was inch forward. So I did, for as long as it needed. A small light broke up the darkness, and got brighter and brighter. I was moving towards it. I relaxed a little, and focused on the goal. Shuffle, pant, shuffle and I made it there. It was another room, smaller than the last, but comfortable. I fell down as I emerged from that sliver of space.

Looking around the room I saw two paths. One was a nice huge inviting doorway. The other was a slit on the ground, resembling a storm water drain in size. I sighed, knowing which path was for me. I stepped over to the slit, lay down flat on the ground and started to move towards it.

It was a lot like the last space I struggled through, only with the added feeling that there was a huge weight on top of me that could crush me at any time. I reached forward to feel my way and hit a solid surface. I carefully felt around and there was no way forward. Trapped in a space only big enough for me, I became conscious of the lack of air and totally lost it. I started hyperventilating and thought I would faint. I struck out my arm again in desperation and felt no resistance. There was even a slight breeze.

I composed myself as best as I could, then continued on. Dragging myself along the ground, cautiously feeling ahead and dreading another blockage. One never came, I'm not sure if that was for my benefit or not. The fear of it stayed with me.

After a time I felt the impression of light ahead of me, and it got stronger and stronger until I knew it was true. I pulled myself forward harder and faster until I could feel the warmth and I was rescued from my tiny prison.

CHAPTER TWENTY-FIVE

DISCOVERY

Amy woke to complete darkness. She felt groggy, but the dream was still fresh. She scrambled for some lights and then her notebook. She wrote down her dream and then began sketching a symbol. Once she was done she stepped back and looked at it.

It was circular and looked like a type of brand, to signify something. It didn't look like a flat design to her. But every other clue had been significant and timely, so she decided to not over think it.

She looked at the clock, it was late - past ten o'clock. She grabbed her room key and stumbled outside, to see if she could find something to eat. There was a pizza restaurant across the road, with lights on, so she headed over. It had only one couple sitting in the corner, sharing a pizza and garlic bread. The decor was old fashioned but very Italian, with red and white chequered table-cloths.

An old man came to give her menus, and provide her with water. She ordered their specialty pizza, then stared off into space. Her thoughts were on her recent dream. She wondered whether the police station incident had triggered it, her fear unlocking something. Maybe it was the fact that she was almost finished following the last clue that she got. Either way, she had something to follow up on after she returned home.

After eating she went back to her room, not to sleep, but to read. She was determined to get to the bottom of the police reports and discover whatever secrets they held. She pulled out the original documents, sat down at a small circular table in the middle of the room, and began sifting through once more.

The pattern she had already established was continuing. All the documents were pertaining to arson. Many were small fires. After examining a few she noticed something interesting. All the documents she had read had something additional written on them. In the bottom right corner of each one, someone had scribbled 'WG'. She flipped through the rest of the stack, and noticed they seemed to be similarly marked up. She filed it away in the back of her mind, hoping that she would work it out later.

Amy continued to scan through the documents, reviewing each one methodically to see what it added. When she reached the end, however, she found something a little different. It was a transcript of an interview. An 'Officer Davis' was interviewing two youths, represented as initials. They were 'WG' and 'RN'. The questions were about fires, and establishing alibis. Amy deduced that all the arson reports were being tied to this 'WG' being interviewed.

She arrived at the end of the interview, without discovering the identities of the suspects. Amy let out a big sigh, not realising that she had been holding her breath in anticipation. She had been counting on this to give her something concrete to follow up. She needed another big piece of the puzzle. It was such a blow, that she started to feel the anxiety of the last day flooding back in one big hit. Amy turned over the page mechanically, and went to collect the documents in a neat pile when she spotted some scrawl on the back of the last interview page. It said the following:

Davis interview with Richard Nelson and Walter Goldberg

Amy didn't know whether to leap up with a triumphant fist, slump back into her chair with relief, or fall off the chair from surprise. She had a link to Walter Goldberg, which also implicated him in the Theatre fire. He was a director in Keystone, and a serial arsonist. He was even a childhood friend of Dr. Nelson! It was an easy case to make that Goldberg had started the Theatre fire so that they could redevelop it. There was an obstacle in his way, so he dealt with it with the tool that he had - fire.

Amy's mind was racing with the possibilities, making the connections. But suddenly she came to an abrupt halt. While she had stumbled on something big, there was still a problem. Both she and Samantha had found no trace of Walter Goldberg. He was like a ghost. It was then Amy remembered, she hadn't called Samantha.

"Ooh I never called her to tell her the change of plans, she would have been expecting me today and I never showed up," Amy said to herself, deciding to call immediately.

She dialled Samantha and heard it ring. Nobody answered. Amy started to worry, then thought that perhaps Samantha had just gone to work. But she still felt uneasy, and wouldn't be able to sleep anyway so she decided to make a start. Amy packed her things, left the keys and some cash in the room as payment and headed out to her car.

The way home was pretty straightforward, she could more or less follow the one highway. As she zoomed down the deserted highway she found the darkness quite tiring. There wasn't much lighting apart from her headlights, and there weren't any other vehicles on the road. The buzz from her discovery slowly melted away, as the reality of the find imposed itself. It was a significant link, but it didn't give her the answers, not yet. But it was a good lead.

Amy played around with the radio, but couldn't find anything worth listening to. Her mind drifted again, but this time it landed on the dream once more. In her excitement she had forgotten the other clue she had - the symbol.

The more she thought about the symbol, the more she was convinced that it was stamped into something. But the problem was where to start? Her first ideas were the museum and the library. They were the most likely people to recognise the symbol, or at least point her in the right direction.

A loud burst, like a gunshot, blared right next to her. Amy panicked, and almost lost control of the car. She looked around frantically, trying to see where it came from. There was still nothing around, so she was puzzled. She continued to struggle with the car, and then realised something was not right. The car was moving unevenly, and steering was more difficult. She calmed herself a little, and tried testing the car methodically.

She adjusted her steering, then let the car drift a bit and noted what happened each time. Her theory was that something on the left side of the car was causing the problem. She passed a sign about a rest area, and decided to start slowing down so she could pull in there and investigate.

She turned the car off, but left the headlights on. The first thing that hit her was the silence. There was no sound around her, just the absence of sound. She opened her door, and stepped out carefully, examining the car as she walked around it. After one loop she spotted the problem: the left front tyre. It had punctured significantly and needed replacing. The closer she looked, the more amazed she was that nothing worse had happened.

Amy knew what needed to be done, but she had no idea how to do it. She had never changed a tyre before, and hoped that the hire car at least had the necessary tools. She opened the boot and scrounged around. There was a spare tyre, and a few tools in there.

"Can't be rocket science," Amy said to herself as she dragged the tyre out and carefully dropped it down. She grabbed the tools and they made a lot of noise clanking together. The stillness of the surrounds accentuated the sound. She knelt down and looked at the tyre. It only had a few bolts or screws holding it on. But then the problem would be the car's weight. One of the tools looked like a lever contraption.

"That must be the jack. Ok so I hold up the car's weight with this and change the tyre - easy." Amy said quietly, even though there was nobody around. She positioned the jack near the wheel and tried to raise the car. She grunted with the effort, but it seemed to be working. When she thought the car's weight was being carried by the jack she stopped and took a short break.

Next she found the tool that looked like it fit over the screws and started undoing one. It took forever but finally she got some traction and it popped loose suddenly. She scrambled to make sure she didn't lose it. The other three were similarly difficult, but didn't stop her progress.

Amy couldn't believe how quiet the road was. She kept looking up expecting a passing car, but there were none. With the tyre unfastened, now was the moment of truth. She tugged at the wheel, but it didn't really budge. She tried again harder, and wrenched it free, almost toppling over backwards. The car lurched as she did so, but rocked back into its position. Amy sat there, clutching the tyre like a baby and breathing hard. Then she saw headlights.

A car was approaching from the same direction she had been going. As it got nearer to the rest area it slowed dramatically, almost rolling past. Amy froze and watched. She didn't think she was visible behind the car, and hoped whoever it was kept going. It wasn't worth the risk that they might be friendly. She sat and waited, her panic rising and falling with her attempts to control it, while she clutched the tyre. After a minute the car sped up and resumed a normal speed.

Amy sat motionless for a few extra minutes, then shook herself out of it and lugged the damaged tyre over to the boot. Grabbing the spare she manoeuvred it over, with some difficulty, and lined it up. With a bit of wrestling the tyre sat in its right position, she just had to fasten it. She grabbed the screws, and the same tool and tried reversing what she had done.

It appeared to be working. Amy lost herself in the job, and ignored her surroundings, the quiet dark. She stepped back when done, and prodded the tyre, testing it. It seemed fine, but the real test would be trying to drive.

The next step was to see if the tyre would support the car properly. She lowered the jack down slowly until she saw the car's weight being borne by the tyres. She carefully pulled out the jack and waited.

Nothing happened. Amy sighed and leaned back against the car to rest. The whole process had been exhausting, but rewarding. She just hoped that it was enough to get home. She stared out into the darkness, testing herself. There was still that uneasiness, of the mysteries of the dark and what could be out there, but not the same fear or panic. If she had to stumble through that black wildness she would, but luckily she didn't have to. Yet.

With that thought, Amy dragged herself to her feet and took the rest of the tools back to the boot. Then she walked back to the driver's seat and sat down. The car still felt normal. She turned the key in the ignition, listening carefully to every sound. But nothing strange occurred. Next she took off the brakes and slowly accelerated. The car behaved as it should, rolling forward smoothly. Amy was quietly confident. She kept increasing her speed while remaining on full alert, straining to find a problem. There were none, and soon she was up to the same speed as before the tyre blew.

Amy waited a few extra seconds then celebrated.

"Yes!" she shouted out and waved one hand above her head. Then she did a little dance in her seat to celebrate. She was back on track, heading home with a successful trip behind her and clues to find. It was a strange feeling, to be hopeful again. But her small success with the tyre was just what she needed to regain her strength after such a draining episode.

The rest of the drive continued without any further incidents. Although Amy was extra cautious and attentive when any strange sounds occurred. She slowly progressed back into familiar territory and then into the city.

"Home sweet home," she said. It was too early to drop off the car however, so she drove it all the way back to her apartment. She was excited to see Samantha and fill her in on all the developments. Thinking of Samantha made her remember the unanswered phone call, so she hurried home even faster.

When she was a few blocks away, Amy had a thought. She had to consider the documents she had with her. Because of that crucial scribble on the back of one of the pages only the original was worth anything, at least for now. She had to put it somewhere safe, just in case. The problem was thinking of a place.

It had to be a place that was open or accessible at this hour as well.

"Hmm, post office, bank, train station, bus depot," she said to herself, listing out places. But only one of them made sense. The bus depot storage boxes were coin operated and always accessible. The drawback was that they were only good for twenty four hours. But it solved the current dilemma, so Amy changed course and drove over.

The bus depot was deserted, with only one staff member prepping for the early crowd. Amy selected a box near the ground, inserted her coins and set a pin code of 1982. She opened the box and only placed the original set of documents inside, deciding to keep the copies with her. After she closed the door she noted the time: 4:44am. If she didn't return before then the door would automatically open.

Satisfied with the outcome, Amy headed for home. She parked a block away and walked to her apartment. She walked up the stairs with caution, and took great care in opening the front door. She inched the door forward, taking a good look inside and remaining alert. The place seemed alright, so she entered and slowly closed the door behind her. Things looked much like they did, which was a relief. She headed straight for Samantha's room and peeked in. It was messy and unkempt, as usual. But nobody was there.

"Maybe she went out after work," Amy said to herself. It was a pretty common event, and pretty likely. But she couldn't shake the feeling that something was not right.

Sleep called, so Amy decided to rest. She had a lot to do, it made sense to rest when she had the opportunity. As she drifted off, she wondered whether she would dream again.

CHAPTER TWENTY-SIX

SEARCHING

Amy awoke hours later, from a refreshing sleep. However it was dream free. She pondered the meaning of that, then got out of bed. Her first check was Samantha's room which was still empty. She forced herself to ignore it for the time being.

Next was a quick breakfast, then she made her plan for the day. She would go to the library and museum to see if she could get a lead on the symbol from her dream. It was the only logical approach, there was clearly something else of importance out of her reach.

The Civic Library maintained a great catalogue of old documents, and Amy's latest theory was that the symbol was a seal of some kind. But something more ancient than the one she had tracked at the police station.

Her first stop though, was to drop off the hire car. She told them the story of how she had changed the tyre, in a very matter-of-fact way for the purposes of informing them, but the woman accepting the car was quite impressed. Amy felt a surge of pride. She knew it was a fairly ordinary thing, but she still celebrated it. She walked out of the car hire office with a spring in her step.

Next she walked to the Civic Library, as she felt in no rush. The sun was out and the day was warming up. Subconsciously she was aware of the various animals she passed on her way but ignored them. It didn't even really register as something she should have noticed. Soon the Civic Library loomed in front of her, its massive roman columns looking quite impressive.

She almost saw her reflection in the polished marble floor, and the echo of her footsteps seemed to fill the lobby area. She headed straight for the customer service desk to ask her question. There was nobody manning the desk, so she stood there and waited. A young man tending to a trolley of books nearby spotted her and walked over.

"Good morning! Can I help you with something today?" he said with a smile. His red hair flopped down in a fringe, giving him a soft and approachable look.

"Yes I hope so. Do you have any old documents here? I'd like some help identifying an old seal."

"We do have quite a few, I've got a fair idea of them. If you show me I can probably give you a good idea at the least." Amy nodded and pulled out her sketch of the symbol, handing it over to the man. He studied it for a moment and then stared off into space.

"Hmm I don't think I've seen anything like that here. But you know, it seems to me like it's probably not a document seal. I expect it to be stamped into something else, like some kind of good. Like a maker's seal," he said. Amy pondered that for a moment before responding.

"That's a good lead. Do you know where I might be able to follow it up?"

"There's a knowledgeable historian at the Municipal Museum, I'd say go talk to her. Her name is Jan. She will be able to identify it for sure."

"Thanks so much for your help."

"No problem, if you are nearby please pop in one day and let me know what you found, I'm curious."

"Of course," Amy said then left the library.

The museum was not far, she only needed to walk fifteen minutes. The library visit had been successful, even though she hadn't gotten the information she needed. The awareness and paranoia she had felt the last few days had begun to fade as well. Amy wasn't sure if it was the change of location to somewhere more familiar, the bright warm sun, or just the passage of time. She did feel like those tense moments being chased and tracked in the police station were far away.

She arrived at the Municipal Museum shortly, and the place seemed the same as her previous visit. However this time she went straight to the reception area, rather than exploring.

"Hi, how are you today?" said a pleasant young woman.

"I'm great thanks. I was hoping to see Jan if she's around today."

"She is, may I ask your name?"

"Amy, she doesn't know me."

"Sure I'll just call her desk now." Amy waited patiently while the woman dialled a number. After thirty seconds she hung up.

"Sorry, she must be out and about, please wait a minute," the woman said. Amy nodded and watched in interest. The woman picked up a walkie talkie from behind the desk and spoke into it.

"Jan to reception please. Jan to reception." After a few seconds the reply came.

"On my way." The receptionist put the walkie talkie away.

"As you probably heard she's on the way."

"Thanks," Amy said and turned her focus to the museum, to watch people and see who was approaching. After a few minutes an older woman walked over, one that Amy immediately recognised.

"Well hello, didn't we meet the other day? I'm Jan," she said.

"Yes we did. I have an enquiry, and I was pointed in your direction," Amy said.

"Well I'll do my best to help. Please follow me and we will go to my office." Amy followed along, and discovered that the museum had been established over two hundred years ago, and that Jan had been working there for over thirty years. Jan's office was compact, just a desk, two chairs and lots of filing cabinets. A bit of natural light filtered through the single window.

"Please take a seat," said Jan as she sat down. Amy sat and then pulled out her notepad. She opened it at the page of her latest drawing, and offered it to Jan.

"I'm trying to track down this seal," Amy said.

"Well I've seen a few in my day, let's take a look." Jan put on her glasses and scrutinised the drawing. After about thirty seconds she put it back down.

"Very interesting, where did you get that?" Amy didn't know how to respond. She couldn't exactly tell the truth.

"A friend gave it to me."

"Hmm well if it's what I think it is, there's probably a good story behind where you got this," Jan said and turned to her filing cabinets. She flicked through the drawers with precise speed, and pulled out a folder. She thumbed through this one carefully, and then stopped on a particular page.

"Is this the one?" she asked as she turned it around and pushed it towards Amy. Amy looked over and immediately knew that it was the same. She leaned forward in anticipation.

"Yes, that's exactly it."

"Now this is exciting," Jan said. She had a big grin on her face.

"That seal we are discussing is very particular. It was only used once, about one hundred and fifty years ago. It was used to stamp the single biggest collection of gold bars this town has ever seen." Jan paused for effect and Amy just stared at her.

"Gold bars?" Amy said, not knowing what to say.

"Yes. The other interesting part is that they disappeared shortly after they were branded, never to be seen again."

"Wow."

"Yes, this is quite an intriguing thing you have stumbled onto. Do you mind asking your friend about where it came from? It's a professional curiosity of mine."

"Sure. I'll update you later," Amy said, unsure of what to do next. She smiled, and said goodbye and wandered out of the museum in a daze. Once outside she remembered something and dug out her notebook again to flick through the pages. And there it was. After the second dream she had drawn a gold bar. At the time she had used it to latch onto the name Goldberg, but now it looked like there was more to it. These particular gold bars were at the heart of it. She had drawn two clues relating to them.

"Is that what this is all about? Greed?" Amy thought to herself. It was a common motive, but still wasn't enough of an explanation. But it was something to anchor her investigation to. She looked at her watch and noticed that it was already one in the afternoon. That reminded her that she only had the rest of the day to find a suitable storage place for the stolen police documents.

"Amy!" a man said nearby and walked over. She was puzzled for a minute, then recognised him as Adam, David's friend.

"Oh hi Adam."

"Nice to see you. How'd you go with Featherby? Going to join the class?"

"He's a bit of an oddball, I don't know what to think."

"Tough but fair. He's a good guy though, really dedicated. Anyway what brings you to my neck of the woods?"

"Your neck of the woods?"

"Yeah my office is around here, I'm on my lunch break." Amy didn't want to mention the museum, so went with the next best thing.

"Oh, I'm looking for some storage space. Just a small space to store documents and stuff, nothing that valuable. It's just good to have a few things stored somewhere else."

"Yeah offsite storage, it's the best practice," Adam said with a laugh. He looked thoughtful for a moment then spoke again.

"You know I think the way to go is a post office box. Fairly cheap, and you can post stuff to yourself from anywhere if you want."

"Great idea, I'll go with that one," Amy said with a smile. He had just solved her next problem. But then he followed it up with something else entirely.

"Hey, so I think David likes you. If you're interested, just let him know," Adam said. That took Amy completely off guard. She stumbled around for words.

"Well, I don't know. We work together, and he's already seeing someone."

"He's not really seeing her these days, trust me you're the one. No pressure, just letting you know."

"Well thank you."

"Anytime. Take care Amy," Adam said and waved goodbye.

"Oh by the way," Amy said. Adam stopped and listened.

"How's your book going?" Amy continued.

"Well I've abandoned it. But by that I mean I finished. That's what they say, you know. Art is never completed, just abandoned."

"Are you happy with it?"

"Yeah, more or less. I'm going to write something new, see how it pans out."

"Writing a sequel?"

"Everybody asks that. I'm not sure, we'll have to see."

"Good luck. And thanks for the advice."

"As I said, anytime. See you later Amy," Adam said and walked off. Amy felt like a mix of emotions, and found herself wringing her hands without realising. She did like David, but she had seen him with prettier girls, and she just couldn't handle it if he said no. She would just die.

Adam had said David was interested, but Amy needed more than that. She needed certainty. It seemed scarier than so many other things she had already faced. She didn't know if that was because of the unknown, or whether it was just that fear of rejection. Just thinking about the possibility made her feel unwell, her stomach churning like crazy. Anything would be better than being in that situation.

Amy put that thinking aside and focused on the job she had to do. She caught a bus to the depot and retrieved her documents. From there she walked to the nearest post office and rented a post box for a six month period. She mentally noted down the number, deposited the original police documents, and threw out the post box registration information. The key for the post box had even come with a tag showing the number, which she almost removed. She didn't want any reference to this location other than in her mind.

With that job completed, she decided to drop in to the Golden Arms and see if Samantha was there. It was a bit early, but the night shift would start soon. Amy decided to walk, as time was plentiful. She decided that she had to walk more, it had a calming effect. Plus since she was less distressed by animals, crowds and other things, there wasn't that potential anxiety to contend with.

She arrived at the Golden Arms feeling quite tired, and relished the opportunity of sinking into a comfy booth. She didn't recognise the bartender, but then she never came in so early. She began to order her usual drink, but then stopped.

"Please show me your cocktail list," Amy said. She scanned the list, and selected a Chocolate Martini. She had a sweet tooth, so why not try something different?

Amy settled into a booth near the corner and slowly sipped her drink. The sweet chocolate flavour and the alcohol kick relaxed her as she let the events of the previous days wash over her. She watched the patrons come into the pub, observing their movements and guessing as to their state of mind. She didn't usually spend that much time people watching, but it was oddly calming and distracting.

She saw men and women flirting with each other, some making propositions and then sheepishly retreating back to safe territory. It reminded her of David, and Adam's suggestion that she show some interest. But she felt detached, like these were other people's struggles and not for her. She glanced at her watch and realised that it was late afternoon and early evening. The night shift should have started, and she expected Samantha to be working.

Amy returned to the bar and looked over the staff. None of them were Samantha. When she did get someone's attention she asked directly.

"Hi, is Samantha working tonight?"

"No, she changed her shifts around," said a young male bartender.

"Was she working last night? Sorry I'm her flat mate and she's been out of contact."

"Oh you're Amy? Let me check with someone else," he said and walked off to talk to one of the other bar staff. He returned a minute later.

"No she wasn't. Apparently she took a few days off recently. She said she'd check back with us in a few days, but to just cover her shifts for the time being."

"Thanks for the information, I appreciate it," Amy said before returning to her booth. She sat down and thought over what the man had said.

It wasn't unusual that Samantha would take a few days off, especially since she had been helping look into things. But it was unusual for her to stay out of contact for more than a day. Amy didn't feel right about it, but decided she had nothing to chase up. Chances were that Samantha was alright. However if Samantha had not come home in the morning, Amy would start worrying and start the search.

Amy went home, and adjusted her detective board to reflect some of the new information she had gained: the previous arsons of Walter Goldberg, and the special gold bars that had gone missing. By reviewing the information, the only logical conclusion was that there was a connection between the construction, the torched theatre, and the missing gold bars. But there was still the question of the mysterious missing man - who was Walter Goldberg? And why couldn't they find him?

While wrestling these ideas, Amy started to drift off. She took herself to bed, and fell into a deep sleep. Her last thoughts were of Samantha, hoping that she would see her in the morning.

CHAPTER TWENTY-SEVEN

DREAM EIGHT

I was standing in a field. I looked around and saw that it was a sports field. Ahead of me there was a crowd of people. They just stood still, doing nothing. I watched them for a time, wondering what they were up to. Finally I walked over and joined them. Standing amongst them seemed to trigger something.

Two men stepped out from the crowd and waved at them. One man put a red arm band on, the other a blue one. The man with red pointed and said something, but I couldn't understand him. A woman stepped out of the crowd and walked over to the man in red, standing next to him. The man in blue spoke next, doing the same action. This time a man walked over and stood next to the blue arm band man.

This process continued, each of the leaders pointing and speaking and being joined by members in the crowd. I slowly came to the realisation that they were picking teams. Then it all began to make sense. I waited patient-ly, observing. One by one the people milling around were selected, their number dwindling. Then there were only two of us left. It was red's turn to pick and he pointed at the man next to me. Blue's pick was next. I somehow knew that the teams were uneven, that picking me would even up the teams. The man in blue looked at me with cool critical eyes then shook his head and turned away.

I almost called out, but stopped myself. I couldn't be-lieve that they didn't want me. It hurt being left out, being rejected. But I knew that it was just a taste of what was to come. I saw another room in the distance, light spilling out from within. I knew it would be harder, but steeled myself and started walking towards it.

I was surrounded by bright lights, sitting down in a comfy chair. People were swirling around me, doing my hair and makeup. I could see myself in the mirror and I looked amazing. I had never seen myself this way be-fore. I was quickly hustled into a lovely red dress and looked and felt like a million dollars. They gestured to-wards a walkway, which led to a stage. I knew what awaited me - judgement. I froze, unable to move. I felt so good, looked so good, I didn't want anyone to take me down. But I knew I had to move forward. So I con-tinued on, fear and trepidation in my heart.

I emerged onto the stage and saw a long catwalk ahead of me. I drew myself up and gathered as much confidence as I could to move forward. I walked up and down the catwalk, trying to fit in and feeling very apprehensive. I thought of walking off the stage immediately but couldn't. I stared at the exit, but saw that it was blocked, and I couldn't leave. But I also knew that the barrage would not begin until I turned around and faced the crowd. I had to make that choice.

So I turned around and it began. I noticed a suited man with a microphone standing expectantly in the crowd, looking at an audience member.

"Excuse me sir, do you find this woman attractive? Would you want to talk to her?" asked the man with the microphone.

"No," said the audience member. He accompanied his reply with a dismissive and disgusted look that hit me like a sucker punch. The man with the microphone, who seemed to be the host, moved on to the next audience member.

"Can you please describe her in one word," the host asked.

"Ugly," said the next audience member. The host nodded and moved on to the next person. I looked up and saw thousands of people in the audience, I felt like it was going to take a while.

After a dozen or so, the blows didn't feel so bad. I told myself that they were just random people, they didn't know me. I kept repeating it, to build up my resistance. At the same time I saw the audience dwindling, until there were no more left. I had managed to combat the assault. I turned and saw that the exit was now available again, and I could leave the stage. I walked off with a tremendous amount of relief, even though I felt I had dealt with the situation well.

I appeared in another room. I could see someone sitting down at the opposite end of it. It was a woman, but she was facing away and I couldn't recognise her. I walked closer and then the woman turned around and faced me. It was Samantha.

"Samantha!" I called out as I ran to her. But something wasn't right. Her eyes were cold, her usual smile was gone and her manner was different.

"Go away, you're no friend of mine," she said icily and I felt it like a dagger through my heart. I closed my eyes to try and make the pain go away. When I opened them again, I was in the same room. It was like the situation had reset. I knew what would happen if I walked closer, and I tried to be brave. I tried to just walk forward, but my feet wouldn't move. I couldn't just push past and ignore the situation, I had to confront it. I clenched my fists and forced one foot in front of the other. I kept Samantha in my sights as I approached, and when she rose I instinctively closed my eyes. I opened them again, and the room had reset.

Again I approached and kept an eye on her. I saw her rise, and waited for what would happen.

"You'll never be my friend," she cried out and it hurt me just the same. I stepped forward.

"I hate you." I stepped forward again.

"You're worthless." I kept going.

"Nobody would ever want you as a friend." I was close now, and I reached out to her. But she faded away into nothing. There was a doorway just beyond where she was standing, so I rushed into it.

I was in a bar, and it seemed familiar. I saw David sitting down at a table. I walked over and sat down across from him. I opened my mouth to say hello but instead said something else.

"Do you like me"?

"No," he said and then laughed. I felt so humiliated, and hurt. Then Melissa sat down next to him and they started making out. There was now a massive lump in my throat and a hornet's nest in my stomach. I spoke again, trying to take it back.

"Will you go out with me?" I said. David laughed even harder and Melissa joined in as well. All I wanted to do was run from the room, my cheeks were burning and I felt horrible.

"In case you missed it, that was a no," David said while Melissa kept cackling. I tried to explain what was happening, but it didn't work.

"Are you free for dinner sometime?"

"With you? No way." I don't know how many times that sequence repeated itself, with minor variations. It could have been twenty, or even fifty. Over and over again I heard him reject me. I kept trying to phrase it differently, to make it noncommittal or even take back the offer, but the right words never came. Every time I spoke it invited another slightly different rejection. Finally I grew tired and I didn't care anymore.

"David, I like you and I'd really like to spend more time with you to see if there's something more than friendship between us," I said honestly, surprising myself. He looked at me strangely, then smiled and faded out. I was alone again, but worn out. I didn't have the energy to even mentally celebrate that victory.

There was a glowing doorway nearby, and I ambled off towards it happy that my ordeal was coming to a close. I stumbled into the light and found myself in another room. There was a woman at the back of the room facing away, much like Samantha had been. But it wasn't her this time. I walked forward cautiously, anxious about what this next trial may be. I felt like I had done enough, but still it continued. As I approached the woman turned and looked at me. I gasped and stopped walking.

It was me, but also wasn't. She looked exactly like me, but she held herself differently, and had different mannerisms. There was a fire in her eyes, an invitation to test her if you dared. Before I could say anything she spoke.

"Look at you. You're just weak and passive. You don't deserve to be me. You can stay here, I'm not taking you with me." She turned and walked towards a glowing door, the other lights in the room winking out. I was left in darkness. But something changed in me. I didn't take it to heart, I knew that she was either wrong, or was testing me. I didn't panic, I just held onto my self-belief and slowly walked forward. The more deliberately I moved, the more she slowed down. Step. After step. After step. Then I was right behind her. She was still facing away. I reached out and hugged her from behind. I felt an amazing warmth which spread throughout me and then everything became white.

CHAPTER TWENTY-EIGHT

STOWAWAY

Amy opened her eyes, and immediately thought of Samantha. But by habit she noted down her dream, and drew another picture. This one was some kind of logo, with an eagle featuring prominently. As soon as the drawing was complete Amy dropped the notebook and ran into Samantha's room.

The bed was made, and an envelope was placed on one of the pillows. Amy quickly grabbed the envelope and tore it open. A photo and a letter fell out. She looked at the photo first. It was Samantha lying on a low bed, asleep. She was surrounded by boxes and other junk. Amy then turned to the letter. It read as follows:

Your friend is safe, as long as you cease your investigation.

Amy was in shock. The letter fell from her hands onto the bed. She fell down and sobbed into her hands. They had taken her, and they had tried a second time and failed. So they had gone after her best friend. Amy started to get angry. But it wasn't a wild rage, it was a slowly burning passion, brimming with determination. She had a task to do, one more important than anything she had done before. She had to save her friend.

Fear, doubt, they played no part. She was pure purpose. Amy picked up the photo again and looked carefully. There had to be a clue in that photo somewhere. There was no view of outside the room to pick up on landmarks. They were clearly too careful to reveal something so obvious. So she decided that the finer details would need to be examined. She took the letter and photo over to her bag and placed them inside. Next she got ready to leave.

Amy had a thought about the message. She would have to appear to be following it, but also be able to disappear when the time was right. She knew that by going home she'd probably gone back on their radar. Therefore her next actions would need to be well thought out. She had to assume that every action of hers would be watched.

Amy left the house and walked to the bus stop. She caught a bus to the nearest shopping centre. She meandered through the shops, until settling on a large department store. Calmly she made her way through to the women's fashion level. After doing the rounds she had purchased the few items she needed. They were a bag, coat, a pink wig and shoulder pads. She took those items to the nearest bathroom and went into a stall. There she did the best she could to change both her appearance and silhouette.

Amy took off her jacket, then put on the shoulder pads and the coat. Next she fitted the wig and then put all of her things (including her normal bag) into the new bag. She exited the stall, straightened up her appearance in front of a mirror, then sauntered out of the bathroom.

She tried to move differently, and act differently. She hoped to be different enough to break any contact, and from there continue on with her plan. Unsure of whether she had succeeded, she took a long path around the shopping centre, ending in a fairly quiet corner. Luckily she found herself at a two dollar store called 'Lucky Dollar'.

Amy first noted the smell, common to all two dollar stores, then browsed the aisles looking for the next item on her mental list. In the third aisle she spotted it - a thick round piece of glass with a metal rim. For good measure she also grabbed a traditional magnifying glass. After purchasing them Amy found the nearest cafe and ordered herself some breakfast and a coffee. After eating her food, Amy pulled out the photo and placed the chunky glass magnifier on top.

Starting at the top left corner, she slowly moved it around over the surface of the photo looking for any special identifying marks. She was in a rush, but forced herself to be slow and methodical. It wasn't until nearing the bottom right corner that she spotted something that grabbed her attention. One of the boxes in the room had a symbol on it.

She picked up the paper and the glass and moved them both much closer to her eyes to get a better look. The symbol was a logo of some kind, but she didn't quite have enough definition and it was a bit distorted. She switched to the traditional magnifying glass to take another look and almost dropped it in surprise.

She looked again, to verify. There was no mistaking it, the logo on the box looked remarkably like the one from her dream. She retrieved her notebook and compared the two. They were a perfect match. Amy sat back in her chair and thought through the revelation. There was a connection between the logo she had drawn and where Samantha was being held. The logo was most likely for a company. The problem for Amy was that she had nothing else to go off, so the company could have been anything.

She looked at the logo carefully. It was an eagle with a fierce expression on its face in full flight. She thought hard and realised that she didn't recognise the logo, and she didn't remember seeing it anywhere else. After a moment of thought, Amy had an idea.

She paid and left the cafe, and looked for a newsagent. She wandered over to the magazine section, and looked for the business magazines. It was only a hunch, but she suspected that if it was a logo pointing back to a company, then that company would be well known. And she could search through the big players with ease. She flipped through a few magazines titled 'Big Company', 'Annual Business Review' and 'Industry Leaders'. Then she found one called 'Fastest Growing Companies'. She opened the magazine and found the index. Scanning through the list of companies one caught her eye - Screaming Eagles. She quickly turned to the page and saw their logo. That was it!

Amy almost danced on the spot, but thought better of it. She bought the magazine and found an empty bench nearby to sit down and read. The company was primarily a corporate freight business. They had doubled in size each year for the last four years. Their head office and distribution centre were both in the city. Amy let the information sink in. She had to investigate them, and discover the link. The most likely angle was that either Keystone or Inspired Planning were using Screaming Eagles for freight services. She had to track them down and follow that lead.

Amy walked with purpose, looking for a phone booth. When she found one she walked inside and opened up the hefty phonebook. She found Screaming Eagles, and saw that their head office and distribution centre were listed. But they were different addresses. She wrote them both down just in case. However the presence of the box in the photo swayed her towards the distribution centre. She felt that was more important than any documents she may find at their head office.

She spent a few moments thinking through her options and settled on a plan. She would infiltrate the distribution centre at night. Hopefully then it would be less busy and she would have an easier time finding something. That gave her plenty of time to make her way there, which was good. Public transport seemed like the best option, to leave less of a trail.

After passing a few hours of idle time and catching a few buses she was mere blocks away from the Screaming Eagles distribution centre. It was a sprawling complex, mostly open with lots of warehouses and trucks. The time was just after six, Amy hoped that it was late enough. First she casually walked around the block, scoping out the potential entrances and the amount of activity. There were two main driveways and a pedestrian walkway that gave access to the complex. There were giant gates that were left open. She didn't sense a lot of activity, but the place wasn't exactly deserted.

Amy prepared a cover story in her head about picking up a parcel as she completed a circuit. One of the driveways seemed much quieter with less traffic, so she chose to walk through there. It was twilight so the sky was getting dark but a lot of the street lights hadn't activated yet. She tried to walk as if she belonged there, but at the same time stuck to the perimeter of buildings and tighter walkways to be less visible and less conspicuous. If she was challenged she had her cover story. If that didn't hold, she at least had her disguise so the incident would not be tracked back to her.

Amy rounded the first main building, and didn't find an obvious entry. It was probably locked up due to the time. She spotted what looked like an admin office at the opposite corner, but wanted to only go there as a last resort. What had promise was a large warehouse with large open doors and light spilling out. As she approached she listened out for voices or other cues, but didn't hear anything. So she strode through the doors like she knew where she was going.

The warehouse was full of boxes, many stacked neatly onto pallets or onto shelves. They all appeared to be stamped with the logo, just like the box in her photo of Samantha. There were all different sizes of boxes, and some were big crates. Amy walked over and inspected some of the boxes. All of the boxes that were sealed had names and address labels attached to them. It looked like they were ready to be shipped out.

Amy wandered around, looking at the labels and trying to work out the system. She wanted to see if any were being sent to Keystone or Inspired Planning. She couldn't find any. Her circuit of the warehouse brought her back to the entrance, but she heard voices approaching. Amy ducked behind a big shelf, and hoped that nobody walked over that way. The voices became audible as they came closer.

"Where's Barry?" the first voice asked.

"I guess he's not here, maybe he's having a smoke," the second voice said.

"Well can you seal up those last boxes and get that pallet prepped, it has to go out tonight. Urgent delivery for our special customer."

"I'm rubbish with the forklift. Best to use Barry."

"I don't care who does it, as long as it's on the truck pronto. Better go find him if you don't want to do it."

"Sure boss." Amy heard footsteps leading away. The mention of a special customer piqued her interest. So she crept out of hiding and had a look at the main pallet closest to the door, which seemed to be a work in progress. There were some shipping labels already applied. She moved closer to read one of them.

"Inspired Planning? Jackpot!" she said softly, not wanting to draw attention. She had to think quickly, as the workers would be back soon. She noticed an open box on the pallet. It was quite large and semi filled with what looked like foam insulation panels. It was an option, although not a pleasant one. She looked around the nearby area and saw a Stanley knife. She retracted the blade and put it in her bag. Now she was ready.

Amy displaced the foam panels then crawled into the box. She placed the panels above her, making it look like the box was full. She had no idea if it was going to work, whether her hiding spot was passable. A nervousness struck her, and the wait for the men to return was slow and anxious. The enclosure of the box was stifling and alarming, but she managed to push those feelings aside.

She felt around with her hand until she had found the Stanley knife and gripped it hard. It made her feel better, knowing that she had an out, or if need be some form of self-defence.

Eventually footsteps returned.

"One last box to seal up," a voice said. Amy tensed up, imagining her discovery. Maybe she could use the element of surprise on them. She heard the box flaps being manipulated above her, and the distinctive sound of packing tape being unwound and pressed down on the box. It was a strange feeling, each piece of tape was closing her in, but also protecting her from being found.

"Alright, pick her up," the same voice said. Amy panicked, running scenarios through her head. Those images were jolted away as she felt everything lurch up, off the ground.

"Easy as she goes," the voice continued. The situation seemed calm, the language more general than suggesting her. Amy calmed a little.

"And set her down, nice work," the voice said.

"Hey this doesn't mean you are off the hook, just because I did it once," another voice said back.

"Yeah, yeah whatever. Hey better leave that in the truck, I bet they ain't there to receive again."

"Yeah, I don't know what kind of operation those guys are running. Pretty slap dash."

"It's just another run, let's get it over with." Amy noticed that her pallet had been placed down in a truck, and she heard the truck doors creak as they swung shut. The sound of the doors being bolted was quite unnerving. She listened closely and heard the door of the truck's cabin slam shut and the engine starting up. She felt everything lurch forward then settle as the truck drove off. She was on her way.

The air in her box became quite stale, despite her attempts at conserving her breathing. It didn't seem safe to open the top up yet, so she just poked small holes into the box to get some additional air. It didn't seem like much, but it was an improvement. Amy tried to judge where they were going and how far it might be, but soon realised it didn't make that much difference and she should be able to find the address at her destination.

To occupy herself she turned her thoughts to Samantha. She had never expected them to go after her friend, although in hindsight it made sense. Amy wasn't sure what would happen next, but she thought she could get Samantha to hide out somewhere. She just hoped that Samantha was alright, and that she could get to her in time.

The truck started to slow down, which prompted Amy to focus. It made a few manoeuvres before backing into a spot. After the engine was turned off she listened out for any activity. There were some door slams and footsteps, followed by voices.

"Told ya, there's nobody bloody here."

"Well lucky we brought the forklift then. Am I driving?"

"Yep, just leave the whole pallet out here. They'll pick it up tomorrow." Amy heard the doors being unlocked, and then swinging open and banging against the truck. Next she heard footsteps and the sound of the forklift turning on. She braced herself for the bump and lift and was slightly less surprised when it happened. She felt herself being carried a short distance, then returning to the ground.

"Job's done," one of the voices said.

"Yeah let's get out of here." Amy heard the forklift move away, the truck doors slam and the truck itself leaving. She stayed still, carefully listening for any signs of life. All she could hear was an empty wind blowing around. She took the Stanley knife and started cutting her way out, starting from the side of the box. The first waft of the cool night air was like heaven. She kicked out at the opening flap and hit something else. She winced with the pain and decided that she had to get out from the top. She squashed the foam panels down enough so that she could reach up to cut at the top of the box. It was hard going, but the influx of extra air from the side of the box helped. As she cut along the top she leaned against the foam even more, compressing it. When at least half the box was opened she wrestled her way up and her hand emerged into the night. She managed to struggle up until she was squatting, half in and half out of the box. She straightened and then felt incredibly exposed. But the freedom, and the feeling of the fresh air on her face was amazing.

Amy clambered out of the pallet and looked around. She was outside a warehouse with multiple roller doors all shut. But it was also part of a larger complex, with multiple buildings. It definitely seemed like a staging or storing area. It also didn't look familiar, so she hadn't been there before. Therefore she decided to explore carefully.

Spurred on by the chatter she overheard about the place being deserted, Amy wandered around the complex trying to find somewhere she could get into. All the main warehouses with the roller doors and truck bays were tightly locked up. The odd building out was a smaller boxy structure with a lot more windows. It looked like an office of some kind. Amy headed towards it, hoping for more luck.

It definitely came across as an office, and she tried the front door but it was locked. There were a few windows nearby, but they were sealed shut and mostly blocked by blinds, obscuring her view of the inside. It was dark inside, so Amy felt like it was safe to investigate more. She circled the building, and spotted a window that was open. The problem was that it was fairly high off the ground, either for a second level or a mezzanine. Amy looked around for something she could use as a boost.

Looking around didn't reveal anything obvious, but gave her a strange feeling. That there was something significant to find. But there was nothing lying around that she could use. However rather than giving up, Amy held onto the feeling and walked back to the pallet she had emerged from. She assumed that the whole thing had been building materials, which meant that there could also be something else useful there.

She prodded and poked around, examining the boxes. It was generally just building materials, and not very useful for getting to high places. She wasn't about to build herself scaffolding. But she did notice something wrapped in plastic wedged in-between some of the boxes. With some effort she pulled it out, dropping it in the process. It made a metallic clank as it hit the ground, and Amy moved closer to have a better look. It was a ladder of some kind, which was collapsed. That had potential.

She picked it up and carried it over to the spot with the open window. By this stage she was convinced that nobody was around. Tearing off the plastic covering, she pulled out the ladder and tried extending it. Surprisingly it extended to a considerable length. She placed it against the wall and assessed the climb. The ladder got her most of the way, but not quite. But she wasn't going to let that stop her.

Amy made sure that the ladder was stable, then started to climb up. She ascended one rung at a time, not rushing and not skipping ahead. As she drew nearer to the top it became more and more obvious that she would struggle reaching the window. Standing on the top step, Amy was still out of reach. But it wasn't far. She took a deep breath, then rolled the dice. She stepped up onto the little shelf at the top of the ladder, to move up even closer. It wasn't designed for anyone to stand on it, so she had trouble steadying herself. With a quick impulsive movement she pushed off of the step and launched herself at the window. With both hands she got a good hold over the windowsill, but her legs were dangling in the air as the ladder crashed down. Amy willed herself inside, dragging herself up with all her might and collapsing into the building in a heap.

Luckily the window was not high, so she brushed off her less than graceful entry. After she felt safely inside her first thought was a panicked one about alarm systems. Amy stayed very still and surveyed the room she was in. It was an open walkway leading to a larger room. She crept forward to the railing and looked down. There was a typical office layout on the level below, with a few couches near the entry and a water cooler. Wondering about alarm systems she looked around, not seeing anything.

Amy crouch walked over to the larger room at her level, and saw it too was a typical office layout with cubicles. But there was also a separate office in the corner. There seemed to be lots of papers and other things to search through, so she made a mental note to return and do a proper look. She turned and went back the way she came, finding the stairs and descending to the lower level. Other than the areas she spotted from upstairs, there was also a kitchen, two bathrooms and a back room labelled 'Storage'.

The rest of the spaces seemed fairly self-explanatory, so Amy tried to open the door to the Storage room. The door was locked tightly. She tried peering under the door but there was no light coming from the room. Rather than ignoring the room, she decided to find a way in. It just nagged at her. So she walked around the kitchen and office areas, looking for any sets of keys. When there were none she started hunting around on the desks, and in drawers.

"I wish that locksmith trick would work again," she said to herself. But at the same time she knew she was lucky it had even worked the first time. With downstairs completed she headed back upstairs.

She repeated the same search upstairs, with the same result. She was left with the separate office with the plain wooden door. She turned the handle, expecting it to be locked. But it opened with ease. Amy slowly entered the room, looking around with caution. The desk looked much the same as the others, but the chair behind it was much bigger and looked like leather. She spotted on the wall a whole block full of key rings with labels.

"Ah ha!" Amy said and walked over to the keys. Each ring had a plastic tag with a handwritten description on it. She looked through them all until she found one which was labelled as Storage. She took it and rushed back downstairs.

There was only one key on the ring, so unlocking the door was no trouble. She tried to open it quietly and slowly, and only had a slight creak betraying her entry.

The room had no windows, so was pitch black. It took her eyes a minute to fully adjust so that she could make out the shapes within. There were things everywhere, so she felt around for the light switch and found one near the door, flicking it on.

The pulse of light temporarily blinded her. When her vision returned she couldn't believe what she saw. It was the room from the photo of Samantha. The bed was there, and Samantha was in it. But there was one other thing. It was a machine with what looked like a drip attached to it, which was attached to Samantha's arm.

"No, not you too!" Amy cried out and ran over to Samantha. She unplugged the machine and carefully removed the drip. Samantha was sleeping soundly.

"Hey, wake up. Samantha, it's Amy." There was no response. Amy slapped Samantha across the cheek. Something registered on Samantha's face. It looked like she was slowly waking up.

"A…Amy?"

"Yeah I'm here. We need to get you up and out of here."

"Where?"

"Just some place you fell asleep." Amy helped her sit up, supporting Samantha when she started to sway. What Amy needed was transport for them both. She had a brainwave and thought of the rows of keys upstairs.

"I'll be back in a minute, don't go anywhere," Amy said with a smile, and dashed out of the room. She stopped to look back, needing to check that Samantha was really there. Once satisfied she ran upstairs to the single office. As she passed one of the windows she saw a light. Startled, she stopped and looked out. There was a truck entering the complex.

"Great, just what we need," Amy said and then rushed off. She found the rows of keys and quickly looked through them all. There were a few labelled 'Truck' so she grabbed those and headed back to Samantha.

She found Samantha in the same spot, looking slightly more alert.

"Hey I'm back, we gotta go," Amy said, trying to be as relaxed as possible and not let the panic seep through. Samantha nodded slightly and tried to get up. Amy stepped in to help, and supported her under one shoulder. Samantha was able to stand up and walk, with help, but not fast. First Amy turned off the light in the storage room and locked the door, hoping that it would buy them time. Together they hobbled over to the main exit of the building, Amy unlocked it with some difficulty one-handed. She needed to head over to where the trucks were parked, but she also knew that's where the men would arrive.

Amy listened out for the signs of movement. That would both tell her where to go, and also what to look out for. She thought sounds were coming from the far corner of the complex, so she headed in that direction. Samantha was slowly getting more mobile, but wouldn't be able to walk unassisted.

"C'mon Sam, let's keep it together," Amy said, more for her own benefit. She took a longer circuit around the pathways between buildings and didn't cut through the common area. Their slow speed made the trek all the more arduous, and Amy broke out into a sweat. She hoped it was just the exertion. She heard voices and saw the flash of the torch being waved around.

"Package should be delivered by now."

"Yeah let's verify, then take it over to manufacturing." Amy froze, realising that they were going to head directly to the pallet she had travelled in. They would know instantly that something was wrong. The other problem was that she wasn't far from that spot. She just had to hope that they went for the office, rather than back to the truck.

"Hey let's keep quiet," Amy said to Samantha, and shifted the hair from her face. The voices became louder, and Amy looked around for somewhere to hide. There was an equipment shed nearby. They wouldn't be able to get in, but there was a space behind it to stay out of sight. Amy steered Samantha in that direction and then they both collapsed onto the ground. Amy was happy for the break, but didn't allow herself to relax. She would need to move again soon.

The sound of approaching footsteps put her on alert. They were decisive and purposeful, not a person idly walking over. She wondered if they had been spotted and prepared herself. She fingered the Stanley knife in her pocket, just in case. The footsteps stopped and she heard the rattle of a lock and the creaky groan of the shed doors opening. Amy held her breath, too scared to breathe. She looked at Samantha, and mentally begged her to be quiet.

The moment passed, the shed doors were slammed shut and the footsteps continued once more. Amy waited for them to get fainter, and then started to pick herself and Samantha up again. She felt her muscles complaining, but ignored them and pushed on. She needed to get as far away from the men as possible. As soon as they saw the pallet they would get suspicious and start searching.

Amy rounded a corner and saw a row of trucks parked neatly near a long driveway. There was a chain link fence surrounding the complex, and a boom gate blocking the exit.

"One problem at a time," Amy thought to herself. She led Samantha over to the first truck and got her to lean on it. Amy fished around for the truck keys, dropping the whole bundle on the ground. The noise alarmed her, and she froze, looking around for any signs of reaction. There were none, so she picked them up and started trying the keys.

None of the keys worked. Amy cursed then grabbed Samantha and moved over to the next truck. She began trying the keys again, taking care to not drop them. After each key she looked over her shoulder, to see if there was any trouble on its way. There was nothing, which really was the best scenario. But not being able to see what those men were up to brought its own worries. When one of the keys turned in the lock Amy almost took it out again to try the next. She stopped herself, and opened the passenger door fully.

"Ok up we go Sam," Amy said, boosting Samantha up into the seat. Samantha mumbled something, and then Amy climbed up after her, struggling with the seat belt. Once that was done, she jumped down and closed the door. She took out the key and went around to the driver's side. A quick glance over the complex told her that things still seemed to be quiet. She jumped into the driver's seat, closed the door and assessed the vehicle.

She never drove manual, but remembered how to manage gears. Experimentally she tried starting the engine, and it spluttered then roared into life. Amy didn't let herself think, and just let her subconscious take over. She turned on the headlights, disengaged the brakes and started driving off. Without a second thought she headed for the exit, accelerating as fast as possible. The truck picked up momentum, crashing through the boom gate. If she had managed to stay off the radar, well now she was squarely back on it. She pushed forward, instinctively closing her eyes and the truck ploughed into the chain link fence.

It buckled and broke away, and Amy forced her eyes open and threw all her weight into the steering wheel to turn the truck. She settled onto the road and continued into the night.

CHAPTER TWENTY-NINE

RECOVERY

The road was mostly deserted, and Amy struggled to think of where to go. She needed a safe place, one that would not be obvious. At the same time Samantha needed attention. Whether it was just some looking after, or a hospital visit, Amy wasn't sure. She glanced over at Samantha, and it seemed like Samantha was breathing fine. For the time being, Amy decided to just find somewhere to rest.

First thing's first, she had to get some distance between her and any pursuers, and then find a way to ditch the truck. It had served its purpose, and would soon become a liability. However she didn't know the area well, and didn't want to ditch the truck without something to replace it. So she drove on, looking for signs of more activity.

She gradually moved out of the industrial area into one that had shops lining the streets and a few parks.

Now the truck was a bit more conspicuous, so she looked out for side streets that might have some business complexes. She spotted one suddenly and took a hasty right turn, instigating a flurry of angry car horns. She ignored them and continued on, albeit slower. She spotted a furniture outlet with a large outdoor car park, so she pulled in the truck and parked it. It wasn't the best option, but it was easy.

Amy jumped out and walked around to help Samantha. Samantha seemed slightly less groggy, which Amy took as a good sign. Again, Amy assisted Samantha and they walked slowly down the street to the main road. They crossed the road and continued walking.

"You'd be loving this if you were actually awake, always the adventurer," Amy said to Samantha. She didn't get a reply, but smiled anyway. They struggled up the street, Amy not quite sure what she was looking for.

"There we go," Amy said as she read the sign for the 'Comfy Lounge Motel'. She quickened her pace, with a goal in sight. Within a few minutes they pushed through the main doors.

Amy saw a lounge to her right and guided Samantha onto it. Then she walked up to the reception desk. A bright young woman in her twenties looked up and smiled, and stopped playing with her curls.

"Hey how can I help you?"

"Hi, I was wondering if you had any rooms available?"

"Sure. For just the night? Twin share?" the woman said, gesturing over at Samantha. Amy paused to think.

"Yeah twin share is fine. How about two nights?"

"Should be good, let me double check. Yup the rate is eighty dollars per night, including breakfast."

"Sign me up," Amy said and started filling out the required paperwork. She wasn't worried about using their real names, as she felt they would be long gone before anyone came looking.

"Is your friend alright?" the woman said.

"Yeah, she just partied a bit too hard," Amy said with a forced smile. The woman nodded and handed Amy the key.

"First floor, last door on the left," she said to Amy and waved.

"Thanks," Amy said and mentally prepared herself for helping Samantha up the stairs. It wasn't as bad as she thought, but Amy was definitely pleased when she opened the door to their room and switched on the light. It was a simple room with two beds, a few bits of furniture, a kitchenette and a bathroom.

"You'll have to let me know how comfy that lounge was," Amy said to Samantha. She guided her to one of the beds, and settled her in.

"Hopefully some natural sleep will sort you out." Amy kissed Samantha on the forehead and then prepared herself for sleep. Just sitting down on the other bed brought a huge wave of tiredness. The day was catching up with her. But she smiled, knowing that she had done the impossible, and rescued her friend.

Amy slept, but didn't dream. She woke several times and checked on Samantha, but there was no discernible change. When morning rolled around Amy didn't feel rested at all, but she couldn't sleep any more. She decided it was time to rouse Samantha.

"Hey sleepy, time to wake up," Amy said, trying to be playful and mask the concern she felt. Samantha stirred a little.

"Rise and shine!" One of Samantha's eyes opened a crack.

"Amy?" Samantha said, slightly slurring the word.

"Yes! It's Amy. How are you feeling?"

"Foggy. Have I been asleep for a while?"

"That makes sense. Yeah you've been out for a bit. What's the last thing you remember?"

"I was at work. No, I left work. I went out after. Some creep bought me a drink and then I blacked out."

"Oh well, business as usual then?" Amy said, trying to laugh it off.

"For you maybe," Samantha said, trying to crack a joke. Amy laughed, mostly with relief. Samantha didn't seem to have any permanent damage. If she had no recollection of her ordeal, then Amy would pretend it never happened. It would be easier for her friend. She also felt like it should never have happened, Samantha shouldn't have been involved. It just showed that they were getting desperate. It meant that Amy was on to something.

"How was your trip?"

"Oh. It was quite eventful. I'll fill you in later."

"You better, or..." Samantha said, trailing off. Her eyes closed again. Amy walked over and checked that her friend was comfortable. She started to ponder about what was next. She didn't have any strong leads, the last one leading her to Samantha. Although that could have been a coincidence, perhaps saving Samantha had not been the right objective. But she stopped herself from going down that line of thinking, she absolutely did the best thing.

Her body and mind seemed to agree on that point. Merely reflecting on the fact that Samantha was safe freed up Amy's conscience. There was more work to be done, but she could afford to rest. It wasn't just Samantha that needed to recover, and regroup. Amy looked over at her bed, and felt the need to sleep. She had been carrying many burdens, fleeing capture and not giving herself time. But it was safe for a time. And a part of her knew, that it might be her last chance.

CHAPTER THIRTY

FINAL DREAM

I was walking in a green and flowery field. The sky was blue, butterflies abounded and I felt a sense of serenity and peace. A gentle breeze brushed my cheeks and cooled me from the warmth of the sun. I sat down in the grass and enjoyed the moment. However I knew it was just a moment and that it would pass. I stood and looked behind me, the ground was desolate, the grass withered and the flowers dried up and lifeless. I felt a pang of fear, and then sadness.

I continued onwards, occasionally looking back. Either death or the inevitability of time was following in my wake. Everything I passed was drained of all energy and colour. I stopped looking back and focused on what was ahead of me. I was approaching a lushly forested area. I was surrounded by the chatter of birds, the swishing swaying of the trees and softness of the ground under my feet. My curiosity got the better of me and I turned to look behind me. It was a dusty graveyard. Lifeless husks where trees used to be, the perfectly preserved skeletons of the small animals and birds of the forest.

Somehow I understood that it wasn't a violent death that they had experienced, it was the cycle of all things. Just sped up before my eyes. Still, I turned my back on it and continued to walk. I passed larger animals, tigers, lions, bears and more. None of them scared me, they were perfectly placid and looked at me with interest. I didn't turn back to look, I knew what I would see and I didn't want to see it. I forged ahead.

I came to the edge of the forest and beyond it was a city. This caused me to stop. I knew what lay behind me, and what would happen if I continued. Yet I felt that I must. Wasn't that how to progress, to keep moving forward? A weariness passed through me and I steeled my resolve. I first passed a small park. It had only a handful of seats, each one occupied by an old couple sharing lunch together. I felt a stabbing pain as I walked past them, having a direct mental picture in my mind of what would happen. I stumbled, and almost fell. Pausing I composed myself and continued.

Next I approached a busy intersection. Everyone was frozen in time, waiting for the lights to change. I stood amongst them, looking at their faces. They had between them happiness, anger, frustration, boredom and sadness. But none of them were at peace. I stepped forward and felt the shockwave ripple through them, unfreezing them from their stasis and putting them in another kind of rest.

With each step I felt more fall. A sea of death. A single tear slowly graced my face, sliding down and then falling. It dropped in slow motion, the air deadening as it descended. As it hit the ground I saw the small splash and the disintegration of it, into nothing. I carried the sadness and continued.

On the other side of the street was a huge high rise building. It had over fifty floors. There had to be thousands of people inside. I tried not to think about it and focused on what was ahead. I walked faster and faster. I left the building behind me, and many more like it. It weighed on me, dragging me down but I stayed on my feet. I felt like I was carrying the weight of all those people. When I caught a glimpse of what lay ahead, I couldn't believe it.

It was a small playground. A handful of children were running around and playing. They were laughing, calling out to each other and climbing all over the equipment. They radiated a special warmth, that cut through the chill I hadn't noticed affecting me. I stood still, unable to move. I couldn't look back at what was behind me, but I couldn't progress.

"It's not fair," I said to myself. I ran forward, wanting to get it over with. I closed my eyes and just ran and ran. I blocked out all noise, all senses and pushed on. Then I hit something and fell down. I was dazed for a few moments, then stood up. I opened my eyes and looked at what was stopping me. I could see nothing, just a vast blackness. I could see a path under my feet, which suddenly ended.

"The end of the road," I said to myself. At first I was confused. Then an understanding hit me. I had been running away, and there was nowhere else to go. The whole time I thought I had been forging ahead I was just fleeing. If only I had embraced the idea, instead of running from it I wouldn't have suffered so much. With much anxiety I turned around and looked at what was ahead.

Rusted and broken play equipment, littered with small bones. Past that was vast ruins, coated with dust.

"If it has to be this way, I'll get it done," I thought to myself. I started to jog back the way I had come, but I couldn't move faster than a stately walk. I had to confront and endure the end of all things. Slowly I trudged through that wasteland of death and decay. Each picture sharply contrasted in my mind with the life and energy that had preceded it. I passed the dense city blocks, which were rubble and bones. The park, the forest and the fields.

After an age I was back where I had started. I was looking at that same spot of timeworn ground. I took my first step past it and I felt a pain shoot through me. My strength drained with every step. A tiredness fell over me. My limbs were heavy, stubborn and troublesome. My mind felt cloudy, foggy and slow. My path started going uphill. Every step became harder and harder, a combination of my degeneration and the difficulty of the path. Soon I was moving on willpower alone. And then I reached the top. I saw a glowing white doorway about ten metres away.

"At last," I thought to myself. However it wasn't over yet. A shadowy figure was standing in front of the door. The figure fired a gun and I put my hands up to protect myself. When I didn't feel anything I opened my eyes and looked at what had happened. The figure was gone, and the bullet was hovering in the air between me and the door. It was turning as it hovered, as if being held in place by some unseen force. I tried ducking and the bullet hovered lower. I tried jumping up and it rose in exact proportion. I knew the deadly potential of the bullet, but I also knew that it was between me and my goal. It was a stalemate.

I was paralysed by fear, of the unknown, of the blackness of death. But I was also aware of the fact that this would haunt me for the rest of my days until I confronted it. Until I let go, and embraced the knowledge that one day there would be an end. I had to set myself free from that burden. Fighting back fear and panic, tears and regrets I stepped forward. I didn't close my eyes, but I didn't look at the bullet, I looked past it. The burning pain as it passed through me was overshadowed by the warmth of the doorway beyond.

CHAPTER THIRTY-ONE

RESURRECTION

Amy gasped for breath and then composed herself. She solemnly wrote everything down in her notebook and drew a detailed drawing of a crest. It looked like a university shield. After a careful examination, she realised that it was for Baxter University. She left a note for Samantha telling her not to worry, and explaining that she was investigating Baxter University. This particular institution was a bit further out from the city, but she didn't want to drive and potentially draw extra attention. So she took the long way, relying on a bus, train and another bus.

Two hours later she arrived at the campus. It was totally different from the University of Technology, boasting a vast expanse of space and grass. Gardens, old stone buildings and a relaxed atmosphere were her initial impressions. She didn't know what she was looking for so didn't over-think it. As she watched the students, she thought that it would have been a nice place to attend. It seemed a lot less crazy than her memories of university. Standing at the campus guide, she decided to start at the Great Hall.

It was the main building, and the path she was on led her all the way there. She walked up the main steps and through the giant doors. The giant room reminded her of a majestic cathedral. There was a mix of old bench seats and newer, single chairs throughout the space. It looked like they would reassemble the configuration to suit the occasion. Amy sat down on one of the benches and waited for inspiration.

Nothing came, so five minutes later she left the building. She thought over what the clue had meant. The one thing that had eluded her so far was the identity of Walter Goldberg. She knew that he was the key to it all, but he was a ghost. Perhaps here she would find a lead to help her solve the puzzle. She was also aware of the fact that it was the last clue she would get. She had faced her last and greatest fear. So this clue had to be a big one, and what she needed was Goldberg. She had come so far, and done so much but he was the missing piece.

On a whim she decided to investigate the Law faculty. Amy felt that she herself was a part of all this somehow, so it made sense to investigate something related to her past. She hadn't been at this university, but maybe the fact that she had studied law elsewhere would trigger something. As she had done when investigating Dr. Featherby she looked over all the noticeboards looking for photos, notes or anything else that would reveal a clue. There was nothing.

"What's the point of this?" she thought to herself. Logically this had to be the most important clue, yet where was it? She walked outside and sat on a bench just outside the Law faculty. She watched the people move about, and felt frustrated. She must have been missing something. The more she racked her brain, the more defeated she felt. She was staring off into the distance when she heard footsteps crunching the grass near her.

"Excuse me," a woman said. Amy looked up at the speaker, a slightly plump brunette with glasses. The woman's features changed dramatically when seeing Amy's face.

"Oh my god, what a surprise. Libby!" the woman said with excitement. Amy looked at her with confusion.

"It's me Becky." Amy just shrugged.

"Rebecca. Rebecca Crowley?"

"I'm sorry, I think you have the wrong person," Amy said. The woman shook her head.

"What's wrong? You really don't remember me Libby? Or do you prefer Elizabeth now?"

"My name is Amy."

"What's happened? We were all so worried after that night. You just disappeared," Becky said. Amy was starting to become unsettled by the discussion.

"I don't know you."

"I'm not crazy, look just humour me and follow me to my office," Becky said. Amy wanted to tell the woman to go away, but she decided to resolve the confusion, so she followed.

"So after graduation, I got a job as a law tutor. I liked it so much I stayed and continued studying," Becky said. Amy just nodded and followed.

"Here's my office. Just take a seat," Becky said as she opened the door. Amy sat down on the designated chair and waited patiently.

"I've got some old photos here. Look at this." Amy took the photo and examined it. It was a photo of Becky with another girl. One who looked exactly like her. But Amy didn't remember Becky, or the photo. She felt a pit in her stomach, but didn't know what to do. She was very confused.

"Oh here. Now this is a good one," Becky said and handed Amy a newspaper article. It was titled 'Law Graduates take on City'. The photograph in the article had both Becky and Amy and some other girls she didn't recognise. Amy read the caption below, 'Vocal Law Students. From left Rebecca Crowley, Elizabeth Edmonds' and dropped the paper after reading the name corresponding to her. It couldn't be possible. There had to be some sort of mistake.

"That article was about our case against the city for their move to tear down the Orphello Theatre. Don't you remember? We held a special fundraiser screening there and it burnt down that very night," Becky explained then bent down to pick up the newspaper article. Amy was trapped in some inner turmoil. Troubling memories were resurfacing, but she didn't know what to believe.

"I'm sorry, I don't feel well. Please keep all these things, I'll come back to see you," Amy said and then ran out. Becky looked out after her, unsure of what to think.

Amy ran through the halls, out into the grounds and kept running. She didn't know what to believe, but something clear rose about the noise in her brain. She had to find Dr. Gary Featherby. He had said not to seek him out until the end, and that she would know when. This had to be it. She needed him to tell her what was going on. Her first impulse was to jump into a taxi, but she thought better of it. The last time she had done so, after seeing Featherby, she had been taken. She stuck to the crowds and got on a bus. She didn't know when he was available, but she was going to wait outside his office until he showed.

Amy felt incredibly unsettled. She had so many unresolved thoughts floating around but ignored them all. The lateness of her connecting train and the following bus trip just made everything worse. Not only that, but her paranoia set in and she saw dodgy strangers where there were just harmless commuters. Her trip back to the University of Technology was frustratingly long but she did finally arrive. Amy ran to the Psychology department and direct to Dr. Featherby's office. She turned the handle but it was locked. She bashed the door with anger. She was completely surprised when there were footsteps behind her.

"I'm sorry but Dr. Featherby is on leave again," the woman explained. Amy turned to leave but the woman stopped her.

"Are you Amy?"

"Yes."

"Well Dr. Featherby left a note for you. I'll unlock the door and give it to you." Amy was too surprised to respond and just watched the woman unlock the door. They both entered the room and saw a plain envelope on the desk with Amy written on the front. Amy took it, thanked the woman, and walked out in a trance. She opened the envelope and read the following message:

Dear Amy,

Sorry for sending you away before, the timing was all wrong. Please come find me at my apartment and I will explain everything to you. The address is enclosed.

Gary

Amy wasn't sure what to believe, but she needed answers so she decided to grant his request. She knew a bus that took her to his area, so she caught that and walked the rest of the way. She found the building without too much trouble, it was an older style block of apartments. She walked up the stairs to his unit and hesitated. Beyond the door would be answers. Answers she desperately needed. Answers she was also afraid of.

Amy took a deep breath and knocked on the door. She waited for a minute but nobody answered. She knocked again and waited. No response. She tried to turn the handle and it opened. Carefully pushing it open further, she eased herself into the apartment. She closed the door behind her as quietly as possible. She stepped into the main room carefully.

Dr. Featherby was sprawled out in his chair, but something was not quite right. His breathing was laboured and his gaze was fixated on something far away. She ran over and checked his pulse. It was faint, but there.

"Dr. Featherby," she said with concern. He slowly broke free from his trance and looked at her. His face took on a look of sadness.

"I'm so sorry," he said thickly, having trouble with the words.

"What's wrong?"

"P…Poison."

"I'll ring for an ambulance," Amy said and looked for a phone. Only Dr. Featherby slowly shook his head. He swallowed, then concentrated on saying something else.

"Don-key Ho-tey," he said with great effort. Amy didn't understand. She was about to ask him what he meant, when he smiled and his eyes glazed over. Amy checked his pulse again, but he was gone. Tears welled in her eyes. He had died for nothing, she didn't have the answers. Just a head full of questions. She pulled herself together and looked around the apartment. It was simply furnished, without much clutter. There was a wall devoted to a bookcase though. She scanned through the titles looking for something useful. It was all fiction. The books varied in age and size. Suddenly one caught her eye. Don Quixote.

"Don Quixote. Donkey Hotey," she sounded out. It matched perfectly. She pulled out the book and looked at it. It was very thick, roughly 1,000 pages. She flicked through the pages quickly found nothing. She shook the book and heard something. That was encouraging, so she opened the book to the middle and found a fake page. She felt along the blank page, noticing something inside. She slipped her hand in and retrieved a small key with the number 20 on it.

"Let's see what you had for me," Amy said softly and then left the apartment. She judged from the look of the key that it was for a garage or storage space. She walked down to the area below the apartment block and found a series of lock-up garages towards the back of the property. She walked along until she found number 20 and tried the key. It worked. She lifted up the door, ducked in and pulled it closed behind her. She felt along the wall and found a light switch, flicking it on. A small fluorescent light buzzed into life above her and illuminated the room. It looked like a lab. There was equipment along the back wall, and a small library of books to the left. To the right was a small desk with chair. There was a notebook on the table. She sat down and looked through it. The earliest part of the notebook was concerned with research into perfecting a trauma drug. One that could be administered to people who needed it, and would effectively block the event in question, allowing them to lead a new life. The drawback that was noted, had to do with how effective it was. It couldn't be released because it was too strong. It caused a temporary disassociation of identity due to the missing event. Amy let the idea sit and read on.

The next section was in almost stark contrast. It was a journal entry in a hurried scrawl.

I relented, against my better judgement, and supplied the compound to be used on a young graduate traumatised by a horrific fire. It was requested by the esteemed Dr. Nelson, and I was foolishly swayed by his flattery and reputation. However in doing some due diligence I found out that not only was it used improperly, but they encouraged the disassociation to create a new identity. That is going too far, there are no circumstances to justify such actions. Something is not right here, but I can't go public on it. I have a plan, but I'm not sure if it will work.

The next section was back to the controlled style of the previous research notes. There were three compounds being tested. One was used to promote dream activity, another to stimulate memory and the last one was for visualisation of fears. Amy skipped through the notes, looking at dates and days.

"He felt responsible, for what happened to me. He spent the next years trying to fix it," she said to herself. It was all true, the conversation with Becky and her previous identity. Dr. Nelson had robbed her of her memories and her identity. He had no doubt amplified her anxiety and kept an eye on her through years of therapy. Then when she had sought Dr. Featherby out, Dr. Nelson had her kidnapped and tried to reset her. Amy felt her anger rising. She reached the final page of the notebook. It was addressed to her.

Dear Amy,

Sorry for everything. If you're reading this, I wasn't able to explain things to you myself. Hopefully my notes tell you enough of the story. I tried to understand why Dr. Nelson did the things he did, and found an answer. It's only a piece though, your memory holds the rest.

Good luck,

Gary

Below the message was a folded piece of newspaper. Amy opened it up and read the headline.

"Whizz kids win science fair," Amy said. She started to read the opening paragraph.

"Childhood friends Richard Nelson and Walter Goldberg win top prize with their project..." Amy's eyes darted to the supplied photo. Her jaw dropped in horror. She recognised the young Richard Nelson, and the one next to him.

"Mayor James Freeman," she whispered.

CHAPTER THIRTY-TWO

ACCEPTANCE

Everything started clicking together, like the pieces of a giant metal puzzle reassembling itself around her. The mayor had changed his name and buried his past along with its inconvenient arson episodes. He had used his influence to push through a major redevelopment project that he personally was benefiting from. Not to mention the mysterious lost gold bars that were tied up in all this. And all the way along his trusty childhood friend Dr. Richard Nelson had been helping him through any and all obstacles. One of which was her.

But that still puzzled Amy. The fact that she still thought of herself as Amy didn't help, or was maybe a sign of damage still done. Her apparent fellow protestor Becky had not been targeted by Dr. Nelson. So what made Amy so different?

She strained her brain to think, but encountered a block. All the things she had discovered about her, were sitting there in her brain like slightly opened cardboard boxes. She knew their contents, but they could still be opened and examined. And while there was still this great disconnect between the person in the memories and her current identity, it made sense in a weird way. But there was something else she couldn't approach, that was unavailable to her. It was something crucial, probably the reason that so much had happened to her. But it was locked away.

Amy lashed out at the wall in frustration. After all she had suffered, after all other people had suffered, there was still a piece missing. There were no more dreams to be had, she had confronted them all. Yet this one thing remained, perhaps the most crucial of all. The facts of her memory were just facts, without the why. Why did this happen?

She tried to calm herself, and it worked a little. She regulated her thinking and analysed the situation. The main outstanding thing was the collection of gold bars. If she had those and a bit of a paper trail she could take down the mayor, even without her locked memory. And she knew there was one place where she could find a lead to one or both: the mayor's private residence.

Nobody knew his real identity, so it was the perfect place to hide incriminating documents because nobody would look there. And if they did, they had other people's names on them.

"Featherby must have realised the same thing," Amy said to herself, and flipped through his notebook. On a page marked with a yellow sticker she found an address for the mayor. It was a penthouse apartment in the middle of the city. If she could get inside, she would get what she needed. A plan started to form in her mind, but it had a lot of missing elements that she would need to fill in. A bit of luck and a bit of determination would see her through.

Amy found herself standing on the edge. She was at the point where if she stepped forward once more, if she took things further then everything would change. She could only act if she was willing to leave everything behind. She couldn't involve anyone else in what was to come, especially not Samantha. But one thing from her old life held her back, one regret. David. But in a way she felt relieved, that she had an excuse for not seeking him out. An excuse that would sound fine, and would satisfy most people if they asked. But she knew it was just an excuse, and that it would remain a regret if she did nothing about it.

She took Featherby's notebook with her, and left the garage. She headed to her work, the whole way trying to come up with excuses about not having to see David. She even played scenarios in her head, showing how she would get rejected. But below the anxiety, and the butterflies was a core of strength in her stomach. Solid foundations that would not let up. It was if the recent revelations had unearthed a strength she did not have access to before.

And so Amy found herself in front of her work building. She looked up and decided to pause for a moment, before going up.

"Hey Amy!" David said with enthusiasm. Amy turned around, stunned.

"Oh hi David," she said, with some difficulty. She hadn't prepared herself.

"How's your leave going?"

"Oh it's good, I'm keeping busy."

"Glad to hear it, the office has been really quiet."

"Well at least I'm not missing anything."

"When do you think you'll be back?"

"Hey do you want to get a coffee?" Amy blurted out.

"Sure, now?"

"Yeah."

"Follow me, I know a good place," David said. Amy nodded and tried to look natural. She was relieved, and nervous and anxious at the same time. She tried internally congratulating herself on a job well done so that she could avoid further complications, but she wasn't buying it. She wasn't going to let herself weasel out of asking him out for real.

The cafe they stopped at was called 'Four Beans' and was originally an old warehouse but had been upgraded with funky modern fittings. They ordered coffee and started with a little chatting. However, David had more on his mind.

"Amy, I have to ask. How are you really doing? What's going on?"

"What do you mean?" Amy said.

"I've known you a little while now, so I can tell that something's going on. You look like you've been going through a lot."

"I have. It's not something I can talk about just yet."

"I understand," David said, but seemed a little off, like he had taken it personally. Amy scrambled to respond.

"It's just that it's too raw, I can't just dump it on someone I want to be with," Amy said quickly, then stopped realising what she had said. David had a surprised look. And there it was, Amy had put herself and her intentions out in the open. Together they floated in limbo, and she felt that fear and anxiety come up. At any moment it could come, the crashing rejection that would destroy her. Only it wouldn't destroy her, she decided. It would mean that David wasn't the person she thought he was. In that fleeting moment that seemed to last a while, she steeled herself and made a choice to be firm and accept whatever he said.

"Wow I didn't expect that. But it was nice, and very honest. While we're being honest, I want to be with you as well. If you need to work through something first that's fine. But don't forget that I'm always here, I'm not going to shy away from anything," David said, with a warm reassuring smile. Amy didn't know what to say, she just grinned madly. She had been accepted, and not rejected. She felt the beginnings of a connection.

"That sounds good," Amy said.

"Yeah, it does. Let's take it easy and see how things go."

"Yeah."

"So, helicopter ride next week then?" David said in a playful way. Amy laughed, but then had an idea.

"Maybe," she said. Then she leaned in for a hug, but instead went in for a kiss. David returned the kiss passionately, and Amy felt a little light headed.

"Wow, well I must be off. See you soon," she said.

"You're not going up to the office?" David asked.

"No, I only came here to talk to you," Amy said smiling.

"Oh. Well see you soon. Take care," David said, his eyes sparkling with delight and happiness. Amy walked off, but once she had reached the end of the block she turned around. It was if she needed to see if he was really there, or if she had imagined the whole encounter. But he was still standing there, and waved when he saw her turn.

Amy felt rejuvenated and energised. It wasn't just the kiss, it was like a weight she had been carrying had finally been lifted. She wasn't sure what the future held, but she knew she could face it. And no matter what she had to go through, it was comforting that there was a lot for her to come back to. David joking about the helicopter though, that had given her an idea. She remembered reading that the mayor's residence had a helipad on the roof, and that there had been some scandals around misappropriation of city funds for his trips.

But to act on her ideas, and continue planning she needed more information, especially her notes from the investigation so far. She didn't dare return to her apartment, so she would have to be creative. And she had just the right person in mind - Samantha's friend Sam, the tech specialist.

Amy called Sam and gave him some explicit instructions to follow, as well as details of Samantha's location. He was happy to help, and promised to start right away. With that the wheels were in motion. Amy stopped by a newsagent and bought a pen, a pad and some pencils. She needed to start drafting up her ideas, because what she was planning was big. And she would only get one go at it.

CHAPTER THIRTY-THREE

RECALL

Amy drew upon information from all her previous research, and Featherby's notes. As it turned out, he had been planning something of his own, just in case. She then decided to rent a separate motel to finish her preparations, leaving Samantha to Sam's care. She spent a whole day and a restless night doing her research, and confirming facts.

The last thing she had to do the next morning was make a phone call. It was something she could only do on the day. Nervously she dialled the number, unsure of what to expect on the other end.

"Yes?" a voice said.

"Death is lighter than a feather," Amy said.

"Male or female?"

"Female."

"Done. The debt is repaid," the voice said then abruptly hung up. Amy gulped, the plan was set in motion.

She would never again have a chance this good, thanks to Featherby's arrangements. Now she had to make the most of it. She spent the morning checking and rechecking her arrangements and information. But it just made her more nervous.

In the afternoon she packed her bag and headed out into the street. The streets were packed with people, all of them out for the annual celebration of the city's founding. There was a parade in the afternoon, followed by a presentation by the mayor and fireworks later in the evening. The festivities provided the perfect cover for Amy, although she had to battle through the crowds.

The train station was even more packed than the streets above. On the platform Amy felt wedged in like a sardine. She was convinced that if she lifted her legs off the ground, the pressure from the other people would hold her up. But she didn't feel like testing her theory, as obvious as it felt. When a train pulled up Amy decided to wait for the next one. But she didn't get a choice, the crowd surged forward and took her with it. She was happy to not get knocked down and crushed.

She was wedged in the main compartment of the train carriage near the doors. She only had to go three stops, so it would be fine. The breath of slightly fresh air from the doors opening first stop was a big relief for her. Midway to the second station however, the train slowed and then stopped. Then the lights went out. Amy noted that she was stuck in a crowded train, with no lights in a tunnel under the ground. Each of those things she ticked off mentally was attached to a fear, causing her to start panicking. But she accepted the situation and calmed herself.

The lights suddenly came back on, and the train lurched forward throwing her off balance. She looked around, confused. But the train was going again so she felt good. Nobody got off or on the train at the next stop, and then the last leg of her train journey crawled by at minimal speed. The driver apologised over the speakers, blaming a signal problem. Amy sighed and just put up with it.

The train arrived at the station so gradually that Amy almost missed her stop. However once the doors opened she switched on and fought her way off the train. However once free of the carriage she just ended up in another other crowd - the people on the platform. The path to the exit was fairly clear, but Amy wasn't heading that way. She had to force her way down to the end of the platform. She squeezed between burly men, avoided bowling over small children, and pushed past women who looked as disoriented as she felt.

Amy looked up at the board and saw that the next train was due in six minutes. The next one after that was four minutes. She needed at least five minutes, so either option didn't seem right. But she couldn't wait forever.

"Please be delayed," she said to herself. She was at the edge of the platform and summoned all her strength and courage. Then she jumped off, landed neatly and started jogging down the tunnel. She heard some gasps and commotion behind her but ignored it. She had to find the right side door passage before the train was upon her. Engine noises startled her, but she couldn't determine where they were coming from so she pressed on. Her heart leapt when she saw a smaller door coming out from the right hand side.

She was making excellent time. She pushed hard on the door and it didn't budge. She felt a dread feeling rise up from her stomach. With a bang she hurled herself at the door, only managing to hurt her shoulder. She pulled out her little torch and examined the door. There was an inscription on it that read 'B-17'. Amy fumbled through her bag and pulled out her notes, scanning for an explanation.

"Dammit I need B-18," she said, and put her things away. She definitely heard the sound of a train now. She checked her watch, and realised that it was due any minute.

"Do I make a break for the next door or do I try and wait it out here?" she thought to herself. She couldn't decide. Amy stepped out to evaluate and saw the train headlights coming down the tunnel. She turned and threw herself into the nook for the door, flattening herself against the door as much as possible. As the train came closer she could feel the wind rushing through the tunnel, and had visions of the train catching her in the back. She could even feel the sensation, as if it were real. With a great whoosh the train was upon her, but passing by fast. As far as she could tell everything was intact, but she just ignored everything, hoping it would pass quickly. And then suddenly the train had moved on, and it was getting softer as it headed away.

Amy released the breath she had been holding, and relaxed. She stepped back and felt around. Everything seemed normal, she had managed to survive unscathed. But she couldn't dawdle, the next train was due in four minutes. She recollected herself and dashed down the tunnel, looking for the next door. She spotted it soon after and threw herself at the door. With a crash the door gave way and Amy fell in a heap on the floor. Feeling relieved, and a bit sheepish, she picked herself up and closed the door.

She was in a passage that was halfway between a tunnel and a room. She ran through the directions in her head, not wanting to make a mistake. It looked like she was in the kind of place where it was easy to get lost. And nobody would come looking for you. She walked but didn't run, taking care that she took the right turns. She also didn't want to make too much noise. She had no idea if there were any other people around. The information she had said these tunnels were rarely used, but she still felt like there could be people around every corner.

She ended up in a plain utility room, with some boxes and storage cages. This looked like where she needed to be. She carefully walked around the room until she found what she had come for. It was a hole in the wall, cut for ventilation and potentially proper air flow and even air conditioning if this area was ever developed. It was tiny, and dirty and thick with dust, but it was her gateway into the mayor's high security apartment building.

Amy put her bag in ahead of her, and squeezed herself into the hole. It was stuffy and enclosed and dark. She thought about getting her torch out and decided against it. As much as she wanted light, it would be too hard to manoeuvre and she was just as likely to drop or lose the torch. So she began her journey, pushing the bag ahead of her and then squeezing herself a little bit further along. The pattern was established early, and she just kept doing it over and over. The passage seemed to slope upwards slightly, but otherwise had no other discernible features.

She battled on, feeling the dust coat her all over. She just wanted to get out and brush her face. But she couldn't and realised quickly that wiping her face now would just result in more dust being caked on. She was sweating with the exertion, but the earth surrounding her and the slight movement of air kept her fairly cool otherwise. The next steps occupied her thoughts, as the stakes would be raised again once she made it to the apartment building.

She noticed some light at the end of the passage, and worked towards it, increasing her speed. She was really looking forward to stretching out and inhabiting a more normal space. As she got closer she slowed down and concentrated on listening for activity. However all she heard was the low hum of machinery. It got slightly louder as she got closer, but otherwise nothing else caught her attention.

The passage was blocked off with a grate with horizontal grills across it. Amy had a sudden moment of panic, but forced it down and assessed the grate. It didn't look particularly well fastened, and was old. She reached out and gripped it, wrestling with the metal. After a bit of twisting and pushing one corner started to move so she used that as leverage to get the whole thing out. It clattered to the ground, but didn't really rise above the ambient noise. With some excitement Amy poured herself out of the dingy passage, and lay on the cold concrete floor feeling a mix of relief and also nervousness. But she had made it inside the apartment building, unless something had gone horribly wrong.

Amy stood up and softly crossed the room, threading her way through the machinery and heading towards the door. She stopped, and returned to where she came in, so she could hide evidence of her entry. After a minute of fiddling the grate looked normal and undisturbed. She returned to the door and slowly turned the handle, easing it open. She peeked through the crack and then when the door was open enough snuck in. She was in a change room. There was a series of lockers and one of them was slightly open. She walked over and opened the locker, her heart rate rising. Inside was a neatly pressed uniform with an access card and a name tag. The tag read 'Stella'. Amy nodded with satisfaction. She could now infiltrate the building as a cleaner.

Amy changed, stuffing some of her clothes into her bag. She took the access card and walked over to the mirror, using it to help her pin on her name tag. She continued looking into the mirror, first to help clean away the dust she had picked up from the tunnel and passage, and then to compose herself. She couldn't just walk around in the cleaner costume, she had to take on the persona as well. She imagined herself to be a disinterested cleaner and then strode out of the room as if she belonged. She found a cleaners cart just outside the change room, as expected. After a quick glance around she put her bag in the under section of the cart and pushed it around looking for the elevator.

As she went, Amy was impressed by the comprehensiveness of her disguise. She wasn't sure how Featherby had organised it, but having a cleaner contact at the mayor's serviced apartment building was very handy. She located the elevator and pressed the up button, but it didn't work. After a mild panic, she realised that there were card readers on the wall. She showed the access card and then tried pressing the up button once more. It worked. Amy waited patiently for the elevator to arrive, hoping that it would be empty.

A small panel above the elevator showed its progress, and Amy watched carefully as the number descended until it read B2. With a ding the doors opened, and Amy gripped the handle on the cart to contain her tension.

Thankfully there was nobody inside, so she pushed in the cart and retrieved her access card once more. She placed it on the reader and pressed the top floor. Nothing happened so she tried again and the floor lit up. Amy let out a sigh of relief and relaxed against the wall of the elevator. She had quite a few levels to go.

Another ding sound aroused her attention suddenly, and the doors opened. Amy looked up at the display, and saw she was only on the ground floor. She grabbed the cleaning cart and pulled it closer to her, trying to make space. A young woman entered the elevator, and Amy avoided making eye contact.

"Hi," the woman said. Amy didn't want to say anything that would make her memorable, but thought she should respond.

"Hello ma'am," she said.

"Oh I'm not that old, but that was very polite of you. You don't see proper manners much these days," the woman said. Amy cursed herself for making an impression.

"Thank you," she said, hoping that would kill the conversation.

"Oh it's nothing. Say, are you new? I'm not sure I've seen you around before." Amy had to think quickly to come up with a reasonable reply.

"Not new, but I only fill in. This is not my usual work," Amy said, quite pleased with herself. She thought she was quite convincing.

"Oh, what's your usual work?"

"Another building."

"Oh, whereabouts?"

"Two blocks over."

"You know, that's the funny thing. I actually organise the cleaning services here, and we don't allow unauthorised people filling in. And the company who does this building doesn't do any others in the city. I'm going to have to ask you to accompany me down to security."

Amy didn't panic, she just reacted. She shoved her cart into the woman, knocking her back against the elevator wall. The woman crumpled into a heap. Amy quickly retracted the cart and checked to see if the woman was alright. She was breathing, most likely unconscious. Amy was struck by not knowing what to do next. She looked around, hoping for an answer. Then the elevator dinged once more and the doors opened. Amy was completely exposed, with an unconscious woman in the elevator and no way to explain it.

Thankfully the hallway looked empty, so Amy blocked off the elevator doors with the cleaning cart to prevent them from closing. Then she grabbed the woman under the arms and dragged her out of the elevator.

"Sorry," Amy said, her voice a mixture of embarrassment, concern and also determination. She propped the woman up against a wall, and stepped back into the elevator. Amy brought the cart back into the elevator and watched the doors close. Then she closed her eyes and leaned back, hoping the rest of the trip would be smoother. However her trip was interrupted once more.

The fateful ding sounded again, and Amy braced herself. An older man in a suit went to get in, but hesitated.

"Going up," Amy said, as disinterested and businesslike as possible.

"Oh my mistake, I wish to go down. I won't hold you up," the man said with a polite tone and stepped back as promised. Amy nodded and then waited for the doors to close once more. The interruption was good though, as it focused her thoughts on what would happen if more people called the elevator. It prevented her from thinking too far ahead.

After a short time she arrived at the top level, the penthouse level. Amy composed herself, and tried to prepare for what was ahead. As the doors opened she pushed the cart out, trying not to look interested in her surroundings. However at the same time she was trying to work out where to go. As it happened, there was only one residence on the level, the rest of the space was reserved for building facilities and the fire escape.

Amy approached the front door, and considered the protocol. She wondered whether to announce herself or just go inside. She decided to announce herself, that way she wouldn't have any surprises once inside.

"Housekeeping," she said and then knocked three times sharply. There was no reply. Using this as her cue Amy unlocked the door and opened it enough so she could push the cleaning cart through. No sooner had she closed the door when a giant black Labrador bounded over barking. Amy froze, petrified.

"Hey there boy, I'm just a cleaner you know," she said. The dog paused, then padded around in a circle barking again.

"He's just being protective, and reacting to my fear," Amy thought to herself, and tried to calm herself and go about her business. She ignored the dog and pushed the cart in further, but did so carefully. She started doing cleaning jobs and changed the sheets on the bed. The dog continued to sniff around her, then started to lose interest. Amy breathed a sigh of relief and finished doing the bed. She left the old sheets lying around so if anybody came home unexpectedly it would look like a regular clean. She looked at her watch: she had thirty minutes to finish up. Probably less, considering the incident in the elevator.

Amy wandered around, looking for the home office. She found a study and walked inside. There was a desk, a filing cabinet, a few book cases and lots of memorabilia scattered around. Amy started with the desk. She examined the papers on the surface, noting that they were just regular boring letters. Next she turned her attention to the filing cabinet and it was locked. That was promising. Amy retrieved her bag and took out a mallet and a screwdriver. She had never done this before, but Sam had said it was foolproof. Amy shrugged and then lined up the screwdriver with the lock and then hammered the lock. She had definitely done some damage, but hadn't opened it or knocked it out. But she had another problem to contend with.

The dog had heard the noise and came running over, barking and looking quite agitated. Amy forced the study door closed and hoped the dog would get the message. Apparently he did, and chose to scrape at the door and bark at her. She turned her attention back to the lock and gave it another go, throwing everything into it. The lock completely gave way, and she threw the tools down in triumph. She opened the cabinet and picked up a file at random.

"Inspired Planning; I've got you Goldberg," Amy said. But she just didn't want documents that may or may not make a case, she wanted the real evidence: the gold. Amy continued to scan through the documents, looking for a lead. She found plans, but didn't know what to make of them. There were also plenty of invoices, and receipts and other things. One of those caught her eye though, and she read the hand written note accompanying it.

Excavation of sub-basement required at Orphello Theatre. Skeleton crew, only trusted people. No destructive force allowed.

Amy thought that was a pretty suggestive lead. But she needed more. She refined her search to only look at documents related to the Orphello Theatre. There was nothing else of note. She was about to close the filing cabinet when she noticed a small folder tucked away at the back. She pulled it out, just for curiosity's sake. It seemed different to the rest. Inside was a small aged piece of paper, protected in a piece of plastic. Amy read it with interest.

Gold safely hidden away beneath the town hall. Awaiting further instructions.

Amy paused, feeling the significance of the find but not quite putting the pieces together. She was after a reference to the gold and she had found it. The mayor had found it as well. And then she remembered her original conversation at the museum, how the old town hall was converted into the Orphello Theatre. And now the mayor was excavating underneath the Orphello.

"The gold's still there!" Amy said with wonder. That was how to catch him red handed. But she took the notes with her for good measure. She turned to go, then remembered the dog outside.

"Here we go," she said to herself then opened the door with great force, feeling some resistance on the way through. She didn't turn to look, and headed straight for the front door of the apartment. She reached it safely, but without her bag. Cursing, she ran back to fetch it from under the cleaning cart. Then the dog was on her. It snarled with anger right in front of her, threatening to attack. Amy imagined the animal leaping at her and bringing her down, but ignored it.

"I'm done, I'm leaving now," she said to the dog in a stern voice, then stepped towards the door. The dog continued snarling, but didn't attack. Instead it continued to shadow her, as if herding her out. Amy let herself be directed and quickly opened and closed the front door. She was outside the apartment, and leaned against the door to get a breather. After a second of quiet the dog started barking loud, which startled her. Then she heard another noise. It was the building evacuation alarm.

"That doesn't sound good," Amy thought to herself. She started running down the hall towards the fire escape. With each step she increased her speed, feeling the sense of urgency in the air. She flew through the exit door, and slammed into a wall of swirling air. The sudden force almost knocked her over, and it was accompanied with driving rain and loud bellows of thunder. The fire escape was on the outside of the building and fully exposed. She headed up, fighting the elements with every step. The metal railings made her think of lightning strikes, but she pushed on. If she didn't hurry, her ride would be gone.

Amy increased her speed again, then slipped and tumbled back against the railing. Only by sticking out her arm to steady herself did she avoid falling back down the stairs. With the storm raging around her she just wanted to find a space to hide and let it die out. But she couldn't. With a sigh she dragged herself up again, and pushed forward. She worked herself harder and faster, but paid more attention to the slippery surfaces and rapidly growing puddles of water.

With a sense of accomplishment she rounded the last piece of stairwell and emerged onto the roof of the building. A helicopter sat there, completely still. It was slightly rocking with the force of the winds, its sides forming tiny waterfalls. Amy was delighted to see it there, but was also assaulted by conflicting emotions. She was worried about how it was motionless, and also scared of actually having to fly in it. It was completely different from flying in a plane, and a lot more exposed. Trying to shield her face from the driving rain Amy sprinted over to the helicopter. As she approached the pilot's seat the door opened and the man inside called out.

"Amy?"

"Yeah that's me," she said.

"Not quite the joyride you were hoping for," the pilot said.

"Well I do have a fear of flying, so maybe this is better?" Amy said, thinking on her feet.

"We'll see. You may be off the hook if this storm continues. My name is Nick and I'll be your pilot today, weather permitting." Amy nodded and then looked around. She had no idea what kind of pursuit was happening, and if they would come looking for her on the roof.

"Can I get in, just in case?" Amy said. She was a bit shielded from the storm, but it was more about keeping out of sight and making it a bit easier to take off if they were able.

"Of course, please excuse my rudeness." Nick jumped out of the pilot's seat and guided Amy into the passenger section. He settled her in and gave her a chunky headset.

"Testing one two three," Nick said into his headset once he was back in the pilot's seat.

"Loud and clear. Over and out," Amy said, having a little chuckle to herself. She was trying to keep things light, and not focus on the fact that armed security could be flooding out onto the roof at any time.

"You've done this before," Nick said, enjoying the joke. He stopped speaking, focusing on his instruments and the weather.

"Do you think we'll be able to fly?" Amy said, obvious concern in her voice.

"I was going to say no, but things seem to be clearing up. It may only be a short window, if we're going to try it has to be now."

"Sure, let's go," Amy said, trying not to be too anxious. She looked around, wondering what was happening elsewhere in the building.

"Hold onto your hat," Nick said and then the rotors started up, and began spinning at incredible speeds. As they started to lift off the ground a group of people ran over, waving their arms madly.

"Some kind of problem?" Nick asked.

"They're just really overprotective, I trust your judgement," Amy said, praying for him to just finish taking off.

"Don't worry, you're in safe hands," Nick said then continued ascending. Amy looked down at the people on the roof, who continued to wave excitedly. Without knowing the context you could have imagined them just being enthusiastic. But Amy knew they were furious and probably also embarrassed at what just happened.

"Normally I'd point out some nice landmarks but it's not really the best conditions and I think you're not along for the view," Nick said.

"Yeah, that's about right." Amy did look out however, and despite feeling very close to being outside at great heights, she appreciated the sensation. There was something cool about it. Almost like they were defying gravity.

"So we have two set down options available today. Our first option is the meadow set down. It's a lovely setting, in contrast to the city. Plus you get to see the classic look of grass being flattened by the helicopter force. Alternatively we've got our base set down. This one caters to a more modern feeling, where you get out at an air facility," Nick said.

"The air facility being where you have to return the helicopter anyway?" Amy said.

"That's right. But it doesn't hurt to dress it up a bit."

"Fair enough. I'll take the meadow thanks."

"Good option, although it's not the best weather for it," Nick said. Amy wasn't worried about that though, she was more worried about irate people waiting for her if she continued on to the helicopter base. The woman who had questioned her in the elevator had seemed quite resourceful, and Amy wouldn't put it past her tracking down the helicopter company and preparing a nasty surprise.

An abrupt turn caused her stomach to turn, but she maintained her composure. It was exhilarating in a way, to see the city from a different perspective. Up high, yet so close. It looked more precious with the weather lashing out at it. A little sad too. Amy had a feeling that there was a big shift coming. There was a stirring in the pit of her stomach, not related to flying. It was that little voice that would whisper to her, that something big was coming. In a way, everything up to this point had been preparation.

Another abrupt turn took them away from the city. After a short flight they spotted way more greenery, with parks and reserves stretching out before them. Suddenly the helicopter started to descend, and Amy looked out to watch the landing. She wanted to get the most of her meadow landing.

"On our way down now. Hope you enjoyed the ride," Nick said.

"Yeah, it was great. Thank you," Amy said.

"I'll leave the helicopter on so you can exit in style."

"Ha-ha sure, I can be an action hero," Amy said, laughing. The helicopter rocked a little as it neared the ground and then settled down. Amy unbuckled herself, removed her headset and opened the door. The force of the wind surprised her, and she had to shield her face. She jumped out and ran from the helicopter, watching the grass bend and flatten from the force of the rotors. She turned and waved at Nick, and he waved back before taking the helicopter up. She watched until it was out of sight, and then turned to get her bearings.

The storm had subsided for a time, and Amy wasn't sure if it was a break or if they had flown out of it a bit. Summoning up her determination she strode through the meadow and out to the street on the other side. It was probably an hour's walk over to the Orphello Theatre. But she didn't mind doing it, it seemed right. This part of the city was fairly quiet, as the rest of the festivities were being centred on the harbour.

The sun was setting and twilight was settling in. The street lights were delayed in turning on, so it became quite dark. And then Amy realised that for some reason they weren't coming on at all. The streets became almost pitch black. Her only explanation for it was a power outage. At another time she would have turned back, and found somewhere with light and safety. But she had a job to do, and the darkness wasn't too bad. There was enough light to walk by at least, without being reckless. So she pushed on, enjoying the walk. It was calming and quiet, unlike the rest of her time lately.

She hadn't really had time to think over what had happened. Or maybe she hadn't let herself think. There were a lot of things to question about herself, and her identity.

"Why do I still think of myself as Amy?" she thought to herself. She came to the conclusion that feeling trumped fact. As well as the fact that there was still a missing piece in her memory and her persona. That gap between her previous self and her current self could definitely be an issue. She thought of Dr. Featherby, and all he had done and sacrificed for her. It had worked too. She had overcome the fear and programming done to her. She had rediscovered her previous identity, and worked out much of what had happened. And she was on the way to expose things. But Featherby had paid a harsh price, too harsh for her.

It was with these thoughts that she reached the Orphello Theatre. It looked spooky and mysterious in the gloom, and as before was barricaded away behind a chain-link fence. The gate had a big padlock on it, and she decided to leave it be. So she walked around the perimeter, methodically checking for any flaws in the fence or gaps. She had no reason to think that there was one, but she just had a feeling. And that feeling was justified, when a few minutes later she discovered a small section of fence that could be bent back and used to gain access. As Amy bent it and crept underneath she had a strange feeling of Deja vu.

"Did I come in this way before?" she said softly. The crunch of her footsteps across the gravel sounded like a processional announcement of her arrival. Trying to walk slower or more carefully made no difference.

The Orphello rose up before her, looking the same as it had. Amy approached the front doors, and carefully pushed one open. It wasn't locked and gave way easily. She stepped inside and surveyed the foyer. There was evidence of fire damage, but it wasn't as extensive as she had expected. In the distance she noticed some stairs down, choosing to walk towards them. After a few steps she felt something strange, like she was being watched. She turned to look but nobody was there.

"It's nothing, just keep going," she said to herself. Amy pressed forward and followed the stairs down. She found a storeroom that matched the description from the police report. It was the location where the fire had been started. The room was cleared, and there was a small hole dug into the middle of the room.

"The gold!" Amy thought to herself. She stepped forward and then quickly spun around, noticing a presence behind her.

"And here we are, right where we started," a deep voice said.

"Mayor Freeman, or should I say Walter Goldberg," Amy said.

"You just kept digging. I tried to help you, make you forget."

"You helped me by brainwashing me and making me afraid of everything?"

"The end justifies the means my dear, it's something you realise with maturity. I was trying to spare you of all this," he said, waving at her and the surroundings with the gun in his hand. Amy watched it carefully. She had a bad feeling about what would happen.

"I'm going to rejuvenate this city, and bring about a new era of prosperity and harmony. You are just a minor irritation, but one that must be dealt with permanently."

"I've seen the records and documents, you're just feathering your own nest. Is the gold your retirement fund?"

"I deserve to be paid for my efforts. That's only fair. The good that I will bring about is worth any cost," the mayor said with an air of finality. He pointed the gun directly at Amy and started tensing to fire. But something happened. Amy froze, but time also froze. She knew that he was about to fire, and that it would be fatal. The fear of death, of the unknown gripped her tight. She was overwhelmed by it, in these final moments. But then she had a revelation. That she had already died twice before. Once, on the night of the fire. The person she had been, Libby, had been killed. And once more in her dream. She did not fear that. But she had unfinished business. And she would complete it. In that moment of frozen time, Amy managed to move slightly, to turn an instantly fatal shot into one that gave her a bit of time.

"Time to say goodbye," the mayor said and fired. Too soon Amy felt the bullet pierce her, and she fell back into the pit behind her. She landed on a large object, and instantly felt her life slipping away. She shoved it aside and looked at it. It was an old treasure chest, locked with a combination padlock.

"Time," a voice echoed in her head. She remembered back to the night of the fire. The giant clock from the Orphello Theatre had read two thirty two. She reached out to the lock and struggled with the combination. First she managed to set zero. Then two. Then four, changing to three. And then two. The lock clicked open and clanged to the ground. Amy reached out and opened the lid. Inside were rows and rows of neatly stacked gold bars. But behind them was a glow, a light that increased in intensity. It extended to envelop her completely.

Before her was a white shimmering door. Or was it a mirror. On the other side she stood, confident and sure. The other version of herself, with all the memories and instincts. Who she used to be. Amy felt a pang of sadness, that she might be lost if she were to regain who she used to be. There was a certain reluctance to take that step into the lighted doorway. But she had done it so many times before, overcoming her fears. She would do it one more time. She dragged herself up and reached out, feeling herself pulled in and then enveloped in a warm embrace. And she realised that her final fear was unfounded. She would be able to take everything with her, and learn from her experiences. She would be stronger and more complete.

EPILOGUE

Libby woke up and slowly took in the room around her. Her eyes didn't want to open, but she forced them. It was a hospital room. Memories flooded back, but they didn't seem right. How long had she been here? A doctor came in as if at her request. He looked familiar somehow.

"Hello Elizabeth, how are you feeling? Do you remember me?" the doctor said. Libby strained her brain, trying to sort out the important information.

"Everything's jumbled, is it Dr. Richard Butler?"

"Yes. Explain how it's jumbled."

"I had a dream. So long, so detailed. I was a different person, a legal secretary called Amy. She was afraid of so many things, but was confronting them in her dreams."

"Interesting. Do you think that there's an overlap between her fears and your own?"

"Probably. There were two doctors, one that helped her and one that held her back. A best friend that went along with her. And a cute guy that she had a crush on. He was a real sweetie."

"Please tell me your full name."

"Elizabeth Edmonds."

"Very good. You've been here roughly 24 hours. You were thrashing around so much that I sedated you. You are very lucky, you escaped any serious burns and deadly smoke inhalation."

"Burns?" Libby said. Then her memory rushed back, her real memory. Her imagined turmoil had been a reflection of her real struggle. She had a job left to do.

"I need to go. It can't wait."

"I'm afraid I can't authorise your release without further observation. There has been, how do I say it, significant pressure on me to keep you here."

"I don't doubt it."

"Unlike the doctors in your dream, I'm not going to help you or hold you back. Did you know that I have a break coming up? I'll be gone for thirty minutes. If that interests you. Rest up I'll come check on you after my break," Dr. Butler said with a smile, and continued on his rounds. Libby waited two minutes and then kicked herself into gear. She unplugged machines, and dragged herself out of bed. Her body was slow and sluggish, but responded. She staggered over to the cupboard in the corner of the room and searched it thoroughly. Her clothes were in there, but blackened with soot. That wouldn't do. She collected her wallet and keys and snuck into the room next door. There was another woman sleeping.

"Sorry," she whispered and tip toed over to the cupboard. She found some floral pants and a white blouse.

"Not my thing, but they should fit," Libby thought to herself. There were even some brown sandals. Libby straightened her hair in the mirror and left the room. She could hear Dr. Butler's voice at the end of the hallway.

"She's still asleep, the same as the last time I told you. I expect her to wake up today, but there's no guarantees."

"I need to talk to that journalist. It's a matter of some urgency."

"I understand that mayor. Once she's awake and lucid then you can get your answers," Dr. Butler said. There were no further discussions and Libby heard footsteps after. She half jogged and half limped in the opposite direction. Her whole body hurt and her head was pounding. Her dream was coming back, mixed in with her real memories. Everything was meshing together. But the one thing she needed to do was clear. It was a beacon in her mind that outshone everything else.

She knew the hospital layout well, and made her way to a side exit. It was only usually used by staff. She didn't relax until she had hobbled around to the next block. She leaned up against a building and took in some deep breaths. She saw several taxis on the roads, but a memory flared up and she decided against it. She had a good look at the street she was on, and realised that her destination wasn't far. It would be a ten minute walk normally, but in her condition at least double that.

"Better make a start," she said to herself. Every step was more pain, but her walk improved and she could pass herself off as normal, although still slower. She felt her head and her feet pounding in sync. As she walked she thought about what the doctor had said. She hadn't wanted to admit it, but he had hit the nail on the head. All those fears, were ones she had held. But they were unacknowledged, lurking in the recesses of her mind. Only coming to the fore in specific situations and forgotten afterwards.

A man walking a dog passed by and the dog barked fiercely at her and tried to jump. Libby felt a pang of fear, which was then recognised and faded as fast. The man apologised and disciplined his dog but Libby didn't notice.

"What just happened?" she said to herself. She continued on, conquering block after block. Suddenly she had arrived. Before her was the smouldering remains of the Orphello Theatre. It was surrounded by police tape and had a guard doing the rounds. The rest of the block was also cordoned off and therefore the only real light coming from the theatre was the guard's flashlight. Libby watched his route, then sneakily approached the building and ducked under the tape. She rushed into a dark corner which was pitch black.

"Thanks Amy," she whispered as she relaxed and let her eyes adjust to the dark. She was in what had been a storeroom. She turned and looked out, trying to form a picture of where she needed to go. It was too dark to get a good idea, so she slowly stepped through the rubble acting on instinct. She heard a loud groaning sound overheard and then a rumbling sound.

"This place could come down on me," she thought to herself. However it was not fear that filled her, but resolve. She had a mission, a purpose. Nothing would stop her from achieving it.

Onwards she forged and stepped into a more open area. She judged it to be the remains of the old foyer. She closed her eyes and imagined the foyer as it had been that night. She conjured up images of the flames and destruction and went back further. A pristine version of the room graced her mind, and she looked around her mental picture figuring out a direction. Opening her eyes helped give her a heading, and she slowly moved forward. She felt something large ahead of her but couldn't quite make out the details in the dark. An errant beam of light shone in from the guard's light and lit up the face of the old clock. Libby smiled. She had found it and it was still intact. She carefully maneuvered around it until she was behind it.

Libby groped the back of the clock until she found the special catch. A subtle door clicked open and she reached inside the hidden cavity. As her hands grasped the document envelope she almost laughed with relief.

Joy surged through her. As she pulled it closer to her she remembered the strain in the mayor's voice back at the hospital.

"Justice will be done," she whispered.

ALSO BY VAUGHAN W. SMITH

Have you read these other books by Vaughan W. Smith?

In this thrilling follow up to Dreamlike, ambitious journalist Elizabeth Edmonds is desperate to break another big story. A spooked informant hands her a tip about the local hospital, but she has no idea that she is about to stumble onto the story of her life.

A man wakes with no memory, just a fake ID and instructions. He follows along and sets off a chain of events that spiral out of control.

ABOUT THE AUTHOR

Vaughan W. Smith is a fiction writer from Sydney, Australia, who explores big life questions through story. His favourite genres are Thrillers, Mystery, Science Fiction and Fantasy.

To connect with Vaughan check out his website: http://www.vaughanwsmith.com

www.ingramcontent.com/pod-product-compliance
Lightning Source LLC
Chambersburg PA
CBHW050509110726
47899CB00005B/1384